# BUSTING OUT

VANESSA M. KNIGHT

*To Julie, my BFF partner in crime, for being there for me in every crazy thing I've done over the years. You are more than friend. You're family.*

## ONE

"WEST ON FULLERTON AT AUSTIN." The instructions crackled over the police radio as Chase Montgomery ran around the corner onto Fullerton. Between the restaurants and the *lavanderia*, civilians lined the noontime sidewalk, creating an impenetrable wall.

"There they are," his partner Perry Flores huffed beside him.

Two teens crossed the road. Why? To get on Chase's bad side. City buses with advertising for everything from Weight Watchers to Oreos squeaked and sputtered as cars whooshed by.

Chase and Perry followed the teens through an extreme version of Frogger. Horns honked, tires screeched, and a car swerved—thankfully dodging right before Chase became a Chevy's hood ornament. More tires screeched. But somehow, they made it across.

Chase craned his neck to get a better look. The

drug-dealing little shits were getting away with, if his intel was correct, a backpack full of heroin. Any heroin was bad, and letting it loose on the Chicago streets was worse.

The epidemic was real, and Chase and his partner were in the middle of it. Deep in the middle of it, chasing low-level runners on the west side of the city.

"Excuse me." He dodged a woman and her stroller, holding her shoulders so she wouldn't fall over. "Sorry, ma'am."

This whole running thing was getting old. It would be so much easier to shoot the drug mules in the leg. Slow them down. But with the people on the streets, it was too risky. Anyway, he couldn't pull his weapon on two unarmed kids. He wouldn't.

So instead, his shoes slapped against the pavement. His muscles ached. The air sliced down his dry throat. Why the hell did he need the gym membership with all this cardio? Or a personal trainer? His PT needed to amp up the miles next visit, or Chase needed to find slower perps.

"They're splitting up." Perry pointed at the shorter of the perps turning east on Wrightwood.

"Follow him. I got this one."

Perry went after the little twerp with the mustache straight out of a seventies porn flick, and Chase turned right on Wrightwood, following the second thug, otherwise known as John Lacik. Chase's shoes pounded against the cracked one-way street. The civilians thinned as he moved from the busy intersection to the residential blocks.

Lacik stopped and turned around. Chase reached for his gun. *Don't do it, kid.* His hand hovered at his holster. "Stop. Police. We need to talk."

The kid's blue eyes widened as Chase stalked closer. The kid looked terrified. Blond spiky hair. Baby face. How the hell had this kid ended up shilling for the Vipers?

"I'm not going to jail."

"No one said anything about jail." But really, if the kid had as much heroin as Chase's snitch thought, there was no way there wouldn't be jail time. He inched closer. "Let's sit down and talk about this." Emphasis on the sit.

"Screw you." Lacik turned his back on Chase. And ran. Naturally.

Chase had really hoped the whole sit thing would pan out. But that wasn't how this worked. It never worked that way. He followed, running through the gangway between the two houses where the kid just disappeared.

Something banged. *Dammit.* He needed to move faster or he was going to lose this kid. Bursting through the wooden gate at the front of the tiny backyard, he sprinted toward the back of the patch of grass and the open metal gate for the alley.

Chase spun around, listening, searching. Garbage and exhaust lingered in the air. Small garages intersected with smaller fences lined the length of the unpaved alley. Overflowing metal and plastic trash bins clustered behind each postage-stamp yard. Spurts of grass peeked through small cracks, the gray corridor's only splash of life.

And the kids blond head bounced along, halfway down the block.

*Fuck.* Chase took off again. When he signed up to be a cop, he never thought "pursuit of justice" meant literally running up and down the Chicago streets.

Yet here he was, crossing Schubert Avenue and making chase down another back alley. Halfway down, a truck was wedged between two facing garages, maybe a foot of space on each side. Moving men sat on lawn chairs in one garage, eating their lunch. Boxes and appliances were piled next to the metal ramp sticking out of the truck bed.

The kid dodged a refrigerator and angled his body to slide past the truck. But it slowed him down.

Chase just had to use that to his advantage. As he slid his way past the truck, his shoulder holster snagged on a piece of metal.

*Dammit. He's getting away.*

---

Maggie Lane drove her car past the alley entrance and parked on the side of the street. She wanted to drive down the alley, but there was a damn moving truck in the way. "How many garbage bags did you bring?"

"Three." Jessica Xu unhooked her seatbelt and leaned into the back seat. "Is that enough?" This was

Jessi's first ride-along. She'd been working the front desk at Busted Detective Agency for the past year, hinting at her desire to be a PI the whole time. She'd proved her reliability—and her tenacity—dropping hint after hint about hitting the streets and leaving the horrible phone system that liked to hang up on customers behind. Maggie really needed to send that thing to the antique graveyard.

"Should be." Maggie poked her head out the window. It was a beautiful day. Sunny. Warm. Not exactly what you expected in April, but she'd take it. Sifting through someone's trash after an April shower wasn't exactly high on her "fun things" list. Although, what part of sifting through trash was high on anyone's list?

Three men carried boxes into the truck blocking the alley. Of course there'd be a truck in back of the house across the way on the day that Maggie and Jessi had to get in and out undetected. That had been the whole point of coming here at eleven AM on a Saturday, when Jillian Hendricks would be out scouring the antique universe for Hummel and Precious Moment figurines. Apparently, there was a whole club that did this every month. Go figure.

"So what are we going to do?" Jessi asked. "Can we make the exchange with the movers around?"

Could they? Yes. Should they? Probably not.

"*Quieres almorzar?*" a deep voice asked from near the truck. Lunch. Was he asking about lunch? Please let him be asking about lunch.

Another deep voice said, "*Por que no? Esto tomará*

*un rato.*" She understood the first part—*why not?* The rest, she had no clue.

Maggie really needed them to stop for lunch. If she and Jessi didn't exchange the bags now, they'd have to wait until sometime next week—or worse, next month, when Jillian went off to find porcelain children again. A whole month. Maggie had already put off this client one week due to Jillian's hectic hospital schedule, and finding a day when Jillian would have a full can and wasn't working had turned into a challenge. Even the boyfriend, Maggie's client, didn't know Jillian's schedule—probably why he hired Busted in the first place.

The moving men removed lunch bags from the front of the truck and disappeared into the garage. Music immediately floated from inside, and Maggie figured this was as good as it was going to get.

"Grab the bags and come on." She waited for a car to pass, and then opened her car door and slipped out, slamming it shut. Noise didn't matter, not on the busy Chicago streets. The mission was speed.

Maggie walked along the right side of the alley, sticking close to the fences and garages. Jillian Hendricks lived on this side—across and over from the open garage with the mariachi music spilling out. The idea was to not let the moving men see them. Not to let anyone see them, actually.

Pausing at the corner of the garage next to Jillian's, Maggie dragged Jessi closer. "Okay," Maggie said under her breath, "give me those." She took the stuffed garbage bags from Jessi and nodded at their target—Jillian Hendricks' trash cans. "Here's what we're going to do. You open the garbage can and pick out the first three bags. I'll dump these in to replace them."

"Why? It's not like she'll notice."

"The garbage men don't come for a few hours or so. What if she brings out another bag? The goal is to catch her before she gets suspicious." Maggie looked toward the open garage. Music. Male voices. Paper and plastic crinkling. It was time. "Let's go."

Jessi popped out and headed straight for the garbage can. Lifting the plastic lid, she heaved out three full bags, flattening against the wooden fence to give Maggie room to dump the proxy-bags without being seen.

Success!

The world shifted. Something or someone shoved Maggie forward, into Jessi. She righted herself with the help of two male hands covered in familiar crude fanged snakehead tattoos above the thumbs. Gang tattoos. The Vipers.

Once she was firmly on her feet, the blond teen turned and ran down the alley, yelling, "Sorry" over his shoulder.

"Hey!" Jessi yelled, as he disappeared around the corner, and picked up a dirty red backpack.

Maggie glared at her, raising her index finger to her lips in the universal shut-the-heck-up sign. They still had to get out of here without anyone seeing them— anyone else seeing them, anyway. She shook her head and leaned over to pick up the scattered garbage bags.

The kid had been like a mini-tornado. It was time to get out of this alley.

Collision. Something or someone slammed into her.

Again.

This time, the air ripped from her lungs when instead of soft Jessi, she hit hard wood. Her feet tangled in the damn garbage bags. Her knees buckled. Nothing stopped her downward momentum. The ground flew up to meet her cheek. Yay, physics.

Someone—not Jessi—rested on top of her, making a very pissed-off Maggie and gravel sandwich. She tried to push up, but the body squashing her was large and male. The hand on her ass? Also not Jessi. Maggie bucked like she was doing the worm, and the five-finger encroacher disappeared.

"Shit," a deep voice rumbled above her as the weight vanished.

Air hit her skin without the human blanket. *Breathe.* It was so much easier to breathe without the weight. She pushed onto her knees. Gravel dug into her palms. What the hell was wrong with everyone, running around knocking people over?

She glared at the man trying to dislodge his foot from one of the garbage bags. *Serves you right.* "What the hell?"

He only grunted. Why she was surprised by his less-than-stellar manners, she wasn't sure.

Maggie stood up on wobbly legs. Her clothes were a mess—jeans covered in a thin layer of dust, black T-shirt now a hazy shade of gray. A few swipes of her hands down her body did nothing; she still looked like Pigpen. "What's with you?"

The guy hopped from one foot to the other, and the garbage bag tore as he yanked his shoe through the neck of the bag. Apparently, it was too hard to answer her questions while being attacked by garbage bags.

"Why are you playing with garbage?" He kicked free and stood to his full height—a few inches taller than her, at least six feet—giving her the perfect view of his face.

That face.

She knew that face. That rugged face. His large nose and the scar curving along the left side toward his lip were the only indication that there might be flaws hiding behind those perfectly sculpted cheekbones. And there were flaws—smoldering brown eyes aside.

They'd fooled her once. Never again.

"Magpie?"

"Maggie." Why was it so hard to remember to call her Maggie? She tried to beat the dust off her jeans. Anything to keep her hands busy, and her eyes from raking over that body of his.

"I'm sorry. Are you okay? Do you want a ride to the hospital?" He stared down the alley, probably hoping to see the teen he'd been chasing. But that kid was long gone.

"I'm fine."

"Are you sure?"

"I'm fine." She felt her eyes roll—of their own accord. It wasn't her fault he was asking dumb questions and her body was responding. Too bad her body seemed to respond to everything he did.

"What are you doing here?" Chase's eyes roamed over the scattered garbage bags and the backpack in Jessi's hand.

"Working."

"In garbage?" Judgement was all over his face. Bad enough she got that from her family.

"Why are you running through the alley like a bat out of hell?" she countered.

"Working." The corner of his lip curled as he stepped away from her. That little curl of his mouth was so darn sexy. A tingle shot straight through her mutinous heart.

"I'm getting the bad guys, Magpie." He leaned in, putting those lips inches from hers.

Gorgeous lips that looked delicious. And if that wasn't bad enough, he smelled. Like man. God, she missed the smell of a man. Spicy. Dark. With a rich woody base. Or maybe that was just him.

He smirked. "Has it been so long since you've taken down the bad guys that you've forgotten what it looks like?" *Jackass.*

Maggie was still catching bad guys, just in the private sector. Not that any of the cops understood. "Don't you have work to do?"

He ran a hand down the back of his neck—had she mentioned what nice hands they were? "I think he got away." The great Chase Montgomery didn't get his man. Must be why he looked mad—no, not mad— maybe upset. The crinkle in his brow couldn't be worry. Chase didn't get worried. He was way too arrogant for that.

Unless this bad guy had done something extra bad—and now he'd gotten away. The urge to make him feel better was both foreign...and unwanted.

He didn't deserve to feel better after what he'd done to her. So why did she grab the backpack from Jessi and shove it into his chest? "Your bad guy dropped this."

"Thanks." Chase took the backpack, and those hands brushed hers.

"And, uh, isn't he a Viper?" Maggie stepped away, wiping her fingers on her filthy jeans.

"Yeah." He stared at her for a long second. "How do you know that?"

"The tattoo on his hand. Don't they have a safe house a few blocks over, on Meade? Ten bucks says he's heading over there."

"Ten bucks, huh?"

She tried to help and all he heard was ten bucks. *Jackass.* She was so done playing his little game, but if she didn't play nice it might get back to her father. So she forced a smile on her face and yanked one of the intact garbage bags off the ground. "Shouldn't you go after him?"

He met her smile with one of his own and slung the backpack over one shoulder. The glare off his perfect white teeth gave off enough wattage to power a small country. "Are you sure you don't need a ride to the hospital? I'm told I give great mouth to mouth."

Maggie didn't bother responding. *Jerk.* She took the garbage bags and walked toward her car.

"Should you be driving?" Those little lines of worry were back around his eyes again. And for a change, he sounded serious. He smiled at Jessi. "Can you drive?"

"I'm fine," Maggie cut in. "Shouldn't you be running?" She turned to him and deliberately rubbed her cheek, where she was sure a bruise was starting to form. He stared at her cheek for half a second before sighing and shaking his head. She was not going to read anything into that. She wasn't.

"Good point." He followed her down the alley toward the end of the block, where he hung a left toward Meade. "See you around, Magpie."

She literally could not take her eyes off him as he made his way down the block and out of sight. Not that she cared. And she most certainly did not watch him walk away because the sight of his round ass in those jeans was an aphrodisiac.

There were an awful lot of *not's* swirling around her head. And *not* one of them was good. Chase was no good. He'd led her on, and tried to destroy her career. He wasn't the type of guy she should be caring about. Or watching. Perfect ass or not.

"Boss?" Jessi stood next to her holding garbage bags. Had she always been there?

This was why Chase was no good. He took Magpie's—Maggie's—focus. He left her mind a frazzled mess. She couldn't even remember her own name. Not that anyone needed to know that.

Best way to show there was nothing going on here?

Pretend nothing was going on here. "Ready? We need to get the bags to the office." She made her way back to the car and clicked open the locks, dumping the garbage bag in the trunk. Jessi added the ones she was carrying before sliding next to Maggie in the front seat.

"After we get cleaned up," Maggie told her, "we'll run and pick up lunch." Pretend. Pretend. Nothing happened back there.

"Thai? I have had the strongest craving for that Thai place in Humboldt Park, by the office." Jessi smiled and leaned against the seat. That was almost too easy. The whole garbage can scene with Chase was obviously forgotten. Or maybe Jessi hadn't noticed the sparks flying.

Not good sparks. Bad sparks.

Maggie started the car and merged into Chicago traffic. She wasn't sure if she should even mention that she'd seen Chase to her partners. Leti and Danni would just get pissed off. In their eyes, he'd screwed her— without actually screwing her. But maybe she didn't need to mention it. Especially if Jessi hadn't noticed anything was off.

"Are we going to talk about it?" Jessi asked two blocks later.

Of course she'd noticed. It was one of the reasons Maggie thought it was a good idea to train her as a PI. Jessi noticed everything. "About what?"

"*Magpie?*"

"Nope." She didn't want to talk about Magpie, or the man who called her that. She didn't want to discuss how she'd fallen in love with him and he had barely known she existed. She didn't want to relive how when he finally noticed her, it was to steal the first case she'd ever been given as a detective—how he'd made her look like a bumbling fool. And she definitely didn't want to talk about how her heart had broken when one minute he kissed her like his life depended on it and the next he didn't want to see her again.

No. She didn't want to talk about it. Any of it.

# TWO

CHASE WALKED down Diversey Ave looking for Lacik, whose blond head was nowhere in sight. Not that Chase was all that surprised. Somehow, he'd managed to lose him. No, not somehow. Someone.

Maggie Lane.

Two words guaranteed to pull his mind off the job he was doing and onto inappropriate things. She was his kryptonite—his Achilles' heel. Always had been.

When Maggie had walked into the twenty-fifth district police department eleven years ago, he knew he was in trouble. Gorgeous blonde hair, curves in all the right places—those hips? They were full. And when she walked, they shook like she was doing the macarena. She exuded sex-appeal.

The only problem? She was the boss's daughter.

Scott Lane had his ass when Chase made a move on his only daughter. Back then, Lane hadn't been the chief of the bureau of detectives, but he'd still been scary as shit. Not that Chase blamed him. Any move Chase wanted to make wouldn't have been father-approved.

A voice echoed from his pocket. "Montgomery, where are you?" The radio.

*Shit.*

"Here." He sounded like a fifth grader in roll call. *Here* didn't tell his partner a damn thing. He checked the signs at the corner he just passed. "Diversey and Meade."

"Ten-four. Be there in five." Flores sounded pissed. He must not have gotten his perp either. Great. That meant the old dog was going to be a new prick.

Chase stared at the church on the corner. It was quiet for a Saturday. No bake sale or church function. Just quiet. He sat on the steps and opened the backpack, squinting at the contents. Tiny plastic dropper bottles. He picked one up and shook it. Filled with liquid. Heroin. Way less suspicious than little baggies, and a favorite among the needle-phobic. Who would question a bottle of eye drops?

Well, not a total loss. At least they were getting the drugs off the street.

A few minutes later, a blue Suburban flew around the corner, and Chase whipped open the passenger door. "Where's the dealer?"

"Shut up, Montgomery." Flores had the car in gear before Chase had a chance to close the door. Yep, new prick. "I don't see you leading no perp walk."

True. Chase dropped the backpack in the backseat. "But I do have their drugs."

"So, not a total cluster." Flores managed a small smile as he pulled away from the curb.

"Nope."

Flores passed Meade, easing through the busy intersection.

"The Viper safe house should be a few blocks north on Meade," Chase said. "Should we check it out?"

"Good idea." Flores shook his head and pulled a quasi-legal U-turn. "I completely forgot about that. I'm surprised you remembered."

They'd raided the house years ago, when Chase first made detective. Which was probably why he didn't remember it. Maggie remembered.

She remembered everything. She knew these streets and how to navigate them better than anyone. Not that Chase could tell Flores that. He couldn't say anything about the boss's daughter.

Although he probably should. If Flores found out that Chase saw Maggie and he didn't say anything, the guy was going to be pissed. On the other hand, if he did say something, the guy would still probably be pissed. No win either way. And Chase didn't want to think, let alone talk about her. Seeing her brought it all back—the way she'd push her golden hair behind her ear when she was thinking, the way she laughed, and the look of heartbreak when she'd been blamed by her father for missing evidence.

She'd gotten the short end of that deal. It hadn't been her fault. It had been her moron partner. But somehow Maggie had been the one who'd paid for his incompetence. People thought she got special treatment because she was the chief's daughter—well, back then her father had only been the commander—but same difference. No one realized being that daughter came with expectations. And for her to not notice the mistake? She'd lost her spot on Detectives.

Chase had seen her old man forgive other cops for less. But they didn't have his DNA running through their veins. So much for *special treatment.*

They parked in front of a small red brick house. It looked normal on the outside. One story. Couple evergreen bushes lining the path to the door. Simple. Clean. Too bad it housed a bunch of lowlifes.

Flores went up the front walk and knocked on the door. Chase followed him, going to the left and cupping his hand on the window so he could get a look through the partially opened drapes.

No movement. No answer.

Flores rang the doorbell. "Do you see any reason to go in?"

Toys were strewn all over the floor, but no people. "Unless an explosion of Fisher-Price toys is illegal, we have nothing." No probable cause and no warrant.

Flores shook his head as they headed back to the SUV. In his usual attempt to stay off the congested main roads on the way to the police station, Flores wound through one-way side streets, swerving to avoid potholes on one block and suited yuppies on another. Chase would have just driven straight there, and the hell with the usual Chicago traffic, but he wasn't the one driving.

They pulled up to the brick station house. There

were rumors that it had once been white, but now it was permanently stained a dingy pale beige. Chase made sure to slide the backpack over his shoulder before crossing the parking lot and following Flores through the glass doors. Small windows lined the walls, letting in the barest of light. If those windows weren't nailed and painted shut, and overall arthritic, they might actually open to allow for a breeze. As it was, the tired building always smelled like mold and stale air.

"Flores. Montgomery. Did you catch Lacik?" Captain Olivia Taye stood in front of her office door, pinning them in place with her dark brown eyes.

Today her black hair was all in long springy twists. Chase's private theory was that the more perfectly controlled Captain Tate's hair looked, the better her mood. He felt safe ignoring the attempt at eye-pinning. Besides, he'd worked here too long to be afraid of any of the brass's looks.

"No, but we've severely pissed him off," he said.

"I don't care if you stepped on his Pop-Tarts. I want him off the street." The captain grabbed one twist and tugged. This was bad. For her to actually mess with her hair meant she was pissed.

Chase tossed the backpack onto a desk next to Taye's office. "Well, we got the next best thing."

Running the zipper open, Captain Taye slipped her hand inside and withdrew a handful of the little bottles. "Heroin?"

"That's what we're thinking. Probably about one liter total."

"Probably?" The captain dropped the vials and

closed the backpack before sliding it toward Chase. "Get this processed. I want an exact amount."

"Yes, ma'am."

"And send it for analysis. Let's find out what we're dealing with here." She stared at the backpack as Chase put it on his own desk. "So it looks like Lacik has moved up the ladder from low-level thug."

"I'm not sure." Flores sat down behind his own desk and began peeling an orange. The man stashed more oranges than Tropicana. And he ate every single one of them. "We would have heard if he was breaking rank."

"Did you just get lucky?" Taye asked.

Lucky? Hell yeah. Taking this much crap off the streets was luck. Chase wished he had this type of luck all the time. "Probably."

"I hate that word." The captain shook her head and walked back into her office. "Don't guess. Find out. If he's moved up in the organization, that's even more incentive to find him."

Flores popped an orange section in his mouth. "Probably."

"And gentlemen, next time you get near him, actually hold onto him. It'll *probably* mean I'll let you keep your jobs." She slammed her door, but there was a small smile on her face. Probably. It might have been a snarl.

"I'll take pictures of this crap and get a sample to the lab." Flores unzipped the backpack and dumped the contents on Chase's desk. "Why don't you start the report on what happened in that alley?"

In the alley. Lots of things had happened in that alley, and Chase hated having to put any of it down on paper. Maggie's name was going to have to go into the report, which would get a whole lot of attention from the chief.

Mostly because Chase had just left her there—left her in the alley with her friend—after he'd basically plowed into her like a steamroller. He should have handcuffed her and forced her to go to the hospital or urgent care or some other doctor-haunted facility. Not that Maggie would let him do that, but that's what the handcuffs were for.

Instead, he grabbed the backpack and ran. *Dick move.*

Hopefully, the friend drove them home. Like that would happen. Control freaks didn't let others drive and Maggie was a control freak—at least she used to be. Maybe he should check in with her and find out if she was okay...

Maybe not. It had taken every ounce of energy to keep his mouth from attaching to hers—from his hands touching the side of her face. All he wanted to do was feel her next to him. How was it that she still had this effect on him?

He couldn't talk to her again. Couldn't see her. No contact.

If he wanted to make sure she was okay, he'd ask her father. Or better yet, her brother. They got along pretty well after fifteen years on the force together. Anything was better than seeing those lips again. Or those hips. He was only human.

Maggie dumped one of the bags of Jillian Hendricks' trash, and papers and random crap spilled onto the plastic tablecloth she'd laid down in the alley behind Busted Detective Agency. Why the alley? She couldn't handle the creepy crawlies in the bags. Why the plastic tablecloth? Did she mention creepy crawlies? And it was garbage. She didn't want to leave trash behind her building and there was no way she'd be picking up each piece—enter cheap tablecloth to catch all the bits of nasty.

"Must you do that out here?" Danni Stein walked out the back door with a laptop bag over her shoulder. Maggie had stolen her away from Chicago PD—not all that hard to do. Danni had her own issues with the bureaucracy of Chicago PD, one of the reasons they seemed to get along so well. They both wanted the same thing. To help people without all the BS. Which was why they decided to open the agency.

Technically it was Maggie's agency, since she was the only licensed PI in the trio, and Danni and Leti were consultants. Consultants entitled to a one-third share of Busted's net profits—Leti swore the expensive lawyer who'd drawn up the contracts knew what he was doing, and since Leti was the financial wizard, Maggie believed her. In spite of all the legal stuff, Maggie thought of them as her partners, because without them backing her up she'd never be able to do this. Maggie was the PI, Leti was the forensic accountant, and Danni the hacker. Maggie's job required stakeouts and garbage and human interaction. Leti played with numbers. Danni performed dark magic with computers. On bad days, Maggie suspected she'd somehow drawn the short straw in this arrangement.

"Where do you suggest I dump garbage? In your office?" Maggie kicked a rolling stray cup back onto the tablecloth.

Danni's lip curled. "Someplace out of the way?"

"This is an alley. How much more out of the way do you want?"

"Suburbs?" Leti Ramirez's perilously high heels clicked on the sidewalk. She stepped down onto the gravel and made her way over to the tablecloth. "This is why you can't find a date."

Maggie glared at her. Old friend or not, that deserved a glare. "I date, and if you don't like my methods, get a license and get your butts out here."

"No thanks." Leti opened her car door and slipped inside. "I'll stick to numbers."

Danni opened her car and threw the laptop bag in the back seat. "Have fun with all that."

"Oh, come on," Maggie laughed. "You know you want to help."

Danni got in and rolled down the window. "Jessi, are you sure you don't want to learn programming? There's no garbage."

"You'll miss all the fun." Maggie grabbed a set of gloves from her back pocket and held them out to Danni, who drove away shaking her head.

Danni and Leti spun their tires as they headed down the alley, each of them tapping their horn when they hit the end of the gravel. It was always good to announce a car's exit. Stopped accidents. At least that was the theory.

Maggie knelt next to their latest hide-and-seek project. Coffee grounds and congealed yogurt covered some of the trash. Gross. The hairs on Maggie's nose curled at the sour smell.

"What are we looking for?" Jessi pulled on a set of plastic gloves and kneeled down at the other edge of the trash pile.

"A signed confession stating she's banging someone else."

Jessi stared at Maggie. Her head cocked. Her eyebrow lifted. "Really?"

Maggie sighed and yanked on her own set of gloves. "No. Although we'd take it if we found it." It was times like these she missed Chase—if she allowed herself to miss Chase. He always understood her jokes. "They never make it that easy. We're looking for anything that will tell us the story. What do we know about Jillian?"

"She's a nurse, works at Saint Michael on the West Side."

"When we talked to Steve" —aka the suspicious boyfriend— "what else did he say that we can use?"

Jessi blinked at her, and Maggie raised her eyebrows and waited while Jessi obviously thought that over. Most people didn't think in terms of how to catch someone doing something wrong. Most people were too trusting, so they didn't know where to look. "He thinks she's cheating? She has all new stuff. A TV and a dishwasher. Um, she says she's working late, and he doesn't believe her."

Maggie was way past the not-believing stage. She'd personally been the better half of one too many cheating scenarios. Even her previous job as a cop had jilted her. The political crap had soured that aspect of her life—which sucked because leaving that job meant constantly dealing with her family's disappointment. Thank goodness for her friends or she'd have no one. "Remember we asked about allergies? What did he say?"

"She's lactose intolerant."

"Right." Maggie pointed to a crumpled milk carton in the center of the pile. "So isn't that odd?"

"Couldn't it be from Steve?"

"In any other case, maybe, but he told us he doesn't drink coffee."

"How do you remember all that?"

Maggie took pictures while Jessi started a list in her notepad. "It's not just about remembering," Maggie said, "it's noticing. Keep your eyes and ears open. Listen to what they say and what they don't say. Focus on what you see, and what you don't see."

The milk carton didn't prove Jillian was cheating, but it was something to put in the report. Every little thing they found would give the client a more complete picture.

"Check receipts." Maggie sifted through a handful of paper. Grocery list. Gas receipt. Junk mail.

"Look. I solved the case." Jessi waved a bent postcard and shimmied in place. "She could save fifty percent on her car insurance."

"That's the key." Maggie laughed. If only it were that easy. "Maybe that's how she's buying the new TV and all the stuff Steve told us about."

"How about this?" Jessi showed her a printout. Fiesta Inn.

"Ooh. That's better. What are the dates?"

"March twenty-third through the twenty-fifth."

Maggie took off her gloves and used her iPad to check the information they'd gotten from Steve. "He didn't mention going away that weekend." She took a picture of the printout. Of course, none of this proved infidelity. Hell, the bill could have been from a night spent with Steve that he just forgot to mention during the initial interview. She hadn't retrieved his whole life history, so he'd know that better than she would. She just gathered the data.

Once they finished sifting through the bags, Maggie shoved all the garbage into the dumpster behind the office. Now was the hard part.

Steve was going out of town for a dental seminar. His girlfriend would be left in the city alone, and when the dog's away the cat will play—or at least that was what he wanted Maggie to prove. "Are you ready for a stakeout?"

"I am." Jessi was way too excited, given what Maggie was proposing. Stakeouts were boring and long —and did she mention boring? Maggie hated the whole thing—endless hours staring at a house. No cell phone or books. No lights, because you couldn't really draw attention to the car. She'd thought about hiring someone else to do them, but that wasn't even an option. If she was on a case, she wanted to be in on every aspect of the case. She couldn't write the report if she hadn't been a part of the evidence collection. Maggie looked up Jillian's address on her phone and handed it to her.

"When do we start?" Jessi asked. She spun the phone in her hands, looking at the back of the see-through case. "Why do you have a business card in your phone case?"

"In case I lose my phone."

"Does that happen a lot?"

"More often than it should." Maggie took her phone back and slid it in her pocket.

"I brought a cooler." Jessi ran inside the office and came out with a red Igloo box. "The right side has sand-wiches, chips, and cookies. The left side is soda and water."

Maggie had to smile. There was a time she'd done the same thing, had snacks and drinks all ready, just in case. After the past couple years and countless stake-outs, her preparation left something to be desired. Mostly preparedness.

She was lucky if she remembered to stop at the Dunkin Donuts drive-through before she parked her butt in front of someone's house. Of course, without the DD coffee, her attention started waning somewhere around midnight.

They packed the picnic gear into Maggie's gray Crown Vic. The car was old. The car was crap. But it ran and didn't stick out, no matter which neighborhood she wandered into. And she'd wandered into some interesting neighborhoods. She'd had her front windshield cleaned by many an entrepreneurial homeless person—some using a dirty rag and water, and one cost-cutting phenom using his spit. She'd run the car through the car wash twice after that one.

Hopefully, today's stakeout wouldn't be spit-wash exciting.

AN HOUR LATER, Maggie eased the Crown Vic down the block from Jillian's Cape Cod bungalow. White stucco, just shy of dirty, windows and doors surrounded by dark brown trim. The cement stairs led to a landing covered by bright green fake-grass carpeting and a white screen door. Wayward trees and bushes lined the tiny front yard. Empty flower pots sat on the paved walk along the gangway between Jillian's house and the one next door, leading to her backyard.

The area was all residential—no convenient coffee shop to hunker down in and inconspicuously watch the house. The one-way street was lined with cars, so maybe they'd luck out and none of the neighbors would notice two women mainlining coffee—they'd remembered to stop at the DD—and staring at Jillian's house.

Time for Jessi's first lesson. "Now remember, we have to be Jane Goodall."

"Isn't she that monkey lady?" Jessi smiled when Maggie nodded. "I love monkeys."

"There are no monkeys. We're spectators. We

watch. We don't get involved. We're like...the cameramen on a reality TV show."

Jessi nodded, turning the radio down until it was a background hum before leaning her head back against the seat.

The sun slid behind the houses, and the air coming through the partially opened windows went from pleasant to chilly. In a little while, men and women wearing business clothes and gym shoes would fill the streets once the typical workday ended. Then things would quiet down for dinner and bedtime.

"Are you okay?" Jessi glanced her way.

"Yeah." Maggie took a sip of coffee. "Why wouldn't I be?"

"The alley incident."

Great. Now the run-in with Chase had escalated to an incident. "There was no incident."

Jessi played with the rim of her mocha latte with a turbo shot of espresso. "You know him." It wasn't a question. She was stating a fact. Well, hadn't Maggie wanted her to observe?

"Yes," Maggie admitted.

"He's a cop." Another not-question.

"Yes."

"You worked together at CPD, then."

"Yes." Maggie could practically see the wheels in Jessi's head spinning. Jessi might not know the specifics of what happened all those years ago, but she knew that something happened. The gossip mill at Busted was alive and churning. Maggie's own family still hadn't gotten over her part in the incident from six years ago. And that was definitely an incident.

Jessi spun in her seat, her voice rising to Chihuahua pitch. "He's the one."

The one? "Which one?"

"The one who broke your heart and ruined your career."

About summed it up. "Yes, he's the one who ruined my career." She wasn't admitting to anything about her heart—not to anyone else. It was bad enough she knew all about the broken heart. She didn't take her eyes off the steering wheel, hiding the only way she knew how. Work.

That was her way to deal. And she had. She'd dealt. She'd busted her ass to get back on the detective's list. She'd worked late, done extra shifts, and took on more than anyone in the precinct. The betrayal didn't matter. Or the way she'd wanted to cry but refused to give Chase the satisfaction. The way her heart literally ached inside her chest.

And when she'd finally made detective, she'd heard a rumor that her daddy got her the job. Not her hard work. Not her sacrifices.

Maggie switched her focus back to her extra-large black coffee. Her past might be painful, but her future was copacetic. She was working toward building a company she could be proud of. She had friends. And right now, she had caffeine. She had everything she needed.

Jessi was staring at Maggie. Just staring. It was

creepy. And Maggie could admit it was one thing she didn't need.

"What?" The opening bars of a Green Day song filled the car. "Isn't this your favorite band?"

"Nice try." Jessi turned off the radio. "No subject change. You loved him."

Maggie had never heard those words out loud before and she sure as hell tried not to think them all that often. The blaring silence as the words lingered in the air made her head hurt. She didn't know how to stop the dead air from sucking up all the oxygen. But somehow it was. And somehow Jessi kept looking at Maggie like she was waiting for some sort of reply.

*Bam! Bam!*

Maggie almost dumped her coffee into her lap when two swift raps hit Jessi's side of the car. An old woman lowered a cane and leaned her lips down toward the partially opened window of the car. "What are you doing here?" The woman's dog barked, and with each bark its little body bounced higher, giving Maggie a brief view of the little bodyguard, a black Miniature Pinscher with a tan snout.

"We're drinking our coffee." Jessi smiled and lowered her window, putting her hand out, probably to pet the Min Pin. The dog snapped at her fingertips, and Jessi yanked her hand back.

"Why aren't you drinking your coffee in a coffee shop like normal people?" The old lady wasn't buying it. Surprise. They never did. The outside world thought private investigators had to worry about the person they were chasing. But no one—absolutely no one—held a candle to the overeager elderly self-appointed neighborhood watch. Their sole purpose was to snoop and therefore drive Maggie crazy.

"Coffee shops are crowded?" Poor Jessi was trying.

"But why else would you go to one of those high-priced places?" The woman pointed at the white cups with pink lettering.

Maggie wouldn't exactly call Dunkin' Donuts high-priced. But then again, there wasn't much she wouldn't pay for a great cup of coffee.

"We... um..." Jessi stuttered as her cheeks turned an interesting shade of dark pink.

It was time to give her a hand.

"I got this," Maggie said as she took a photo from the center console and stuck it in her pocket. The lost pet was as good an excuse as any. She stepped out of the car and went around to the sidewalk. "We needed the caffeine to help us deal with a problem. You might be able to help. You seem like an animal lover."

"Why yes." The lady picked up her mini-Cujo, and Jessi's window rolled all the way up. Maggie didn't blame her, given the display of pointy teeth now at eye level.

Jessi leaned forward, and right away, Green Day whispered through the glass. At least she was keeping the volume down. Jessi was known for cranking it all the way to eleven.

The dog licked its owner and then growled at Maggie. "Hush, Stanley," the woman snapped at the dog. "I love all God's creatures." You'd have to be an animal lover to cuddle with that snarling beast.

"I thought so. We're looking for our Burmese cat. Goes by the name Kono." Maggie slid the stock photo of a cat from her pocket. She kept it handy for exactly times like this. When all else failed, go for the sympathy. "My girlfriend accidentally left the back door open when she was bringing in the groceries, and now Kono's missing."

"Oh dear." The old woman took the photo and ran a wrinkled thumb over the cat's adorable face. The cat was ridiculously cute. If Maggie had time for an animal, she'd love to get herself a little Burmese. "You must be so heartbroken."

"I'm trying to stay positive." Maggie tried to look sad, but not too sad. Tears would be too much. She deserved an Oscar for today's performance. "But she is absolutely distraught."

Maggie turned to her so-called girlfriend, who was shaking her head and singing about American idiots. Speaking of idiots... Maggie glared at Jessi, but her long straight black hair was flying, and the air guitar obviously blocked her from seeing anything.

The woman tsked. "You're very strong, dear. You are obviously a very caring person." She glared at Jessi as she handed Maggie back the photo. "I'll keep my eyes out for Kono."

"Thank you so much."

"But honey?" The woman rested a hand on Maggie's arm. "You can tell a lot about a person by how they treat their animals, and how they treat the one they love. You might want to find someone your own age. Someone who wouldn't dance around when your pet is lost. You deserve better."

Maggie tried to keep her expression somber, but it was hard. There was actual thumping coming from the car as Jessi slapped the dashboard like a drum. "You are so kind. Thank you."

"You're welcome, dear." The woman looked inside the car and pursed her lips. "You could do so much better." She put her dog back on the ground and started down the sidewalk. "By the way, there's a park down the block that Kono might have found."

"Thank you. We'll head over there next." Maggie went back around the car and slid into the front seat.

"How'd it go?" Jessi hit the stereo, and Green Day slid to a quiet hum.

"Fine. You would have heard if you'd kept the window open and the music down."

"For real? It's like freezing out there and Green Day is my jam." Jessi went to turn up the music, but must have realized Maggie was contemplating handcuffs, because she paused. "With the baby, I don't get to really rock out anymore."

"No problem." Maggie wanted to be mad, but she couldn't. Jessi was busting her ass to care for her three-month-old son, Matty. The baby-daddy was another story for another day—especially since it was a story that Jessi absolutely refused to share.

"So, how did you get her to go away?"

Maggie quickly rehashed the whole scene. "It's just a matter of finding the best way to get them to go about their day—preferably without calling the cops."

"I can't believe she said you could do better. It's the boobs, right?" Jessi palmed her chest and attempted a jiggle. "Even with milk-boobs, I'm heading the itty-bitty-tittie-committee."

"I doubt it was your chest."

"It's because I'm Chinese."

Maggie rolled her eyes, and froze as a shitty car parked in front of Jillian's house. A guy with blond spiky hair jumped out of the jalopy and ran up to the front door.

Maggie reached into the backseat, and dislodged her camera bag from under an empty Butterfinger wrapper and the bag from last night's take out. With all the crap she kept in the car, it was a miracle she could find anything. Sliding out the expensive DSLR—whatever the hell that meant—she popped off the body cap and screwed the telephoto lens in place. The camera was supposedly the best, which was why she nearly had to take out a second mortgage to get it. She sat up. "Lean back."

Jessi and her self-described flat chest melded with the front seat. "What do you think, delivery?"

"Maybe, but there's no bag or pizza box."

"True." Jessi help up her phone and hit record just as the screen door swung open. Jillian stood there, her brown hair in a ponytail. Jalopy dude wrapped his arms around her and hauled her out onto the landing.

"Brother? Old friend?" Jessi guessed.

Jillian turned around and locked the door while her blond "friend" didn't keep his hands to himself. If this was her brother, it was one twisted family. When he looked out at the street, Maggie got a good look at his face.

"Shit." The bulldozer with the Viper tattoos. Maggie pressed into Jessi, inches from her face.

Jessi's eyes grew to cartoon size "You know we're not really dating, right?"

If Maggie wasn't so worried about being made, she'd find it comical. "The blond is the guy who ran us over in the alley."

"No shit." Jessi craned her neck, trying to get a look past Maggie.

"Stop. I don't want him to see us." Maggie lowered the camera. "Okay, look now, but do it casually."

Jessi tipped her head at a weird angle, a constipated look on her face. They needed to work on defining *casually.* "They're heading to his car."

Sure enough, Jillian and her date jumped into his car. "We've got a field trip," Maggie said, starting the ignition.

Poor Steve. The cat was definitely playing, but what was the game?

# THREE

CHASE FOLLOWED John Lacik's piece of crap car toward the heart of downtown. The thug was going on a date. *A date.*

Well, it looked like a date.

The kid had lost something like a key of heroin this afternoon. He should be freaking out. He should be lashing out and making mistakes. Not heading down North Avenue with some woman. Who was she, anyway? If that scene on the front steps was anything to go by, she wasn't just some random girl where Lacik got lucky and swiped right. Or maybe that's how it started. Hell, maybe he did find her online. He might just be looking for a distraction tonight.

"Do you see that?" Flores asked.

"See what?"

Flores pointed to a gray sedan in the next lane. "The Crown Vic is following Lacik."

It looked familiar. Same dented rear door. Same

cracked bumper. Same car Chase had passed when he'd chased Lacik. "How do you know that?"

The gray car swerved in front of them, and Chase hit the brakes and shouted a few choice words as Lacik merged into the left-hand turn lane. The Crown Vic's turn signal flicked on, and the driver practically embedded its cracked bumper into Lacik's ass.

Dammit. How had he missed this?

As the two cars went through the intersection, a streetlight bounced off blonde hair in the driver's seat of the Crown Vic. Maggie. It could just be a coincidence that he ran into her this afternoon in that alley, not a hundred feet from this exact car. But something told him it wasn't a coincidence.

Something also told him she was messing around where she shouldn't be messing. This guy wasn't some shmuck who diddled the secretary in the broom closet. This guy was a gun-carrying idiot who sold drugs to kids.

"Shit. They're after Lacik." Flores picked up his phone, probably to call in the plate number.

"Don't bother calling it in." Chase didn't want to have this conversation, but he didn't have a choice. "I might have seen that car earlier—when I ran into Maggie Lane."

"The boss's daughter? You ran into the boss's daughter? Please say you ran into her figuratively."

"More like literally, in the alley when I was chasing Lacik. She was standing back there with garbage."

"With garbage. What the hell was she doing with

garbage?" Flores shot one eyebrow up. "And you're just telling me this now."

"She was working." Chase tried to keep his voice light. "It wasn't a big deal." At least he hoped it wasn't a big deal. "She barely got a bruise."

"Not a big deal?" Flores slammed his fist onto the center console of the car. "She sees Daddy and tells him what happened and it's not in our report. And she has a bruise. You actually bruised the boss's daughter. Fantastic."

"I put it in my report."

"So, you just didn't tell me."

"I didn't want to have the conversation."

"What conversation?"

"You know." And he must have known. Chase had partnered with Flores shortly after he became a detective. Flores had been there when Maggie had been shit on by her partner. He'd watched Chase try to save her, only to get hit with the backsplash. He also knew about Chase's small yet inadvisable crush on the woman.

Flores sighed. "Is she okay?"

"We didn't exactly have time to talk, but yeah."

"Is that why you lost Lacik?"

The look Chase shot his partner was supposed to instill fear or at least absurdity. But Flores didn't appear to understand—or maybe he didn't care. "Is that why *you* lost your bad guy?"

Flores huffed. "I lost mine because he was part monkey. I'm not scaling no six-foot fence."

"What if we brought along a trampoline? Or I could give you a lift." Chase used his knee to drive as he clasped his hands together, miming a hypothetical boost over the wall.

A hand flew to the steering wheel. "Quit playing around and drive the damn car. You make me crazy."

Chase couldn't help but smile as they followed the caravan to a parking lot outside a local sushi bar. Making Flores crazy was a perk of the job. Chase parked along the curb across the street.

Lacik pulled into the small lot, stepped out of the car and waited for his girlfriend. The only restaurant along the strip was a small hole-in-the-*mall*. Sushi Palace. Bright light shone through the storefront window between the menus and pictures taped to the glass. Not exactly romantic, but you couldn't tell from the way the two of them were draped all over each other. Their hands groped places that should only be fondled in private.

Flores cringed as they watched the amateur porn movie. "We can't grab him. Not with that many civilians."

Chase agreed. Even from here, he could see the tiny restaurant was packed. By the time they hit the front door, Lacik would be out the back door.

The love-birds walked inside, and Chase briefly lost sight of them as they followed a hostess to the back of the restaurant kant. He caught a glimpse of the two love-birds as they sat down, and as long as he could tell they were still there periodically everything was good.

Or not. Blonde hair came down the sidewalk. Well, the blonde hair was on a woman. The woman he'd been thinking about on and off all day.

She strolled along the empty sidewalk with her partner-in-garbage. The partner wrapped a black jacket closer around her shoulders, and her black hair hung in a straight plank down her back as she tipped her head toward Maggie, who did the same. What were they plotting now? The two women turned toward the restaurant.

Not the restaurant. They wouldn't actually go into the restaurant. Would they?

"Montgomery, we have a problem..." Flores might have said more, but Chase didn't hear it. He was out of the car and running across the street. *They had a problem? No shit.* And her hips swayed as she crossed the parking lot.

Didn't she realize that Lacik had seen her? He'd run right into her. He'd probably seen her face. He'd probably felt her body.

Chase wanted to kick the shit out of the little hoodlum for that reason alone.

Lacik would recognize her the second she walked through that front door. The little shit might not be the brightest bulb, but he was quick enough to know when something was off.

Chase crossed the sidewalk, intersecting Maggie and friend before they reached the windows of the sushi joint. "Excuse me, ladies." Stretching his arms out, he nudged them toward the darkened insurance office next door.

As they all stepped back into the shadows, Maggie's lips curled in a snarl. She looked pissed off. Convenient. They matched.

"Where do you think you're going?" he snapped.

"Dinner. Are meals illegal now, Detective Montgomery?"

"You cannot go in there for dinner."

"Why? Are the Chicago Police so bored they're concerned about my eating habits? I promise not to eat the spicy green stuff commonly thought to be wasabi." Maggie crossed her arms at the same time she eyed Chase's arms.

"It *is* wasabi, and who says I'm here for you? There are almost three million people in this city." The irony wasn't lost on him. Three million people in the entire city and he ran into her—twice. Her eyes kept roaming his arms. He'd like to think she was checking him out, but the spark in her stare told him she wanted to run past him. Bad idea. "He'll recognize you," Chase pointed out.

"Do I look stupid?"

He really wanted to answer that, but any response he gave, one, wouldn't have been nice, two, would have pissed her off more, and three, would guarantee she'd push past him and four, enter that restaurant blowing his chance of getting Lacik. So he said the only thing he could. "What's your plan?"

"I'm not going to let him see me. I was just going to slide in the front and get a few shots." She held up a professional-looking camera. "We wouldn't actually get close enough for them to see us."

"Have you seen this place? It's as big as a lunchbox and they're both looking right at the front door."

She hooked the camera's strap on her shoulder. "I'll figure it out." She slipped around him.

"No." His arm shot out, stopping her again. He probably looked like a spastic crossing guard.

"Are you going to stop doing that?"

"Are you going to stop trying to get to that restaurant?" See, he could ask dumb questions, too.

"I need pictures of her with him."

"I'll give you the mug shot after we pick them up. Just stay out of it."

She stared at the building, probably wishing herself in front of it. But then like a flash of lightning, the look disappeared and she was all business. She turned to him as her lips quirked into a poor excuse for a smile. "Fine."

"Fine?"

"Jessi, let's go." She spun on her heel, headed for the sidewalk. "We have a report to write—and when I say we, I mean you."

Maggie's partner scurried to catch up. "Can we write it without all the pictures?"

"I guess we'll have to." It was pretty damn dark on the street, but the glare Maggie shot over her shoulder told Chase who she blamed for their lack of photographic evidence.

She might be walking away, but it so wasn't *fine*.

They disappeared around the corner. The headlights sputtered on the Crown Vic, then shone against the brick wall of the building. The lights narrowed and bent as the car left the parking lot.

She'd actually done what he asked. She was staying

out of it. He didn't think it would be that easy to change her mind. She never changed her mind. But the lights merging and melding with the city traffic said she'd left and given him the space he needed to make his arrest.

Just when he thought he couldn't want her any more than he already did, she walked away from her collar and let him have his.

Chase walked across the street toward his car. Her sacrifice almost made him want to look her up, see her again. Busted Detective Agency had to have an office. He could bring a fruit basket or a bottle of wine.

A bottle of wine. That would only lead to fun...no. It would lead to bad choices. Job-losing life-fucking choices that he'd be too stupid to avoid—he always had trouble avoiding stupidity when she was around.

Thank God she drove away. He didn't have to see her again.

At least that was the plan.

## FOUR

MAGGIE DIDN'T SLAM on the brakes once, and she'd only called one non-driving motorist on the street an ass. That was pretty good, considering all the swear words swimming around her head. All of them technically directed at Montgomery.

Montgomery.

Back on the street, she'd wanted to knock him on his ridiculously hot ass. Bossy jerk. She didn't know which was worse, his complete lack of faith in her or his craptastic attitude.

Like she'd let herself be seen. If Jillian or her boy-toy saw her, there was a good chance Maggie would get made as a PI. Nothing like finding out you're being followed for a person to stop doing all the bad stuff. Then, where would Maggie be? Without proof. Without evidence. Without a paycheck.

Her fish liked to eat way too much for her to miss out on fishy-flake money.

"Are you okay?" Streetlights illuminated Jessi's pinched face.

"I'm fine." So not fine, but she would be. Decision made, Maggie drove back toward the restaurant. She wasn't missing this opportunity. If Chase was throwing that dirtbag in jail, this was her only chance to get a cozy couple-shot.

Jessi pointed toward the back of the car. "The office is that way."

"Yeah, but we're getting those pictures." She went around the corner, looking for the alley behind the restaurant. They'd park out of sight—go through the back—and get the hell out before Chase even thought about chasing them. Well, her.

"You said you wouldn't go in there."

"I never said that. I said fine."

"And then you drove away."

"I'm calming down and re-approaching the scene from a new direction." Maggie found the alley behind the sushi place and eased into it. A small graveled lot —lot was generous, it was a small rectangle of space, a hundred feet to the left of the back door—sat deserted.

She squeezed the Crown Vic as close to the back door as she could and retrieved her camera from the backseat before getting out. The cool evening breeze met her skin. Felt good on her overheated cheeks.

"Umm... Maggie?" Jessi tried the handle on the door, but there was no room to swing it open.

"Do you want to wait here, or would like to crawl across?"

Jessi huffed and slid across the car's front seat, angling out of the door. "I should get hazard pay."

"Me too." Maggie shut the door with a click. Not that anyone could hear her all the way in the back, but it made her feel stealthy to keep quiet. And she needed stealth. "We're going in through the kitchen. Keep your head down, and try to slide in without being seen."

They crept up to the building. The back door to the restaurant was propped open, an OSHA-violating box fan sitting right inside. Galley kitchen. Narrow and small. Lots of angry Japanese coming from the men crowded at the stainless-steel counters. *Crap.*

Jessi bumped her arm. "How are we supposed to get through there—unnoticed?"

Good question. The men were filling plates and bouncing into each other like a pinball in a field of bumpers.

A server came in through a swinging door at the front of the kitchen, grabbed a couple plates, and slid out the way he came. Another door swung open, at the back of the kitchen. A busser with a loaded plastic tray dropped off clean dishes. He yelled something. The counter people yelled something. The busser walked toward the back door, an unlit cigarette hanging from his fingers.

"He's coming outside." Maggie pulled Jessi behind a dumpster and crouched down.

"This dumpster stinks like bad fish." Jessi crinkled her nose and whispered, "Does anything in this job not require close proximity to trash?"

Maggie pressed her index finger to her mouth. She

didn't bother answering. Because everything in this job *did* require close proximity to trash.

The man dug out a cell phone and began talking. Cigarette smoke circled his head as he walked down the alley, away from the door.

Maggie slid her hand through Jessi's. "Okay, let's go." They scurried over to the back door and inside. There wasn't much space, so Maggie took both a hop and a sidestep to walk around and over the box fan at the same time. The staff didn't notice as Maggie towed Jessi a couple steps into the kitchen and slid through the door the busser had used.

They ended up in a small dingy space filled with stacks and stacks of dishes lined up on drying racks. A huge sink sat in the corner of a small counter. But what Maggie really wanted to see was to her left. Another door. And from the clinking and muted voices coming from the other side, this was where she wanted to be.

Maggie inched the door open and peered around. Young couples filled the tables, and an elderly couple stood at the front door waiting to pay their bill. The soft hum of conversation, but nothing else. She leaned out the door a little further... *Jill*-pot.

It was a weird angle, since the cheater and her beau were sitting off to the side of the door, but if she could just inch out a little further, she could get a shot of Jillian. At least that was what Maggie banked on. She stepped back, letting the door swing closed. Jessi sat on the edge of the small counter next to the sink, dangling her feet and checking her phone. Maggie raised her eyebrows. "Comfortable?"

"Not really." Jessi hopped down. "Are they out there?"

"Yep." Maggie took the lens cap off and stuck it in her pocket. She had to do this fast. "I'm going to take a quick set of pictures, and then we're out of here." Maggie hit the power switch and slid the camera viewfinder in front of her eye. "Keep a watch out for Smokey the Busser."

Maggie slowly slid the door to the dining area open, propping it in place with her ass. Through the viewfinder, Jillian and her bulldozer were leaning in close. Jillian ran her hand down his arm as sympathy played across her face. Bulldozer must have had a bad day. Little did he know there were two cops out front making sure his day didn't get any better.

*Snap. Snap.* She took multiple pictures of the two of them talking at the table. The angle wouldn't show the hand-holding. Darn it. That was the money shot.

She slid further out. Still no hand-holding. Just a little more. She slid all the way into the room, the door closing behind her, and now she was at least a foot away from a quick getaway. But she needed the shot. One more shot.

She lined up the camera. Hand holding. Yes. She spun the focus spinny-thing and their hands came into view. Bingo. She snapped the picture at the same time something slammed into her back and threw her forward. It wasn't like she had time to think—she dropped the camera and tried to catch herself. Her hands landed on a metal tray, flipping it up and tossing full plates right at her. Food soared and dive-bombed right into her face. Something cold and wet slapped her cheek. A raw fish facial. Lovely. Rice lodged in her hair as the tray clanked on the floor.

Someone yelled in Japanese. Someone yelled in English. *Wait.* That was her. Clumps of rice flew when she shook her head. Cold seaweed fell into her shirt. *Ewww.* She flapped her shirt, watching as the green stuff left her cleavage and landed on her camera. Her camera, which was covered in raw vegetables and fish. *Shit.*

She picked up the camera that Danni swore Maggie needed to have. The camera she was still paying off. The one that was probably now an over-priced paperweight. She turned the thing over in her hand as she righted herself. It looked okay. As long as she didn't lose the pictures she already had, it should be okay.

The pictures.

Jillian and her boy-toy were staring at Maggie. Everyone was staring. Why wouldn't they? She had maki sticking out of her hair.

Jillian and friend had that look, that *just can't place where I saw you last* frowny thing. Not a good look. Ducking her head so her hair slid forward, Maggie spun around.

"What are you doing here?" A man in a fancy suit came out the door from the kitchen. "I'm the manager."

Maggie smiled as inspiration struck. "I'm a...a...food blogger, and I just needed a few shots."

"Oh, no, I'm so sorry. You eat." The manager

guided her to a chair and made her sit down. "I'll get you some food, on the house."

Maggie took a deep breath. All she wanted was to get her pictures and run. She didn't want free food. She didn't want to pretend she was a blogger. It had worked though, so now she was stuck.

She set the—hopefully still working—camera on the table and tried not to stare at her prey. But her eyes kept roaming back, which was why she saw the moment recognition crossed the bulldozer's face.

He jumped up, clutching Jillian by the hand and dragging her out of her chair. Proving that she was not entirely a stupid bimbo, all Jillian did was squeak when he wrapped one arm around her waist and pressed a gun to her head with the other. "Get back!" His eyes were locked on Maggie.

She slowly stood up, hands straight in front of her, palms out. "I'm not coming any closer. I just want to talk."

"Fuck talking. I'm getting out of here." His eyes flicked toward the front door, where the elderly couple were still at the counter—were they paying with pennies? Everyone else just stared at the crazy with the gun, at least until they realized what was going on. Then there was screaming and diving under tables. There might have been crying and flailing. Maggie was too busy trying to keep from getting shot to notice the details.

Crazy slid sideways, toward the back door. "Move out of the way!" He waved the gun at Maggie, indicating she should move toward the front.

So, naturally, she did. "Don't do this. You're scaring everyone. You're scaring her." Maggie took another step closer to the door, bumping a chair. Without thinking, she gripped the back of it to keep herself from tripping over the darn thing.

*BAM.*

A bullet passed by her head. A bullet. Her head. She stopped moving. She stopped breathing. She was pretty sure even her eyelids were permanently glued in their current position.

The front window blew out in a wave of jagged shards.

Maggie stood perfectly still as everyone else flattened under the tiny bistro tables. The gun was—again—pointed at her. Bulldozer shuffled backwards toward the door Maggie had used earlier, pushing it open and disappearing.

*Jessi.*

Maggie waited a beat and then shoved through the door, finding Jessi sandwiched between a drying rack and the wall.

"Are you okay?"

Jessi slipped from her hiding spot. "I think so. Does that happen a lot?"

"More than it should, but no." The last time Maggie had been fired at was by a biker named Skip. Anyone could see how she might have underestimated him. His name was Skip, for cripes sake. Of course, his biker name was Blade. Had she known that, she might have used more caution. You'd think with a name like Blade, he would have carried a knife, but nope.

A deep male voice that Maggie recognized right away came from the other side of the door. "Is everyone okay?"

She didn't want to see the face attached to that voice, but if she ran she'd probably be looking at obstruction charges. Hell, she might be looking at them already. But Jessi wasn't. Maggie couldn't let Jessi end up in jail on her first stakeout.

"Did you see anything when they came through here?" she whispered to Jessi.

"No, it happened too fast."

"Good." Maggie dug in her pocket. "Here are my keys. Go home to your son. You can pick me up for work tomorrow."

The camera. *Dammit.* It was still in the other room. Maggie couldn't exactly go get it now.

Jessi clutched the keys. "Shouldn't I wait here?"

"I'll take care of things here. You have to leave now."

Jessi ran out the back.

Maggie heard the engine roar to life, and the car tires crackled on the gravel. While she debated sidling back out to join the diners, the door in front of her flew open, and another gun stared her in the face. This one was solid and sure, and attached to one very pissed-off detective. A familiar pissed-off detective.

"Clear." Another familiar detective, also with his weapon drawn, appeared on Maggie's other side, propping the kitchen door open. Of course Chase's partner Flores—who was Maggie's father's lifelong friend—would be there to see her hair caked in sushi. Why not?

She hadn't seen him in months, so naturally she'd see him now.

She pointed past him at the open door leading to the alley. "He went that way?"

"Who did?" Chase asked, still wedged in the door to the dining room.

"The guy with Jillian. He had a gun."

Chase and Flores looked at the back door. The fan from earlier was unplugged and lying on its side just outside—not violating OSHA rules any longer. Chase shouldered past her as the Flores ran for the alley.

Maggie stood there and watched them leave. She shouldn't have given Jessi her car. She should be leaving. But everyone saw her. And now Chase saw her. And Flores, too. There was no way she'd get out of this mess.

She walked through the door to the dining room and sat down. She'd made this mess, now she was going to have to lie in it.

---

Chase sprinted around the building to the lot where Lacik had parked his car, just in time to nearly get run over as Lacik backed out of the space. Chase raised his gun as Lacik slammed the car in drive and gunned the accelerator. No civilians around. He shot at the tires. One shot. The tire hissed, but the car whipped out of the lot and onto the busy street. Chase couldn't risk another shot. Hopefully, tagging the one tire would be enough to slow him down.

Flores lumbered over to Chase. "Dammit. He got away."

Of course, the little creep got away. All that was left was lop-sided taillights.

Sirens rang out in the distance. They'd called in shots fired before they'd run in to secure the scene. They'd been told to wait for backup, but they couldn't risk losing Lacik.

Which didn't work out as planned. Well, at least they had a BOLO out on the guy. Every cop from the city would be looking for him. And with his tire-impaired car, they just might catch him this time.

"Let's start interviewing witnesses." Flores reached for the small notepad he kept in his pocket for just that reason.

Chase wanted to interview a witness, all right. One witness in particular. Just in case she had any ideas of slipping away before he had a chance to interrogate her, he used the back door of the sushi joint and went through to the front. If she wasn't there, he was going to charge her with obstruction, fleeing from the police, and just being an overall pain in the ass. There wasn't a statute for that one yet, but there should be.

"Should I start with Lane?" Flores asked. Chase didn't bother answering. He was too busy stalking closer to the person who'd fucked up his op—well, probably fucked up his op.

"We need to talk." He looked her in the eye and nodded to the kitchen. Depending on her answers, what he had to say might or might not be appropriate in front of civilians.

He opened the door and waited for her to get all the way into the tiny room. "What happened?"

"That psycho started waving a gun."

Psychos generally didn't just start waving around their guns without provocation. "What provoked said psycho to wield said gun?"

Maggie stared at her hands, and Chase finally took a moment to look her up and down. The woman was covered in food. Rice clung to her hair. Sauce was all over her shirt. Whatever had happened, she was obviously in the middle of it.

She let out a breath. "I came in to get one picture..."

He heard the rest of the words, but barely. He was having a hard time keeping his mind on what she was saying when he had this incredible urge to handcuff her —and not in a good way. His way included a paddy wagon and interrogation room.

"...the manager wouldn't let me leave, and then the bulldozer recognized me and went all crazy. He tried to shoot me, but missed—"

"Wait. He was shooting at you?"

"Yeah. I tripped and went to catch myself, but the gun was already out and he was twitchy, and it missed me and—"

"Slow down. Do you always talk this fast?"

"No." Her fingers clasped and released as she stared at them. "But this is my fault."

He wanted to argue, but given everything she'd said, it was her fault.

"You were right." She audibly gulped and looked up from her finger steeple with huge sad eyes.

*Fuck me.* He wanted to be mad. He was mad. Except every mental replay of *you were right* from her lips—soft lips, if he remembered correctly. Lips that held their own against his—well, how could he stay mad when all he saw were those words on those lips?

Maggie shook her head, and rice tumbled onto her shoulder. "I shouldn't have come back, but I knew you'd take him to jail, and I'd never have another shot at the proof I needed."

There was that anger. He'd found it again. "So you fuck up my op for your proof? You let a drug dealer roam the streets so, what, you can get a picture? Are you kidding me? We have rules and regulations. Rules put in place to separate us from the gorillas."

"Montgomery." Flores stood in the doorway. "Chief's here."

"Fuck me." Today was turning into a *fuck me* kind of day. "Why?"

"Apparently, he heard his daughter was here."

"How? Who would've called him?" If Flores called the chief, Maggie wasn't the only one on Chase's shit list tonight

"Someone named Jessi has her cell phone—and her car."

Jessi. The woman she was with earlier. He hadn't gotten a good look at the dining room, but he would bet that her friend was nowhere to be found. Chase eyed Maggie. "Where is the woman you were with earlier?"

Some of that attitude he knew and hated came to life in Maggie's eyes. "She went home. Wasn't feeling well."

"With your phone? How were you expecting to get home?"

Her eyes popped open wide, like she hadn't realized she had no phone. "I don't know if you've heard, but Chicago has an amazing mass transit system."

"Officer Montgomery, what is going on here?" The chief strode into the narrow kitchen, wearing jeans and a T-shirt. Even in street clothes he demanded respect. And he got it. He'd earned his title with years on the force and a healthy dose of take-no-shit.

"Lacik was in the restaurant," Chase said evenly. "Took his girlfriend as a hostage and ran out the back."

"Why is my daughter here?" The chief's glare nearly split Chase in two. The old guy was intimidating on a good day. Right now, playing overprotective Dad and Chief? He was downright scary.

"Why don't you ask her?" Maggie stood up, saving Chase from having to rat her out. "I was here to take pictures on a case I'm working. Your perp saw me and thought I was a cop."

"Where were you?" The chief moved his attention back to Chase.

"Waiting for Lacik. Outside."

"Outside? If you were watching the building, why the hell did you let her in here to take *pictures*?" The way he said the word spoke volumes on what the chief thought of his daughter's new job.

"He didn't *let* me in." Maggie stepped in her father's line of sight again. "I'm an adult. I made the decision to come inside. I entered through the back so Lacik wouldn't see me, but that didn't work out."

"Didn't work out." The chief pinched the top of his nose, probably trying to stop a headache brewing. Chase could understand. He was planning on having an intimate relationship with a few Tylenol when he got home tonight. If he ever got home.

"Go to the front, Margaret. Give your statement to Flores."

"I've given my statement to Chase...Montgomery."

"Just go out front. I need to speak to him alone."

Maggie's chin lifted. "Why? He didn't do anything wrong. I messed up the operation. It's my fault."

Fighting with the chief was futile. Chase knew it. Maggie had to know it. But he couldn't help but think it was the sexiest thing he'd ever seen.

"Oh, I understand, and I'll get back to you and this...this distraction you've concocted. Your hobby is not only ruining your life now, it's affecting others. We will talk, but right now, get your ass up front."

Maggie gave Chase the briefest look. Pity. Apology. It was sweet. It was quick. He wanted to give her the same look. Her father obviously thought the detective thing was a game. Anyone who knew her, knew it wasn't a game. She loved her job.

She walked through the swinging door and left Chase alone with the chief.

"Is what she said true?"

Chase stopped himself before he shrugged. "Yes."

"Why didn't you try to stop her?"

He had tried to stop her. But Chase didn't think saying that would go over real well. It would just make Maggie's life more difficult when she tried to wiggle her way out of this with her father. No matter how much he wanted to arrest Maggie, or at least make her life hell, he would never mess with a father/daughter relationship.

He would have given his left nut for any relationship with his own father. But the guy had run out on them years ago, leaving Chase with his mother. Then after his mother died, with his grandmother.

"We had no indication that this was anything other than a casual dinner," Chase said. "We watched Lacik enter through the front door, and kept an eye on the door the entire time. We were only made aware of the issues when Lacik discharged the gun."

"Why did he discharge the gun? Who was the intended target?"

*Your daughter* sat on the tip of his tongue, but Chase couldn't say it. The chief would figure it out—from the reports or from Maggie. But by then he'd be much calmer and there was a better chance he wouldn't put his daughter in a plastic bubble.

Instead, Chase said, "We're still trying to determine the sequence of events."

"You discharged your weapon." It wasn't a question, it was a statement. But Chase still found himself shaking his head.

"Outside the building," he explained. "I hit a tire on Lacik's car."

"I expect all mandatory paperwork on my desk by tomorrow morning."

"Yes, sir." The mountain of paperwork on that one act alone was enough to empty an arboretum.

The chief looked around the room, sighed, and shook his head. He must know something wasn't right with Maggie's story. He always knew. His bullshit-meter was probably on overload right now. "I'm disappointed. I expect more from you. This was your operation—your mistake. We'll discuss it Monday."

"I'm sorry, sir." And he was sorry. Chase hated disappointing the chief. Hell, the chief had been more of a father to him than any other man in his life. Not meeting his expectations was like a dagger to the chest.

"All right." The chief pinched his brow again. "Wrap this up and give me the report Monday."

"It'll be on your desk first thing." Chase followed the chief through the swinging door into the dining room.

The chief passed his daughter with a nod, but kept walking, out into the night air. And just like that the chief was gone.

Chase walked over to Maggie, who was talking to Flores.

"Can't I just get the little cardy thing?" Maggie asked. "You can keep the camera."

"This is evidence." Flores had a large plastic bag with the camera inside.

"I'll take care of this," Chase told him, "if you want to see whether we've missed interviewing any of the witnesses." Chase took the bag and pulled out the camera. Turned it on. "Did you get any pictures we can use with this thing?"

"No." She held out her hand. She seemed to think he had the intention of giving this nuisance back to her.

Chase sifted through the pictures. Shot after shot of Lacik and his woman. "I thought you said you only got one picture before all hell broke loose?" There were so many, she must have set up residence.

"I took a few. Can I please have that back? You can keep the damn camera, I just need the card."

He sifted through till he hit one of Maggie at a... baby shower? "Whose shower?"

"Jessi's."

"Was this the only camera at the shower?"

"Why does that matter?"

"Just asking." He twisted the camera so Maggie could see when he got to someone familiar. "Didn't she work for CPD?"

"Yes, she was in computer forensics, and yes, there were other cameras at the shower. Is the interrogation over?"

"Yep." He flipped the camera over and slid the memory card free before dumping the camera in the bag.

"Thank you." She lifted that hand again.

He sat the bag on the table right before snapping the memory card in half.

"What the hell, Chase?"

He smiled and placed the two halves into her hand. "Next time we agree for you to stay out of it? Stay out of it. Flores has more questions." He walked away. Didn't turn back. Didn't look at her face. He could imagine she was pissed. Good.

She could have died, and for what? A damn picture.

FIVE

THE STREETS WERE dark when Maggie was finally let go. The last few people were filing out of the restaurant into the cool night air. The other storefronts were all dark, metal bars covering the windows, except for the club down the block which was just getting going. Bass thumped and knocked against her ears as she adjusted the camera hanging from her shoulder. She couldn't believe Flores let her have the camera. But he probably felt guilty after Chase's shitty attitude.

The temperature had dropped a few degrees since she'd first walked into the sushi joint. She'd only been inside the restaurant for four hours. Four hours? Felt like *twenty*-four. She squeezed her jacket closer to stop the chill nipping at her bones.

She'd answered questions, listened to stories, and took every chance to glare at Chase. What a jackass. She still couldn't believe he broke her cardy-thing.

There was no reason for that— other than because he was a complete and total jackass.

It was eleven at night. Too late to call Jessi—her son would be sound asleep, and given all the sleeping problems the little one inspired, if Maggie woke him up she was sure Jessi would hunt her down and run her over. It might get Maggie's car here, but she'd have a hell of a time driving it with the bumper lodged in her spleen.

Not that it even mattered. She could call Danni and Leti, who didn't have the baby issue, but Maggie didn't even have a phone. True, she was only a fifteen-minute bus ride from Busted, but that meant she'd have to sleep on the lumpy pull-out couch in Danni's office. A forty-five-minute commute would get her back to her house on the north side.

Alone. On mass transit. At night.

Lumpy couch or mass transit? Somehow, sleeping in her own bed seemed worth the long ride on a bumpy bus with woozy junkies. If she was lucky, they'd pass out, and she wouldn't have to listen to rambling stupidity the whole way.

But it would be so worth it for her soft pillow and firm mattress. And her quilt. Oversized and cottony-soft and warm enough to make her forget what a shit night this had turned out to be.

She moved toward the thumping bass of the club and the bus stop. Forty-five minutes. She'd gotten through the past four hours of crazy. What was another forty-five minutes?

She kept her feet moving over broken sidewalk squares. The dark streets of Chicago, with shadowy corners and shady figures looking to take advantage of a woman walking alone, was no place for a nighttime stroll. She just needed to get on the bus, with its fluorescent lighting.

Crappy lighting, but it was still lighting. No shadows.

Something grabbed her right arm. Someone. Strong grip, enough to hold on to her when she yanked. Her heart hammered in her chest. Her breath thundered to a stop. All outside noise stopped.

The fingers of her left hand curled, her arm snapping back and rounding on the face attached to the owner of the grip.

*Crack.*

Her fist hit skin. The crack was her fist. And dammit, did it throb. They let go, and she finally got a good look at who she'd hit. She'd know the scar over that lip anywhere.

"Maggie." Chase looked more concerned than hurt.

She needed to work on her left hook.

"Where are you going?" His voice cut through the thumping backbeat from the club, and the banging of her heart slowed to a normal rhythm.

Where was she going again? "My house."

"How?" Chase ran his hand along her neck, slowly tracing up to her face.

Just a soft brush. But that brush said warmth and caring and home. Her eyes fluttered shut for a second before snapping open as heat sizzled along her skin. Home? Ugh. Why the hell was he affecting her at all? It must be the late night. She was too damn tired to fight him and his mojo. Tomorrow. Yes, tomorrow she'd be better. What were they talking about again? "How what?"

"How are you getting home? You have no car."

*No kidding.* That he remembered Jessi had taken her car might have been sweet if he wasn't such a jackass. "Magical broomstick."

"I'm not touching that one."

She smiled. She might have set herself up with the broomstick comment, but so what. How did he think she'd get home? "Bus."

"You're not taking the bus alone this late at night."

Maggie could admit it wasn't high on her to-do list, but she couldn't exactly rack out here on the sidewalk. "I don't have much choice."

"I'm driving you home."

The concern in his eyes was like a drug. It pulsed through her veins and swirled around her head like good scotch. "I live on the North Side," she pointed out.

"So does Flores." Chase's thumb slid along her cheek. He didn't even seem to notice he was doing it, or maybe it didn't affect him the way it did her. "I have to drop him home, so it's no big deal."

Maggie leaned into his strong hand. With each swipe of his rough finger, her pulse jackrabbited. Her heart squeezed. She shouldn't let him touch her. Not like this. Not when he didn't mean it like that.

His eyes moved to her face and his thumb stopped. That didn't make the feelings disappear. Not even when he snapped his hand away. The feelings never went away. *Dammit.*

She had to make them go away. It wasn't healthy for her heart to crumble over and over again like a crash-test dummy during a safety experiment. She needed to hit her own brakes. And fast.

Maggie rocked back. "I should probably just ride the bus to the office. Sleep there."

"Fine. I'll take you to the office." He stuffed his hand in his pocket.

Probably for the best. Although it was nice to have someone show this much concern over her well-being. Her heart swelled inside her chest.

"You don't actually think I'm going to leave you here alone? The chief would have my ass."

Her heart sputtered and snapped as it deflated, leaving a small ache. The chief. That was who he really cared about.

She was such an idiot when it came to Chase.

"C'mon, Chase, let's go," Flores called from a partially opened door. "Raquel's waiting up."

"Fine. Take me home." Maggie nodded and headed toward Chase's car. She couldn't say no to Perry Flores, or his wife Raquel. He was a good guy. He'd partnered with her father back in the day. He'd been a permanent fixture in her life, especially when she'd dealt with all the stares and whispers.

She opened the back door and slid inside. The leather seats offered a chill, but it was still warmer than it was outside. This might not be the worst idea she'd ever had. She could handle being in the same car with Chase—she was a grown-ass woman.

As Chase drove, light from the street lamps illuminated the car in broken intervals. His eyes met hers in the rearview mirror. "Are you comfortable?"

Why did she sit behind him? Not that she could hide from those eyes—no matter where she sat. "Yes." She nodded and slipped the camera strap off her shoulder, settling her camera on the empty seat next to her.

Perry huffed. "You never ask me if I'm comfortable."

Chase glared at the windshield. "Probably 'cause I don't care."

"I'm heartbroken, kid. We'll see if Raquel makes you any more of those brownies you like."

Chase grunted. "Like you could stop her."

"Amen to that." Perry laughed. "You bat your pretty lashes at her and she's a goner. I'd get upset, if I didn't know what a dick you are."

Maggie couldn't help but laugh. They fought like they were married. And they kind of were. They were each other's backup, their shadow, for at least eight hours a day. There was an inherent bond with that much together time—that much trust.

It was like her and her team. Or at least what she was trying to build her team into. It was the one thing she missed from her policing days—having someone she could count on. Not that she couldn't count on her team, but something was missing.

Maybe she just needed a little bit more. That one person. That one person who'd make her brownies.

Too bad Raquel was already taken—because she didn't think Chase would make her a brownie—or even know how. But he sure had other talents.

A shiver slithered up her spine. From her thoughts or from the cold? She wasn't sure. She wrapped her arms around her body and huddled in the leather seat.

"Are you cold?" Those eyes found hers in the rearview mirror again. And she felt the weight of them down to her core. His care was her catnip. She really needed to stop acting like a puss...cat—like a cat. No matter how much she wanted to take a nip.

She nodded, and he turned up the heat.

Flores snorted. "You never ask if I'm cold."

"For cripes sake, Flores, are you cold?"

Perry rubbed his hands together. "Nope, I'm keeping warm by the heat of your hostility."

Chase huffed as he parked in front of Maggie's house. "This is it right?" He pulled the keys from the ignition.

She nodded, clicking off her seatbelt. "What are you doing?"

"Walking you to the door." Chase jumped out before Maggie could argue.

*Jackass.* She leaned over the front seat. "Nice to see you again, Perry. Say hi to Raquel." She slid back over, and found her car door open, with an asshat standing in the opening.

"Yeah, uh, Maggie." Perry reached back and rested a hand on her arm. "Next time I see you, can it not be because someone is shooting at you?"

She smiled at him. "I'll sure try."

"Good." He patted her arm, and she angled out of the car.

Chase slammed the door shut, and Maggie didn't

wait for him. "You don't have to walk me to the door." She kept walking, down the sidewalk and up the front steps. She stopped when she got to the door.

"What's wrong?"

"Jessi has my keys."

"Shit."

Yeah, shit. "No, wait." She stepped around him, and tilted the large metal flower pot on the bottom step of the porch. Her shoulder ached as she propped the large thing up and dislodged a small magnetic box from the bottom.

"That had better not be a hide-a-key."

She glared at him in a silent plea to shut up. He ignored her.

"You live in the city of Chicago. You were a cop. Why the hell would you keep a key to your house out here?"

She squinted at the little steel box, barely able make out the numbers on the tiny dials in the dark. 4-3-6. The last three digits of her badge number. "You know you can leave. You don't need to be here." She popped open the box and removed the key inside.

"I don't have to, but I want to. You were shot at by a known drug runner. Who, after today, has become Chicago's most wanted."

"Why is he most wanted?" She used the key to open the first lock on the front door, and used the keypad to enter the security code for the second. Her family were all cops, security was practically hard-wired into their DNA—despite what Chase had just said.

"Lacik had over a key of heroin in that backpack. He's either breaking rank and trying to strike out on his own, or he's moved up in the Vipers. Either way, if he hasn't figured out he's a target for other dealers and the cops, he will. And then he'll really be dangerous."

She opened her front door, walked around the couch and clicked on the light. *Please let him not notice the clothes everywhere.* Or the pillows on the floor. Wardrobe emergency. It happened. "I'm home. I'm safe. Thank you."

"Were you robbed?" Chase went for gun as he followed her into the front room.

"No. Put your gun away." She'd had a date. *Sue her.* She'd wanted to look good. Little had she known the guy would end up barely worth putting on lipstick.

"I don't remember you being such a slob."

"I've changed." And she had changed. After she lost her mother, all the girly touches that made her happy were taken away. The pain in her father's eyes when she wanted to buy her first training bra or any other "female" thing made Maggie just stop asking. Being one of the boys was less painful.

When she lost Chase, she decided to focus on herself. Her wants. Her girly side. She didn't want to be one of the boys anymore. She wanted to be better.

Chase's eyes caught on something, and he stared and gulped.

Maggie looked down to see where his eyes had rested. Her bra. Her red lace bra. And the matching panties, right next to the couch on the floor. *Crap.* She snatched them both from the floor and shoved them between the cushions.

"Sorry." Why did she say that? She had no idea. It wasn't her fault. She had no idea he'd be bullying his way into her house tonight. She might have cleaned up had she known. She definitely would have put her damn underwear away. "What?"

"I just never knew you were a red-underwear kind of girl."

"There's a lot you don't know." Heat crawled up her neck and scorched her ears. This night—this life—couldn't get any more awkward if she tried.

And she wasn't about to start trying.

DAMN ADORABLE. There was no other way to describe the red crawling up her neck as she stuffed her underwear in the couch. Once his mind stopped picturing Maggie in that damn red lacy bra and panty set—and nothing else—Chase walked the one-story ranch. The house was quiet, the closets empty of perps. He checked the windows. All locked. Smart. He couldn't count how many women he'd dated who left their windows open all day—for the fresh air.

He liked fresh air as much as anyone, but leaving the windows open was like a big red sign. *Burglarize Me.* Why stop at leaving the windows open? Why not prop open the front door? Better yet, just put all the furniture and the TV in the front yard. Why make the bad guys work for it at all?

Of course, there still was the problem with the hide-a-key. It might have a combination lock, but it made him nervous.

"Is the house to your liking?" The red had receded from Maggie's cheeks. Tragic.

"A little girly." He ran his finger over the pink lace curtains in the living room. Pink lace. "Were you hiding your girlish tendencies when we were...?"

He didn't say the word together, but he didn't have to. Their being together had been short-lived and was over way too soon for his liking. Not that she'd tried to find him after he'd left. She must have known it was the right thing to do back then.

"When you grow up in a house full of testosterone, the minute you get away, you tend to lash out in girly ways."

"Is this you lashing out?" He pointed to a throw pillow with bright pink tassels and the silhouette of a unicorn stitched into the fabric. "Because this looks like a cry for help."

She picked up the pillow and wrapped her arms around the middle. "That is not a cry for help." Her fingers twirled around the tassels in slow, even strokes.

Her teeth pulled on her bottom lip as she slid her hand up and down the pillow, then returned to fondling the tassels.

Each touch, back and forth, made his heart jump. The damn thing was about to lodge in his throat and choke him. Which didn't take away from the pain—he swore his jeans were shrinking as he stood there watching the show.

Between the bra and that pillow...

Her wearing the bra while stroking the pillow...

*Ugh.* He blew out a breath. That was officially his favorite pillow. Unicorn and all.

Her bottom lip popped out as her teeth showed in a smile. "This pillow was a gift."

He could argue what she was doing to that pillow was a gift, but he didn't think that would go over very well. "It's a nice pillow."

*It's a nice pillow.* He sounded like an idiot.

"Really?" She dropped the thing to the couch, joining with its multitude of pillow friends. How many pillows did one person need? He looked over at the chair in the corner. More stuffed cubes. "Is this a Gremlin thing?"

Her eyebrows arched, looking confused. Join the club.

"Do these things multiply when you put them in water or something?" He lifted a blue one. It might have been blue. It was a weird blue-green thing. "Are you not allowed to feed them after dark—but you did— and they put your cat in the microwave..."

"I don't have a cat."

"Not anymore you don't."

She laughed, a tinkling sound that lightened the air around them. She didn't laugh much, but when she did... "You are such an idiot. My pillows don't multiply, kill cats, or try to smother me in my sleep."

"I hadn't even thought of that." He flicked the blue-green thing to the chair. "Are you sure you should be outnumbered by them?"

"Go." That laugh kept going.

*Go?* He could do this all night. He could play the idiot if it meant she kept that smile on her face.

"I need to go to bed." The red crept back up her neck as she watched his face. It's like she could read his mind. "To sleep. I need to go to bed *alone* to sleep."

*Yeah.* She might've been reading his mind.

"Fine. Call me if you have any problems?"

"Sleeping?"

"Well, I was thinking more like if Lacik shows up or you need backup. But if you need help sleeping or getting your daily allotment of cardio, I would be willing to help."

"How generous."

"I'm a giver." He walked to the front door. He didn't want to leave.

A horn honked out front. Apparently, Flores wanted to leave.

"Thanks, Chase. Goodnight."

"Anytime." And he meant it. Anytime at all. "And Magpie, I'm sorry about breaking your memory card. I just— don't want to see you get hurt, so be careful. Stay out of trouble."

She nodded, but didn't say a word.

"Good night." He walked out of the house and heard the locks click into place behind him.

"About time," Flores said as Chase slid behind the wheel.

"I had to secure the building." Chase started the car and rolled away from the curb, heading toward Flores' house.

"Secure the building or secure Maggie?" Flores didn't live far, and at midnight there wasn't a lot of traffic. Which was good. He had that judgment-police look about him. "Did you find anything?"

"Nope."

"Good."

Chase turned and stopped with the flow of the lights and traffic before pulling down the block where Flores and his wife lived. He'd managed to make it here without a lecture.

Flores opened the car door. "Not gonna walk me in?"

Chase shook his head. He might've rolled his eyes. Flores was acting like a jealous girlfriend. And no matter how much Chase loved the man, they weren't in that type of relationship—not the type he'd like to have with Maggie. Chase would love to see her in those red, lacy underthings. Flores' old wrinkly ass—not so much.

"Be careful."

"What do you mean?"

"Really, kid? She's the chief's daughter. You almost got burned by this before."

He had. He had been burned and his wounds were still cooling. But this was different. "There's nothing to worry about." And that was true. He wasn't going to see Maggie again. There was no reason to.

Flores kept his eyes locked on Chase before nodding his head. "Okay. But stay away from her. I don't want to break in a new partner. I'm used to your brand of asshole."

That was a compliment—in Flores-speak anyway.

"I'm used to your brand of asshole, too."

"Don't get all sappy on me. I'm driving tomorrow. Go home." Flores slammed the door and disappeared around the corner to the back of the house.

Home. Chase had to go home. So why his car started toward Maggie's house, he had no idea. Or why he didn't stop himself.

Again, a mystery. Or maybe it wasn't. All he could picture was lacy red. And all he wanted was her. But Flores was right. If he went to her house, nothing good would come of it.

A red light stopped him a few blocks from Maggie's. He checked the rearview mirror. Nothing. No eyes. He listened, but there was no laughing. He missed her—which was beyond ridiculous and not even worth thinking about.

He liked his job—hell, loved his job. That's why he worked the twelve-hour days and sacrificed dating and —well—plain old living. He'd lost blood, sweat and years to the job. He was proud of where he was, and nothing and no one would ever take that away. No matter how well she fondled a unicorn pillow.

Chase passed the street where he would turn to get to Maggie's. He could do this. He'd stopped himself from doing anything with her before—granted, it hadn't been his choice, but her father could be very persuasive.

He could walk away again. He had to.

# SIX

MAGGIE COULDN'T BELIEVE it had already been two days. Two days since the sushi incident. Actually, it had soared past incident and was officially logged as a debacle. In fact, that's how she ended up here—sitting at her father's dining room table listening to the intervention going on around her and trying not to gouge out her own ears.

A literal intervention. Her brother Kyle and his wife Tatiana sat across from Maggie, on the other side of the table. Her father directed the onslaught from the head. The only ones missing were Kyle and Tatiana's daughter Michaela and Kyle's twin, Kevin, who was in the Middle East driving tanks for the US Army.

She generally didn't covet her brother's overseas life. But right now, she wished she was knee deep in sand, sweating buckets—although, he always complained about the shit coffee. That would be a deal breaker.

"We're worried about you." Kyle puffed out his chest and put his cop-voice on. Normally he was an annoying Cabbage-Patch-stealing pain in the ass. But today he was all interrogation and concern. The interrogation bit came from channeling his inner cop. The concern was probably because Tatiana was here. He tended to attempt human decency in front of her.

"Margaret," her father said. Tag teaming. *Yay.* "This private investigator thing was supposed to be temporary. You were going to come back to the precinct."

Did she mention she hated the name Margaret?

"It's Maggie, and who said this was temporary?"

"Now, Margaret, don't get all upset." Her father could be a patronizing jerk sometimes.

The name she hated and a condescending tone. *Bonus.* Was it so hard to call her Maggie?

"It's just that this little escapade is now affecting our job." Her brother was so damn arrogant when he thought he was putting her in her place.

And *this little escapade*? Now it was an escapade? The vein above her right eye twitched. What did her job, or the overall enjoyment of her life have to do with her father or her brother? "How is my job affecting *your* job?"

"Are you kidding me?" Kyle got up and paced, running a hand through his thinning hair. She had to wonder if he chose the military-style buzz cut because it was harder to tell he was losing his hair, although that was probably giving him too much credit. He was a mountain of stress, always had been. Which was weird, since Kevin was the opposite. He was a mountain of Zen—well, he had been until he entered the service. Now his calls were more stilted, but that wasn't the issue right now.

Kyle kept pacing. "Your run-in with Montgomery and Flores was the icing. You've been the joke of CPD since you left. I can't go a week without someone asking if my washed-out sister got a real job yet."

Maggie grabbed the underside of her chair so she wouldn't launch herself over the table and strangle him. She had a real job and she was damn good at it. They'd know this if they took two minutes to talk to her—and not in an A&E reality show kind of way. Take a minute to ask her about her job, and actually listen to her reply.

But why ask when they could assume?

"Kyle." Tatiana laid her smooth hand on his pasty, white one. Her dark brown hair was pulled back, away from her perfectly symmetrical face. She was gorgeous. Model gorgeous. And what she saw in Maggie's tool of a brother, Maggie had no idea.

"I'm sorry, but she has to know." He was such a jerk, but one look at his bride and he went all mushy. It made him almost likable. "She needs to know how her actions don't just reflect on her, but on us. Dad's the chief, and it makes him look bad that he can't control his own family."

Almost likable, but not quite. "Are you five?" Maggie raised her eyebrows and glared at him. "What, you can't handle a little ribbing from the guys? When did you become such a candy ass?"

"Now, kids, no name-calling."

"He called me a joke and washed out." Wasn't that a name? God, now she was the one who sounded five.

"Enough." Her father leaned back in the chair. He might look laid back, but that was his power position. This was where he took control. "Kyle, you and Tatiana go pick up the pizza."

Power position and time alone. Never a good combination. Not for Maggie. All of a sudden—or maybe not so suddenly—she had this urge to run. Really far and really fast. Too bad her feet wouldn't cooperate.

"We'll be back." Kyle jingled his keys before leading his wife outside. Tatiana managed to give Maggie an *I'm sorry* cringe before the front door shut with a thud.

She really liked Tatiana, but Tatiana's husband— he'd been a pain in the ass since Maggie was six and flushed his GI Joe. In her defense, he'd taken the last cookie, so he deserved a water-logged toy and so much more.

"Margaret, I'm not quite sure what to say to get you to listen." Her father leaned forward, concern arching his brows—well, she'd like to think it was concern but it was probably more like confusion. He acted as if she really was from Venus, and spoke a different language. "You do understand we're worried about you."

"I get that, but there's nothing to worry about."

"You can see how we might find that suspect. You left a good-paying career, with benefits and stability— for what? To sit in that rundown car and tattle on adulterous grown-ups. You were performing a service in the world. You had a purpose."

"I have a purpose." Why did everyone in this family think she had no purpose, no direction? She did everything but show them a prospectus.

Her detective agency was a good idea. It wasn't just about cheating spouses. Maybe at first it was, but once she got the agency's name out there, she'd been getting calls for everything from stolen cars to missing people. And she wasn't tied down by the rules and regulations that held the police back. She didn't have to wait forty-eight hours for missing persons. She didn't have to go through pre-ordained channels. Her and her staff did what was necessary to solve the case. Why did everyone but her family and former co-workers seem to understand?

"What purpose?" Her father scowled.

"I give people peace of mind. I help people find out the truth—just like you do."

"No. You had a job like mine." His voice ticked up a notch. Between that and the red sliding up his neck, he was inches away from full-blown tantrum. "You have the talent and the temperament to be a great cop—no, a great superintendent. But instead of excelling in law enforcement, you chose mediocrity."

"I tried, Dad. I did. I just don't want to sit behind a desk dealing with the bullshit and bureaucrats. I'm not like you."

"Since when?" He stood up, shoving his chair back. "Kyle is not like me. Kevin is not like me. *You* are like me. I've watched you handle the mayor, the city council—there is nothing you couldn't do. You have the potential to go so much further than I ever could. You have nothing and no one holding you back except yourself. Dammit, Margaret."

Every time. The same BS every time. He'd been held back so, somehow, she was ungrateful because she didn't want what he could never have. Tears poked at the back of her eyes. Back in the day, twenty years ago, her father had been next in line for the Superintendent position. But then he'd taken time off to care for Maggie's mom while she battled cancer—and lost. And then he'd had three kids to raise on his own. Not really a surprise that he got passed over. And then when everything settled down and her and her brothers had moved on, grown up, he'd basically had to start from scratch. He had new management to canoodle. But the Mayor wanted an old friend appointed as superintendent, so her father lost out again. How did you live with being the reason your father's dreams went up in smoke?

The real problem was that his definition of success wasn't hers—which was why they had the same conversation every time he tried to push her to make something of her life.

"How the hell can you throw away your future like this? You're inches away from sitting at home eating bonbons all day, and watching soap operas." Her father didn't swear often. He didn't pace, either, but that was exactly what he was doing.

Right this minute, sitting at home with bonbons all day sounded pretty darn good. "I'm not throwing away my future. Dad, I couldn't do it. I didn't make any difference on the force. No matter what I did, the good guys lost and the bad guys won. And every time I tried to change the system, I lost."

"So you gave up? The daughter I raised was not a quitter."

"I'm not quitting, I'm doing what I do best while representing people—not the police force. I make their lives better. It's not just about finding cheating spouses." Aggravation curled in her stomach, twisting with every word she used to defend living her life, her way. "I find lost merchandise. I investigate fraud, and cases the police are too busy to take. I get closure for victims."

"I get closure. You play a game. After everything I've done to get you here, why would you risk it all?"

Why *wouldn't* she risk it all for what she believed in? "I never asked you to do anything."

The pain on his face was unbearable to watch—he was her father, her family, her everything. She wanted to tell him everything would be all right, she'd changed her mind, she could handle sitting at a desk barking orders and puckering up to kiss the asses of the higher-ups for years and years to come. But...she couldn't do it. That wasn't who she was.

"Margaret." He said her name on a sigh while his shoulders hunched and he pinched the bridge of his nose. He was pissed. She got that. So was she, so they matched. The sad thing was, they probably did. He wasn't lying when he said they were very much like alike. Not that she wanted to admit it.

She took a deep breath. "Maggie."

"*Maggie*, please be reasonable."

"Dad, I can't go back—"

The front door flew open. Her brother came in carrying an extra-large pizza box, followed by Tatiana carrying a salad. "Dinner is served."

"We'll talk about this later." Her father walked into the kitchen. His words probably weren't meant to be a threat, but somehow they felt like one.

She didn't want to talk about it anymore. She wanted her father to accept her choices. Trust her. She had a good thing going.

He just needed to see it.

## SEVEN

"WHERE THE HELL WOULD HE GO?" Chase sat at his desk in the center of the precinct and leaned back in his chair. He and Flores had called in every favor and reached out to every snitch, but no one had seen Lacik in two weeks. Not since the sushi joint disaster.

Not since Chase had seen Maggie—the only part of that night that hadn't been a disaster. Not that he was thinking about Maggie and not seeing her or anything. That would be stupid. He was keeping his distance, so naturally, he hadn't seen her.

Of course, he wasn't looking for Maggie. He *was* looking for Lacik. Every rock he overturned had been annoyingly Lacik-free. The little shit was hiding, and doing a damn good job of it.

They'd sat on the girlfriend's house, but nothing. Either she didn't like being a human shield and had dumped his ass, or he was long gone. Or maybe both.

"If I knew where he was, do you think I'd be sitting

here listening to you whine?" Flores peeled a wedge from the orange on his desk. It was too damn early to fight about whether or not Chase was actually whining.

Captain Taye stepped out of the main conference room. "Meeting time. We need to talk." Today her hair was drawn tightly back from her face, making her scowl more obvious. She waved her hand once—motioning for the detectives in the room to follow. She only needed to do it once and they all came running like addicts to crack. She might be short, but her voice was loud and she could be scary as shit.

Inside the conference room, the Chief and the Medical Examiner sat at opposite ends of the long table.

Chase hadn't spent a lot of time with Chief Lane, not since the old man made Chief. Now he'd seen the man three times in two weeks. Not necessarily a good thing. The chief getting in everyone's business meant one of two things: he was suddenly micro-managing the shit out of the twenty-fourth ward, or he was pissed that Lacik took a shot at his daughter.

Chase could admit he was pretty unhappy with that little fact as well, which was why he'd tipped over all those rocks. He had to get that asshole off the street.

Chase and Flores both snagged one of the crappy metal chairs with the ratty brown fabric seats around the large metal conference table. The room itself wasn't bad, maybe a bit old. But that pretty much described the whole building. When all the seats were filled, the rest of the detectives leaned against the painted-shut windows lining the far wall

"Doctor Maelstrom, what brings you across town?" Chase had worked with the man off and on for years. Mostly on. Chase's DOA's tended to end up in the doctor's care on the other side of town.

The Medical Examiner sat at the head of the table, the fluorescent lights sparkling off his bald head as he adjusted his glasses. "It's very bad. Very bad."

Well, that didn't sound good. Bad repeated twice was usually doubly bad. And when the ME talked about bad shit, it usually meant people were dying or they were going to die.

Captain Taye gave the room full of detectives an evil glare. It was her "no bullshit" glare. The one saved for her staff and her toddler grandchildren. "Doctor, let's get this started. Can you repeat what you told us?"

Maelstrom moved folders from one side of the table to the other, looking for something, pushing one side of his slightly crooked glasses to even them out. He picked out one folder and opened it up, turning a page of graphs around so the detectives lining both sides of the table could see the numbers.

"I know it's not normal for us to come to the precinct, but we thought you might want to know about this. We've been seeing an uptick in heroin overdoses—namely, deaths from a combination of heroin and fentanyl."

"Hasn't this been an issue for a few years?" Chase had found his share of users DOA after they played with that combination. It was an ugly way to go. And from the graphs, it was getting worse.

"Yes, but this is new." The doctor ran a hand over

his head. "They're synthesizing a new combination—one that's more fentanyl than heroin."

"Sounds addictive." Chase hadn't meant to say that out loud, but the idea of a more addictive combination on the streets scared him shitless. More deaths—more lives ruined.

"Oh, yes. Yes, addictive." Maelstrom poked the bridge of his glasses. "But what's worse is that it's easier to overdose. It takes a lot less to be lethal."

"Someone has to be putting it on the streets. Where's the drug coming from?" Flores obviously understood the ramifications of this as well. No one wanted these drugs on the street.

"Oh, I don't—I don't know who's putting it on the streets. All I can say is we've found a condensed population here on the West Side, focused on..." The doctor sifted and moved the file folders again. He found another one and pulled out a stack of pages. "...the twenty-fourth ward. I know there was a large bust a couple weeks ago that passed presumptive tests for a controlled substance, so I suggest that you run more definitive testing."

"We sent it off already." Chase was glad they'd written it up and sent it for processing as fast as they did. This was a disaster.

"Good. Good. I believe the lab already has a calibration curve from previous samples, so make sure they use that." The ME's eyes sparked, like they were discussing a recipe. "I'm curious to see if this is the same formulation."

Chase was not going to tell the crime lab how to do their job. It didn't matter how curious the doctor was.

A more deadly drug. Like they needed that out there. Just the idea had some guys in the room joking around and some had gone quiet—but all of them were probably trying to figure out if their caseload would be affected by this new information.

And Chase's case might be in the center of all this crap. Not surprising. Lacik and the Vipers liked to peddle the latest and greatest.

"All right, guys, meeting's over. Get back to work." The captain nodded to Chase and Flores. "I'll get with Forensics and check the status. If they're not already processed, we'll make sure the drugs from Lacik get fast-tracked." Captain Taye hit a few buttons on her cell phone as she left the room.

Except for Flores, the other detectives filed out the door, leaving silence behind as they went. Chase stood up. "Thank you, Doctor."

"Yes, yes. Thank you for your time." Doctor Maelstrom collected all the paperwork and shoved it into the folders. "What I don't know is where they're getting the fentanyl. That's the real question."

"They find a way." Chase knew that for a fact. If there was a new high, a better high, people always found it.

"Well, I guess they do." The doctor picked up his stack of paperwork and adjusted the side of his glasses. "It's just a shame."

"Yes it is."

The doctor scurried out of the room as the captain

came back. "The test results are in. They're going to email me the full report today. But from what they said, we might need to rethink this case."

"Rethink?" Chase sighed. Rethinking never meant good things. It was like when someone told you, it's not you it's me. All bad.

"The drugs you confiscated are a weird combination of fentanyl and heroin. It's cut with baby formula, but there's a higher concentration of fentanyl than usual. If this had hit the streets, we'd have an epidemic on our hands."

Chief Lane rubbed his temples with his thumb and index finger. "What type of epidemic?"

Yeah. Even the thought of a fentanyl epidemic was giving the chief a headache. At least Chase assumed that's what it was, because he was feeling the start of a rager behind his eyes, too.

Taye shook her head. "According to the lab guys, the makeup of this batch is off—too much fentanyl for a single dose. If they split the bottle into two hits, they might be okay, but how many addicts think that way?"

"Even Lacik has to know that killing your customers is bad for business." Chase couldn't wrap his head around it. What kind of businessman kills the hand that pays you?

The captain sat back down next to the chief. "Maybe he doesn't know what he's got there."

Chase twisted his neck, relieving the tension that snapped and popped. "We need to find Lacik. Make sure he's not making any more of this crap."

The chief nodded. "The sooner the better."

"Where do we start?" Flores huffed, pushing back from the table.

"He's getting that fentanyl from somewhere," Chase said. "We find the fentanyl. We find Lacik."

Flores looked thoughtful. "What about the girlfriend? She's a nurse over at Saint Michael."

Chief Lane stood up. "Go down to the hospital and check it out. If she is stealing fentanyl, their inventory should be off." He paused. "Chase, can I talk to you for a minute?"

Chase nodded as Flores and the captain walked out into the hall—leaving him alone with the chief and wondering what in the hell he'd done wrong. Chase had flirted with Chief Lane's daughter, but there was no way in hell the chief had seen that. Of course, Chase thought the same thing last time, and Lane had somehow found out about their kiss.

The man was psychic or some shit.

The chief shut the door. "I'm recommending that you be sent to Staff and Command next month. I think it's time. The Lieutenant of Detectives put in his papers. He's retiring at the end of the year. I'm going to need someone I can trust in that position."

Chase's heart thudded to a stop. Too bad he wasn't psychic. If he was, he'd have brought the defibrillator.

"Are you interested?"

*Interested?* Was he kidding? Apparently, the chief wasn't psychic either. If he was, the man wouldn't be asking the question. This was everything Chase had been working for. It made the long nights, early mornings, and lack of social life worth it. "Yes, sir. I am."

"You've done well, son. You've been instrumental in ensuring this precinct adheres to the mandates." He shook Chase's hand. "Congratulations."

Pride about burst out of Chase's ears. All he wanted to do was tell someone. Okay, not someone, Maggie. Where that urge came from—he had no idea. "Thank you, sir."

The chief let go and headed toward the door. Turned around. "One more thing. I read the file. I know my daughter is following this nurse." The chief shook his head. "I need you to keep me posted. If this is going to turn more dangerous than it already is, I need to know."

"Of course, sir." Chase nodded. He had no problem keeping him posted. Maggie chasing that nurse was something he'd planned on addressing as soon as possible. Of course, that meant he'd have to see her.

Seeing her never ended well—or started well. Hell, everything in between usually went to shit, too. But the feeling of her skin on his—of her lips. That kiss was so long ago, yet he couldn't seem to think about anything else.

He wanted to do it again—see if it was as good as he remembered or if he'd built it up in his head. He had a feeling he hadn't built it up, which was scary as hell, the way a huge roller coaster was scary—and made you get on line one more time. He'd get on Maggie's line anytime.

Either way, after visiting Lacik's girlfriend at St. Michael he was going to find out.

"So you haven't heard from him at all?" Jessi leaned over the center console like Maggie had some hot gossip to drop.

Maggie had no gossip—nothing TMZ-worthy anyway. "No, and it doesn't matter." Not a lie. It didn't matter. She and Chase happened to cross paths while working two separate cases. It was barely a blip.

No reason to tell Jessi, who'd tell Maggie's best friends-slash-partners, Danni and Leti. They'd freak out. Which was understandable. They'd both been there when Maggie had fallen apart.

And it had been ugly tears—sad—and just to the right side of pathetic.

"It does matter." Jessi just wouldn't let it die.

And it really didn't. After the sushi tsunami, Maggie hadn't heard from him. Not once. Which was probably for the best. Did she mention the history of ugly crying and being pathetic...?

Maggie concentrated on watching Jillian's house. They were on stakeout duty again, although it wasn't producing a hell of a lot. Jillian's boyfriend was back in Chicago, and Lacik was keeping his distance. Maggie hadn't seen the two of them together since the sushi place over two and a half weeks ago. Which sucked.

The footage they'd shot on the phone turned out fuzzy and useless. Her camera had a brand new— empty—memory card. They had nothing. Nothing but their word. And although Maggie's word would probably be enough for the client, it wasn't to Maggie. She wanted to offer proof, something tangible so he could make a decision about how he would proceed with the relationship. This was a big deal. These types of things ruined lives, and she refused to do so on hearsay.

Music played. Click. Music stopped. Click. Music played. Play. Stop. Play. Stop. Jessi fiddled with the radio.

"What are you doing?" Maggie wasn't gritting her teeth. Much.

"Finding something to listen to." Jessi clicked on a station and a grin spread over her face. "Now this is epic. Do we have to sit out here all day?"

"No. We just need to put the tracker in her purse." Maggie checked to make sure she had the small round black box. She'd charged the thing last night after Leti retrieved it from the last adulterer. They always retrieved the little buggers after a case.

"Why didn't we just put one of these on her from the beginning?" Jessi rolled the tracker between her fingers. It looked innocuous—about the size of an Oreo —and cheap. It wasn't.

"All of the trackers were in use."

"Can't we get some more?"

"If you have an extra two hundred dollars laying around, sure, we'll buy another one."

"This thing is two hundred dollars? I'm in the wrong business." Jessi dropped the faux cookie into Maggie's palm.

"You and me both." Maggie slid the powerful magnet off the back. Normally, this tracker would go on a car, but since Jillian didn't own a car, they needed to get this on her without her noticing. Her purse was the best option. Jillian carried it wherever she went, and the bag was large enough for this thing to get lost in the bottomless pit.

The problem was getting the device into the purse. Maggie was an average pick-pocket—and no, it was part of her training, not a hobby—there was no way she wanted to get caught.

"Who's that?" Jessi pointed toward Jillian's house. A man—more like a teen with a mustache—approached her front door and rang the bell. Then he knocked. His baggy pants dragged on the ground as his feet shuffled back and forth. His head never stopped moving. Neither did his feet.

He knocked again, this time with what appeared to be more force. Impatient much? "He's in a hurry."

Jessi turned down the radio. "Is Jillian home? I swore she didn't leave."

"I didn't see her leave. Why isn't she answering?" Maggie found her cell phone and snapped a few quick pictures. "Get the camera."

Before Jessi did anything, the front door flew open and Jillian stood there in her bathrobe. Her fists immediately planted on her hips, and the decibel level as she yelled at the man went to earsplitting right away. Mustache guy pushed her back into the house and slammed the door.

*Shit.*

Jessi sat back, eyes wide. "That didn't look friendly." *Way to voice the obvious, Jessi.*

Maggie shoved her phone in her pocket. "Nope."

"What do we do?" Jessi glanced at the house and back to Maggie. "We can't leave her alone with some crazy guy, can we?"

"We're Jane Goodall, remember?"

"Fuck Jane Goodall." Jessi's head whipped around at a crash from inside Jillian's house.

*Shit.*

"No, we can't." Maggie slipped her hand behind the seat and palmed her Glock. She hated going in alone, but she didn't have a choice. Jessi was right. Maggie couldn't sit in the car and let Jillian get hurt —or worse.

"Do you have one of those for me?" Jessi asked, and swallowed hard.

Maggie slid out the clip, just making sure. Full. "Do you have a FOID card?"

"Do I need one?"

"If you want to carry anything stronger than a Nerf gun, yes. Stay here. Call the cops." Maggie slipped handcuffs in her pocket before jumping out the car. Another crash came from the house, followed by a scream.

Maggie ran across the street and flew up the stairs to the front porch.

"...I don't know... I don't know..." a woman's muffled voice said.

"Where is the bag?" That voice was male and loud.

Maggie leaned over the handrail to see inside the front window. Jillian was on the floor, a guy bent over until his face was inches from hers, with a fireplace poker in his hand. "Where is it?" he snarled. When all

Jillian did was whimper, he slammed the poker across her back.

Maggie tested the front door knob, slowly twisting it open. She put her ear to the door and listened.

"I'm not asking again." His voice shook and rumbled in the otherwise quiet house.

Scraping, off to the right. The jingle of metal against glassware, followed by a huge tinkling crash. "I swear, I don't know," Jillian sobbed.

"Useless bitch!"

Maggie pushed open the front door. "Stop pol—ease. Don't move." She aimed the gun at the angry little man who was hitting Jillian's face with one fist. Jillian was curled in a ball. She wasn't fighting back. She wasn't moving. Blood streamed down her face.

"Step away from her," Maggie ordered.

"Who the fuck are you?" The guy dropped the fire-place poker, and the metal clanged as he raised his arms above his head, turning a little to face her. She finally got a good look at him. Dark greasy hair matched the creepy mustache. But that wasn't what drew her atten-tion. It was the eyes. Shark eyes.

But she didn't have time to analyze what that really meant. "Your worst nightmare, now back the fuck up."

"You a cop?"

She moved closer. "It doesn't matter. Just shut up and stay back." She needed to get him in cuffs and pat him down, because anything could happen before she had the scene locked down. She'd learned a lot in over ten years on the force, and cuffing the perp was rule number one.

Keeping the gun leveled at creepy-stache, Maggie shuffled left to right, side-stepping the Jillian ball until she stood in front of him. "Turn around." She reached in her pocket for the handcuffs, and they snagged on her jacket. She pulled harder, and heard the rip. Ugh—her favorite jacket. Another tug, and the cuffs came free, accompanied by a thud by her feet.

Damn phone. She couldn't reach her fallen comrade. Not yet. Secure the scene.

"Turn. Around," she barked at the gaping bad guy. He didn't seem like Mensa material, but this was pretty bad.

A hand snaked around her ankle. "Help me." Jillian yanked on Maggie's leg, putting her off balance at the same time Creepy-stache shoved at Maggie's chest.

No way was she going down. She lunged, grabbing his long greasy hair.

He yelped when she twisted, trying to keep hold of him, and something hard rammed into her stomach. She let go on reflex, and he stumbled back a step, going down on one knee before turning and running for the door.

Off. Kilter. Jillian's hand stayed adhered to her ankle, and Maggie lurched, hampered by the Glock stuck in her right hand. There was no way she'd drop the damn thing—she was not giving Creepy a weapon. Her free hand hit the wall and she kept herself upright. Somehow.

Sirens clanged in the distance. Jessi had called the cops while Maggie played a human Weeble. Thank goodness.

"Jillian, it's okay. You can let go."

Jillian stared up at Maggie through puffy eyes, her blood-soaked five-fingered vise still locked on Maggie's jeans. She needed help, and quick.

"The police are coming. You're safe. Relax."

After a second, Jillian's head drooped, and the white knuckles at Maggie's ankle released. But somehow Maggie couldn't move. She was neck-deep in the middle of another crime scene, and the bad guy got away. Again.

Chase was going to be pissed.

## EIGHT

CHASE WALKED the long corridor of Saint Michael hospital. The smell of antiseptic and bleach stalked him with every squeaking step. The fluorescent lights bled the oxygen from the air.

God, he hated hospitals. He'd spent so many days and nights watching his grandmother deteriorate. He'd smelled the odors and breathed the unbreathable air, all while watching the cancer eat away at the only constant in his life.

Not a good time. Sixteen years old and watching his whole world disappear to nothing. And every sight and sound in this place made him relive it.

Followed by Flores, Chase walked under the sign for the surgical center and up to the moon-shaped reception desk. A man sat at the desk with a phone in one hand and a pen waving in the other. "...Of course, Mrs. Waverly, your husband can eat whatever he wants after the procedure, it's just before he has to stick to the diet—no, Mrs. Waverly…"

Chase tuned him out. He'd worked with his share of Mrs. Waverlys in his day to know this conversation would keep repeating.

Flores shook his head as he angled himself into a chair against the wall. Yeah, they were going to be here awhile. A woman stepped behind the counter and aimed a high-powered smile at Chase. "Have you been helped?"

"Not yet. We have a meeting with the Director of Pharmacy."

"You a patient?" She leaned against the counter and licked her cherry lips. Ran a hand through long blonde hair as her eyes slid down his body. She was his type. All blonde and gorgeous, but for some reason he wasn't in the mood to flirt. Not with her.

Now, another blonde who was a severe pain in his ass—yeah, he could go for some serious flirting…and other things. Not that that would ever happen. He couldn't let it.

"No, Chicago PD." He flipped open his wallet and showed her his badge. "Detectives Montgomery and Flores. She should be expecting us."

She cringed, picking up the phone. "I'll call." She turned her back and spoke into the receiver. "Doctor Lee, there's a cop here for you." The way she snarled cop told Chase she didn't like his kind much.

Luck of the draw. Sometimes you got the badge-bunnies who chased anything with a gun. And sometimes you got the cop-haters who wanted to chase you with a gun. He preferred the ones in between.

"Detectives." A pregnant woman waddled up to the counter and held out her hand to shake. "I'm Doctor Debra Lee. I understand you're here for a quick tour of our pharmaceutical management. Before we can perform any tour, I need to see your ID's."

Chase pulled out his wallet and flipped open the worn leather. She stared at the badge and then the picture. She nodded.

She took Flores' wallet and looked from his ID to his face. His picture had been taken a while ago, before the gray hair. She squinted at the picture again before she handed back the wallet. "I'm sorry, but we have to be careful, Detectives. Please follow me." Dr. Lee appeared to be walking for two. Not that Chase would say that. He'd learned long ago to never comment on or question a seemingly-pregnant woman—unless you positively knew they were expecting.

She paused at a steel door. "I'm sorry. I'm eight months pregnant, so I'm not walking as fast as I once did."

The doctor waved a card at a security pad, and when the door popped open, Chase and Flores followed her into a small, square room behind the nurses' desk. It wasn't huge, but it was big enough to allow the pharmacist, Chase, and Flores to stand inside comfortably. A computer monitor sat on top of a large white cabinet with multiple drawers. There was a narrow refrigerator with glass doors to the right of it, and another cabinet with more metal drawers on the left.

"What is this?" Flores looked around the room. "Where's the pharmacy?"

Good question. Chase looked around as well. He'd been in his share of hospitals because of his grandma and then because of the job. He'd never been behind the scenes, though. This wasn't exactly what he had in mind when he thought *pharmacy*.

"This is the secure medstation that the nurses use to access all medication. It's more efficient and secure than a pharmacy. No one can access this machine without an ID, and every transaction is saved in a database identifying what medications were taken and when."

"Can they get fentanyl from here?"

"Yes. Everything."

"We have reason to believe that a hospital employee has been taking fentanyl for personal use. Could that happen with this machine?"

"Anything can happen, but we have processes to ensure it doesn't." The doctor rested her hand on her belly and shook her head. "Although, shorting patients is one of the hazards we combat daily."

"This is more than shorting patients," Chase said. "They would have needed to steal large quantities. Multiple vials."

"Let me show you how the system works." Dr. Lee brought up a menu on the computer monitor and typed in a code. "It would take months to steal that much without us noticing. This room is always under surveillance." After selecting more options on the screen, a lock clicked on one of the drawers to the left. She opened the drawer, revealing multiple partitions, each with a locked cover. One of the covers popped open. "This is the CUBIE system, which restricts access to one medication at a time. This CUBIE holds fentanyl." She tapped one of the vials lining the small drawer.

"Couldn't someone steal two vials?" Flores leaned over.

The doctor shrugged. "Perhaps, but not without the cameras seeing. And these vials are inventoried weekly. We haven't had any shortages in years."

Chase asked, "After a nurse selects the medication and the drawer opens, what do they do?"

"They go to their patient."

He selected one vial from the tray and read the side. "One patient needs two milliliters of this stuff?"

"No. That's way too much for any patient." She held out her hand, staring pointedly at the vial in his hand. She didn't look happy. Apparently, she didn't like him playing with her stuff—which Chase couldn't really fault her for. They were here to see if this stuff could have wandered out the door. The ease with which he got his hands on said stuff showed it could be done.

He dropped the vial in her hand and she replaced it before closing the drawer. "What would a nurse do with any extra?"

"They waste it."

"Waste?" He really hoped that was just an expression.

"Basically, they draw the remaining contents of the vial into a syringe and dispose of it in a locked waste receptacle. The receptacles are attached to the wall, and can only be accessed by the disposal service. Once the nurse wastes the medication, they sign into the machine and verify that the overage was wasted. A second nurse must vouch for all wasted medication."

This wasn't sounding as easy as he thought. Between the cameras and computer, how would she get the medication out the door? "So, each vial of Fentanyl would have two nurses monitoring it? It's dispensed, and brought right back for wasting?"

Dr. Lee hesitated for a second. "Not necessarily. In a perfect world, yes. In the real world, the nurse takes the vial and administers the dose. Afterward, she'd probably have a laundry list of things she had to do, so she might hold onto that vial for an hour or two. And then there's the witness—you can't waste until you have a witness on hand because they both have to enter their ID into the system before verifying the medication was wasted."

Chase cocked his head. "So what's to stop someone from replacing the medication in the vial with water before wasting it?"

"It's a risk," Dr. Lee said, nodding. "As long as there's something to waste, the witness and the cameras won't know the difference. Pills tend to be easier to verify, since they're stamped or embossed. But with a clear liquid, there's no way to tell."

After exchanging a look with Flores, who shrugged, Chase said, "Well, thank you for your time."

"Please contact me if you have any other questions." Dr. Lee handed him a card as they left the wing and headed for the elevators.

Once they made it out the revolving lobby door and into the sun, Flores said, "So, it would seem a go-getting drug dealer could easily stockpile unused fentanyl." It was the simplest explanation.

Chase nodded, but before he could say anything, the phone in his pocket chimed. "Montgomery."

"Sir, this is Officer Poole. I'm at Jillian Hendricks house. I know you were working on the case with Lacik and all."

He didn't say anything. Poole was nice—just off probation—and the whole crush thing was sweet. But he could never start a relationship with her—no matter how much she wanted it and how easy it could be. If anything, he'd learned a lot from being with Maggie. Don't shit where you eat.

"She's been beaten."

"Who's been beaten?" He really should pay attention.

"Jillian Hendricks."

Chase looked over at Flores. "The nurse was beaten." Given that information, the simple explanation was looking pretty damn good right about now.

"We have a witness," Poole added. "A PI was posted outside the house."

Chase's heart skipped a beat. Maggie. "Is she okay?"

"I'm not sure. Lieutenant told me to give you a call since this could be related to a case you're working." Poole gave a breathy laugh. "Well, I volunteered to call."

"Thanks." Chase disconnected the call. "We have to get to the nurse's house." He ran toward his car, chirping the doors open. "Maggie's there."

Flores whipped open the passenger door. "Son of a bitch."

Chase couldn't agree more.

---

CHASE WHIPPED OVER POTHOLES, ignored red lights, and basically stomped the vertical pedal on the right into the floor of his car. The removable cherries on the roof flashed.

"Shouldn't you slow down?" Flores asked at one point.

Chase grunted. At least he thought he did. Dumb questions didn't get answered. He parked on the block of nurse's house in record time. Well, he couldn't actually get his car down the block, so he parked at the corner. Squad cars and ambulances lined the street. Multiple ambulances.

Multiple. Ambulances. One of them drove away with their lights spinning, the wail of the siren echoing between the houses. Someone was probably inside. *Maggie.*

Chase jumped out of the car, barely taking time to

pull his keys from the ignition before his feet hit the ground.

"Montgomery?"

Chase heard Flores, but he didn't have time to listen to whatever he had to say. He had to find Maggie.

"Excuse me?" He leaned into the back of the first ambulance, flashing his badge. "Who's in this bus?"

"We're in the middle of stabilizing her." The EMT didn't look up. He ran the tube attached to the woman over a hook and checked a clipboard. Hanging a tube. Eyeballing a clipboard. Were they really too busy to answer a question?

He'd said "her" though. Her. Her. It was a woman. He strained his neck and tried to see past the blankets and tubes and wires. Her hair was covered in blood, and too hard to see the color. Chase stepped up, and the ambulance shook as he attempted to stand in the small space.

"You can't be in here," the EMT snapped.

"Who is she?" Chase flashed his badge. He might not be allowed back there, but what were they going to do, call the cops? All the guy had to do was answer a question.

The EMT huffed. "Jillian Hendricks."

"Who was on the ambulance that just left?"

"I don't know, I was handling my job here." EMT guy glared scalpels at Chase. "Now get down."

Chase wanted to have words, maybe explain how they were all on the same side, but he didn't have time. If this wasn't Maggie, where was she? Jillian looked awful. *Please, Maggie, be all right.*

There were no more ambulances to check. That might be a good thing. He ran through the obstacle course of police in front of Jillian's house, and showed his badge to the cops before ducking under the police tape and walking inside.

Evidence markers were everywhere, and a photographer was taking pictures of a pool of blood staining the hardwood. Glass and broken pottery covered the floor. It looked like a hurricane had hit. A female cop walked through with bagged blood-covered clothing and gym shoes—as well as a few other bags. But the shoes were what caught his eye. They looked like the same ones Maggie had on the other day in the alley.

"Hey, where's the owner of those shoes? The witness?"

"She did more than witness it. She nabbed a handful of the perp's hair." The cop held up a bag. Either this guy was hairy like an ape or Maggie had scalped the guy bald.

Pride in her evidence-collecting ability warred with concern—his need to see her. "Where is she?"

"Kitchen." The cop looked at the bag with awe as she tucked the sneaker-filled one under her arm and hooked a thumb over her shoulder.

He walked—although he really wanted to run— through the doorway into the quiet kitchen.

Maggie sat at a small kitchen table wearing light pink scrubs, a V-neck shirt and matching cotton pants. Not exactly the jeans and gym shoes she normally wore. Not even the size she normally wore. The only explanation for the Pepto-Dismal outfit engulfing her was that her clothes were the blood-stained ones in the evidence bag.

Her sushi friend sat next to her, in jeans and a tee, holding her hand. Nothing seemed to be wrong with her outfit. Which meant Maggie came in here alone—*imagine that.*

He wanted to yell. She should have known better. She shouldn't be putting herself in danger. So many words crowded his throat as his eyes swept over her body. No blood. The blood on her clothes hadn't been hers.

Not one word hit the air as he stepped up to Maggie and dragged her into his arms. She was okay. He took a deep breath as her body lined up with his. They always did seem to fit together perfectly. "Are you okay?"

She felt okay to him. She felt solid in his arms. Her heart pounded against his chest, deep and fast. Although that could be him—she'd scared the shit out of him.

"Yeah, I'm fine." She rested her head on his shoulder and the familiar scent of berries washed over him. She must bathe in them or something. Not that he was complaining. He loved the way she smelled. He loved that she wasn't hurt.

He exhaled as his muscles relaxed. She was okay. He'd never been so glad to see someone—to smell someone—in his life.

"Did he hurt you, Magpie?" he whispered, his hand roaming down her back and up her bare arm, more caress than examination. Her skin pebbled. Soft skin. No injuries.

"No." The word was breathy, sexy. Like the woman saying it.

His hand kept searching. Up her middle back. Down her side. Feeling for anything wrong. Enjoying everything right. His hand slid lower.

His body reacted as his fingers found only silky skin and warm willing woman beneath his palm. And she seemed willing. Her arms locked him close. Her hips melded to his. Her heart jackhammered in her chest. Her tongue slid out and drifted along her lower lip.

Every part of him throbbed to be with every part of her. Her hips. Her heart. Her lips. He wanted them all. He wanted her. He brought her into him. His mouth so close to hers—he could practically taste her. He could almost feel her.

Somebody cleared their throat and Maggie's eyes popped open. She pulled away—far away—like, he couldn't touch her any longer, far away. In other words, she might as well have moved to the moon, she was so damn far away. Sushi-friend had a huge grin on her face.

Dammit. He'd forgot about sushi-friend.

Jessi held out her hand. "I'm Maggie's employee-slash-friend, Jessi. It's so nice to finally meet you. I've heard so much about you."

The cold creeping into his bones from Maggie disappearing suddenly didn't feel all that bad. "She talks about me, huh?" He shook Jessi's hand and smiled. "What does she say?"

"What an arrogant pain in the ass you are," Maggie said, smirking, but he could tell she'd felt something when she was wrapped around him.

Chase gave her a smirk right back. "Well, I'm glad she hasn't embellished."

"I don't have to. You take asshole to all new levels."

"Funny, I was saying that same thing last week," Flores said as he walked into the kitchen and wrapped Maggie in a quick hug. "You okay?"

"I'm fine." Her loaned flip flops smacked against her feet as she walked the two steps back to the chair at the table and sat down.

"We really have to stop meeting like this." Flores sat next to her and reached for his notepad.

Maggie laughed, that deep tingling laugh that lit up the room. "I agree. We need to meet under more pleasant circumstances."

Chase could admit he was a bit jealous. He thought —more like hoped—that laugh was reserved for him. Chase went around the other side of Maggie, past Jessi, pulled out the chair and sat down across from her.

"So, how did you end up here tonight?" Flores asked.

"Jessi and I were sitting on Jillian's house waiting for Lacik, since we no longer have any usable photos." She glared at Chase. She'd be off this case if he had just let her keep the pictures from the restaurant. He was an idiot.

"Did you see Lacik?" Flores prompted.

"No. He hasn't been here in a while." Since the sushi joint. Maggie didn't have to say it. He and Flores were having the same issue finding Lacik.

She turned her attention to her hands, resting on the table. Something seemed off in her voice. He couldn't pinpoint what.

"This young guy, with a mustache, came to the door. Jillian yelled at him but he forced himself in. I couldn't sit by and let him kill her—or whatever his plans were." She shook her head, like she was shaking off unpleasant thoughts. "No. I couldn't sit on the side-lines and let a woman get abused. I had to go in."

Flores nodded. "So, you went in. Did you call for backup?"

"I don't really have backup." Maggie laughed. Laughed like walking into this trap alone was some-thing to joke about. "But I have a fantastic apprentice who called the cops, while I came inside and dealt with creepy-stache."

"Apprentice?" Chase looked over to Jessi, who was smiling as she watched Maggie. The way these two watched out for each other was rather fantastic. He liked she had someone like Jessi in her corner.

Flores looked up from his notebook. "Creepy-stache?"

"Young guy, maybe late teens, with long black hair in a ponytail and a black mustache. He looked like the villain who was going to tie Jillian to the train tracks. Weird. But worst of all, he had shark eyes." Her face went pale as her eyes unfocused. Chase was betting her body was here but her thoughts were back in the living room. The guy she was talking about was way past creepy from what he could tell. He'd seen eyes like that before. Hollow. No humanity. It wasn't something you could forget.

"I know what you mean." Flores kept writing. Thank God he was here; Chase didn't think he could distance himself in this situation. He was having a hard time concentrating on what should come next. Flores looked up. "Do you remember anything else about him?"

"No. I had my gun on him, and he shoved me. I pulled out a handful of his hair."

Her gun was drawn and this guy was not only close enough to touch her, but close enough that she was able to grab his hair. Seriously? "Why did you let him get so close?" He might have said that out loud and might have said it with a little more volume than he intended.

The look on her face told him all of that, and that he was an ass. She didn't even have to say it.

Flores coughed. "I think what my partner means to say is, that it's impressive you kept your gun out of his hands."

Maggie's eyes narrowed. "I was a police officer for ten years. I think I can handle my weapon."

Wise man that he was, Flores stuck to the details. "So, you grabbed his hair and he ran away."

Maggie let out a sigh crossed with a growl. "Basically, I had Jillian attached to my leg and holding on for dear life. I couldn't go anywhere. All I could do was hold on to my piece and try to keep him in the building.

His hair was closest, so I held on tight. But he still got away. That's it."

That's it? He doubted. Somehow it felt like she was leaving something out. Maybe because she always left something out. Chase needed to know everything if he was going to get this guy. And he was going to get him. "Are you sure that's it?"

"Are you sure you need to be here?" Her voice had returned to its natural strength. The fear was gone.

"Yep. I like it here." He wasn't going anywhere anytime soon. She could try her worst, but he wasn't going to let this guy get another shot.

"You did everything by the book, kid," Flores said, a proud look on his face, "but sometimes the book doesn't account for half-crazed women grabbing your ankles and screaming."

Maggie dropped her eyes to the table, smiling at the same time red bloomed on her cheeks. Compliments always seemed to bring out a blush. "One would think that would be in the appendix or something."

"One would think." Chase nodded when Maggie looked up into his eyes. Soft hazel with rings of blue. Beautiful. And something else. Maybe the fear was back. Either way, she had to be exhausted.

She ran her hand around the back of her head, scooping her hair up and over her shoulder. "Anything else? I'd really like to get home."

"No. I think we're done." Chase wasn't sure Flores was done, but he didn't care.

"Thanks." She looked up and smiled. Actually smiled. No amount of sadness could dull the way her eyes sparkled with that one movement. She was gorgeous. And with that look, he remembered all the reasons he wanted her.

Flores punched him in the shoulder and gave him a look. A look that said *cut that shit out*. Or maybe it said *we have more questions, why'd you let her go?*

Right now, Chase would be hard-pressed to find someone who cared. Because his gut roiled and his head ached. With that one look from Flores, Chase remembered all the reasons he couldn't have her. Too bad his body hadn't gotten that message, because watching her, listening to her only made him want her more—made him want to hold on and keep her safe.

No matter what looks he was getting from anyone else.

NINE

SOMEONE YELLED "COFFEE" from the front of
the house, and Maggie watched Chase get up from the
table. "I got it." He walked out of the kitchen, leaving
Maggie alone with Perry and Jessi.

The look on his face when he'd walked into the
kitchen almost made it seem like he cared. And the way
he'd held her...? Oh man. There was more of that
concern of his. And what had she done? Rubbed
herself on him like he was covered in catnip.

She was so pathetic.

Chase came back into the kitchen with a tray of
coffees. He tilted the cups, probably to read the names,
before putting them in front of the owner. When he
placed the extra-large black coffee in front of her,
Maggie almost jumped him—right here in front of
everyone. But since she'd already done that once today,
why give everyone a repeat performance?

"Margaret!" Her father's voice was unmistakable as

118

it roared through the tiny house. That was one way to keep her from jumping Chase. Her father was a natural hormone blocker.

Flores got up and went to the doorway, waving her father into the kitchen. What the heck? He didn't even give her time to make a getaway.

"What happened?" First words out of her father's mouth. Not *how are you...* Not *are you hurt...*

"Don't worry, Dad. We're fine. Thanks for asking."

"We?"

"Jessi and I." She nodded to Jessi. Why she was getting Jessi involved, she had no idea.

"Don't you have a son?" Her father aimed the question at Jessi, but there was an undercurrent of judgement toward Maggie. She'd put her employee in danger.

"We're fine, Dad."

"I can see you're fine." He sighed. "What I want to know is why you were here in the first place."

"I was watching Jillian Hendrick's house because her boyfriend has me on retainer."

"I thought you were done with this nonsense —this case."

"Why would I be done?"

"After your run-in with Lacik, I figured you'd be smart enough to recuse yourself from further contact."

"Nope. Me not smart, me like eating food and paying bills." Maggie wanted to be mad, but her father had mentioned her lack of intelligence so many times over the past year, what was one more time? Of course, that didn't stop her from snarky responses and Neanderthal speak.

She *was* only human.

Her father's glare moved from her to Chase to Perry. "How did you let this happen?"

Hello? She said, "*They* didn't let anything happen. *They* weren't here. I was. A woman was in danger. What was I supposed to do—sit outside and let him kill her?"

"Call the police."

"I did. Well, Jessi called the police while I handled things in here. Jillian is alive. I'm okay."

"Where's the perp?"

"He got away."

Silence. He couldn't very well tell her that she should've waited for the cops. Well, he could, but that would be ridiculous. Waiting for the cops might have given the bad guy time to really hurt Jillian, maybe even kill her, and chances are the perp would still have gotten away.

Her father's eyes narrowed. "Where's your gun?"

"On the counter. They wanted to run a residue test to ensure it wasn't fired." She smiled her most sweetest smile. *Can't get me.* "Oh, I forgot. I even got some pictures of the perp." *Take that.*

Maggie stuck her hand in the pocket of her jacket. Shit. She had no jacket. No pocket. The last few seconds of her exchange with creepy-stache rolled through her mind—including the thump of her phone hitting the floor. She'd never picked it up.

Her mind replayed the events—yet again.

After she'd removed Jillian-with-the-kung-fu-grip from her leg, she'd worked on stopping Jillian's bleeding, using a blanket to put pressure on the wound. The phone hadn't been on the floor. She'd talked to Jillian until the ambulance came. The phone wasn't there.

But who could've taken it? There was no one here. Just her and Jillian—and Jillian was way too out of it to five-finger a cell phone.

And then they'd taken Jillian away. The phone still wasn't there. Not underneath her. Not under the shards of glass.

Creepy-stache must have taken her phone before he left. But why? Why was irrelevant. She was so screwed.

"Where's the picture?" Her father looked at her with soft eyes. The glare was gone.

"On my phone."

"Where's your phone?" Chase had that look—that terrified look he'd walked in with. The one that Maggie was probably sporting right about now.

"He took it."

"He took it." Her father's scowl had returned. "Please tell me you locked your phone and all the information."

"Of course I did." Her phone and all of the information was safe. The phone wasn't the issue.

"Good, then the phone can't be tracked back to you."

"What about the card?" Jessi asked—ever so helpfully. Maybe no one would notice.

Her father picked up on that question right away. "What card?"

Jessi looked from Maggie to her father. Something on Maggie's face must have told her to keep her mouth shut, because Jessi leaned back against the chair, lips thinning until they practically disappeared.

"What card?" Her father was never going to let this drop.

The air left Maggie's lungs in a whoosh. "I put a business card in my phone case, so if I lose it they know who to contact."

Her father just stared at her. He didn't say one word. The muscles in his face didn't move. None of his muscles moved. Maybe he was having an aneurism.

After a painfully long moment he said, "So, what you're saying is that the thug who beat this—Jillian— into a coma has your name and address." Her father's face didn't move. It was like he'd gotten a shot of Botox while she wasn't looking. His voice, on the other hand, was low and horror-movie worthy. The calm before the storm. Or with her luck, the calm before the heart attack.

"Give us a minute." Her father looked at Jessi, Chase, and Perry. Only his eyes moved. His face and body remained still. *Crap.*

They all left the room. Maggie wanted to reach out and get them to stay. Surely, he wouldn't kill her if there were witnesses. Right? But they didn't stop. They left her alone with her father.

"What have you done?" he ground out.

"Dad..."

"Don't 'Dad' me, Maggie." *Crap.* He used the right name. He never called her Maggie—well, not without a condescending-smile chaser. "Do you realize what you've done. You have given that thug your name. Your address. He knows exactly where to find you. He knows exactly where to hurt you."

"I know." And she did. It wasn't exactly something she was proud of, but it happened.

"You can't go to your office. You can't go home."

"Why can't I go home?"

"Because the Vipers will find you, Maggie." He father's voice slowly rose to a dull roar. "They'll find you and kill you. Do you understand the assholes you are dealing with?"

"Yes."

"You obviously don't. If you did, you'd have been smart about this and kept your distance."

Did she mention how much she loved when her father questioned her intelligence?

"You're coming home with me." He turned around and started toward the living room.

"To hell I am." She felt the words leave her throat before her mouth could close to prevent them. But she didn't want to go to her dad's house. She didn't want to get sucked into his helicoptering judgmental ways. When she was too close to him, she wasn't herself.

She just wanted to be herself.

"What?"

"Chief." Perry walked into the kitchen, followed by Chase. "Sir, we were just talking, and if you'd like we could get Maggie to a motel. We'd drop her off and sit on the room if you'd like."

Maggie glared at him. Was this a conspiracy? "No. I'm not some child that needs a babysitter."

Her father didn't sneer, but it was close. "Apparently, you do. Come on, Margaret, let's go. My daughter is not staying at a motel."

Maggie kept her butt in the chair. Juvenile? Yes. Necessary to prove she was an adult? Absolutely. "No."

Chase added his two cents. "We can keep her safe." *Et tu Chase?*

"No." She was so tired of fighting them on this.

Her father pinched the bridge of his nose. Apparently, so was he. "Choose. Either you come home with me or you go to a hotel with them."

Great choice. Her bossy father or her bossy—Chase —whatever the hell he was to her.

She took a deep breath. "Fine. I'll stay at a hotel tonight."

"Fine." Her father turned to Chase and Perry. "Use the hotel that has the CPD's account. It has security, and you'll blend in. Make sure the rooms are adjoining." He pulled out his wallet. "Here's what I have on hand, that should cover a two rooms for the night. If you spend any of your own money, I'll pay you back."

"Are you sure?" Perry asked as her father handed over cash. "She's a witness. You could use departmental funds if you wanted."

"No. Not for this." Her father looked her up and down before stepping over to kiss her forehead. "I'm glad you're safe, Margaret."

"Thanks, Dad."

Her father walked out of the kitchen, and she heard him talking to the techs and cops as he left the house, leaving her with her babysitters—exactly what she didn't need. What she really needed was a plan. She'd go to a hotel, but she was perfectly capable of keeping herself safe.

Her car. She'd passed the driving portion of the police academy with one of the best scores. She could probably outrun the cops. Maybe. It was worth a try. "I need my keys."

Chase eyed her like she was dangerous. "I gave Jessi your keys. She's taking your car home."

"What do you mean you gave her my keys?" He gave away her damn keys. "Those are my keys. My car."

"Yes, well, since you've been so quick to give her your keys in the past, I didn't think you'd mind giving them to her today," he said slowly. "That way your car won't sit here all night."

"It wouldn't sit here all night. I'd drive my car to the hotel." She wasn't gritting her teeth. Not really.

"What hotel? You don't know where we're going." He wrenched out his keys and twirled them on his finger. "I'll drive."

She widened her eyes and tried for a smile. "If you tell me which hotel, I can drive there. Myself."

"You could, but why? That would be wasting gas. We're all going to the same place, right? Do you not like trees? I'm trying to be green."

Chase? Green? "I'll give you green. A swift well-positioned kick would make you green all right." She swung her foot and the damn flip-flop fell off. It was so hard to appear bad-ass in oversized flip-flops. Then again, the fact that they'd had clothes and footwear to give her at all was amazing—anything to get rid of the blood-sport outfit. "A good kick would make you green *and* singing soprano."

"Ow." Chase winced. *Bingo.*

"Don't incapacitate my partner." Perry looked a bit green himself.

Maggie couldn't help the laugh that bubbled out. Well, she probably could have, but why bother. "You never let me have any fun." She stuffed her foot back into the flip-flop and walked out of the kitchen.

A night at a hotel. With Chase. Should be interesting.

CHASE PARKED the car in the underground garage, a few blocks from Millennium Park. The flickering lights made the concrete cocoon only slightly less dark than the streets of Chicago. During the day it was overrun with people going in and out. Right now, it was quiet. Empty.

Chase liked it that way. He liked quiet. He'd gotten used to it over the years. He came home to an empty house every night. It was relaxing after dealing with all the BS of the streets.

They left his car, walked to the elevator, and made their way up to ground level.

They were so out of place, Chase and Flores in T-shirts and jeans—Maggie in scrubs with shower shoes. The hotel was all modern luxury, with white walls, huge windows, black counters and pale wood. Thank God the chief was footing the bill; Chase would never be able to afford the smallest room for one night—let alone two adjoining rooms.

After they checked in, they rode the mirror-walled elevator to the twenty-seventh floor. Chase stepped out to the quiet hallway, holding the door open while Maggie slid out.

"Thank you." She headed down the hall, stopping at her room.

"Wait," Chase told her before she swiped the keycard. "We need to go in first."

Maggie tried the usual heated glare, but she must have been getting tired because the fire was cool around the edges. "Why?"

"I need to make sure there's no one in the room." He handed his emergency duffel off to Flores.

"How would anyone know I was here?" She didn't appear too tired to keep asking questions, though.

"Humor me." He took the keycard, swiped, and entered the room, pulling his gun at the same time. Bright blue carpet, white bedspread, white desk, and a white chair. The white walls glistened in the light from the lamp. The pristine bathroom and closet were empty. No one was in the room.

Better safe than sorry—at least that was Chase's story. "Come on in," he called into the hallway as he holstered his gun.

"We'll set up right through here." He pointed to the adjoining door. "Once it's open, keep it that way."

"What exactly am I supposed to wear? I have no clothes."

On a good day, he could barely control the thoughts running through his head when Maggie and no clothes were brought together in his mind. This was not a good day. He was tired, stressed, and way past the point where he could control the images floating around his head. So Maggie without clothes was not something he should be thinking about. It was not something that should get his body all excited.

Yet here he was.

"I'm not sleeping in this," Maggie snarled from in front of the bathroom mirror. The thin scrubs left little to the imagination. Which would have been hot if it wasn't for how she'd managed to be wearing said scrubs.

The adjoining door rattled. Chase unlocked it, and opened the door to Flores' smiling face. "What's taking so long?" Flores asked.

"Don't you have your better half to call?"

Flores looked Chase up and down, but he nodded and handed over Chase's duffel before disappearing into their room.

Chase put the bag on one of the beds and unzipped it, prying out a pair of shorts and a tee. "This is for you." He dropped the clothes on the bed.

Maggie scowled as she walked out of the bathroom. "Can't you run and get my clothes tonight?"

"Tomorrow. I'll take you tomorrow." They had no

idea if anyone was sitting on the house and if someone was—who, how many, the hardware they'd be carrying.

"Fine." She huffed, and yanked the clothes from his arms. "I'm taking a shower and going to bed. You can go now."

"I love it when you get bossy."

She rolled her eyes and pointed to the next room.

"Sleep well, Magpie." He walked through the adjoining door, telling himself she'd be fine.

Flores sat on the queen bed closest to the window, holding his phone in front of his face. Little whispers and cute giggles came from his side of the room. The wife. They'd be at this awhile. Not that Chase was jealous—well, not much.

Raquel was a good woman, and she was perfect for Flores. Their relationship just seemed to work. Even after twenty years, they still did little things for each other. Heck, they actually seemed to still like each other.

Chase would love to find something like that someday. But right now, a shower and bed sounded pretty good.

Flores laughed as his cheeks turned a bright shade of red. More giggling.

"Taking a shower." Chase grabbed his duffel and ran into the bathroom. Once he was behind closed doors, he could breathe. He was alone. No one was making googly eyes. He should have told Flores to just go home—not that he would.

The old man probably worried about leaving Chase alone with Maggie in a hotel room, or hotel rooms, as it were. Not that Chase could blame him. He *couldn't* be trusted alone with Maggie. If the scene at Jillian's taught him anything, it was that he couldn't be trusted with people in the room either.

None of that mattered now. He'd jump in the shower and hope the love-fest going on in the next bed was over early enough for Chase to get a good night's sleep.

At least that was the plan.

A half hour later, Chase put on a pair of sweatpants and a T-shirt, walking out of the steamy bathroom into a dark room. It was too damn dark to see anything, which normally would be fine. But tonight, he was working. He was keeping Maggie safe. He reached back into the bathroom, flipping on the light and closing the door most of the way. Now he could just make out Flores, on his side, turned toward the window. The next room was black, too. If Maggie had managed to fall asleep, he wasn't going to wake her by turning on the lights. She'd had a rough day.

Anyway, Chase wasn't afraid to be alone in the quiet. He actually liked having some time at night to decompress—time to think about all the events of the day. Time alone. It was his time to deal with all the crap that had happened. Time to just relax.

Flores sighed. "Hrlch...Shoo..."

Chase set the duffel next to the bed and slid under the soft sheets. Nice bed. Comfortable. Not as good as his bed back home, but a bad back for a day would be worth making sure Maggie was safe.

"Klerpcha...Skoo..."

Chase glared at his roommate, but Flores was out cold—and apparently channeling the noises of a Mack truck with a shoddy muffler.

Not really helping the whole relaxing thing.

"Tycherybu...Shoo..."

Staring at the ceiling, Chase tried using his arm to cover his ears. Maggie could probably hear the noise. Hell, she probably thought a bear was coming to get her.

He should check on her. Make sure she wasn't worried. See if she could sleep, because Chase was having a hell of a time.

"Sgechjalfujda...Skoo..."

Flores' snoring was gradually gaining more syllables. By the end of the night it would be one continuous mix of vowels and consonants. *Something to look forward to.*

"Chase?" A soft voice came from the doorway. Although he couldn't see her, he knew that voice.

"Yeah." Chase threw off the blankets and made his way over to her.

The light from the bathroom haloed her head as she stepped inside his room. She looked good, if not exhausted. "Are you torturing innocent cubs over here?" White light washed over smiling lips. Even in this light, she looked downright edible.

"It sounds like it, doesn't it?" He leaned in close, resting his fingertips on the top of the doorframe. Cool air tickled along his stomach as his shirt rode up.

Maggie's eyes travelled down his body, her attention stuck to the edge of that shirt. The look she gave was torture. Pure lust. He had a feeling he'd given her a look similar to that once or twice.

Her tongue slid along her bottom lip. Okay, maybe he was giving her that same look right now.

"Do you want a drink?" She bit at her lip almost like she didn't know the answer to that question was going to be yes.

He nodded. "I would love a drink." He followed her into the room, closing the adjoining door with a quiet click.

"Thank God for the mini bar." She hit the light switch before opening the refrigerator, selecting the first tiny bottle. "We have whiskey."

"They'll charge you for that if you lift it. It's weighted."

"Crap." She put the bottle back. "Then they probably already charged me for this." She pointed at the *Pleasure Box*. Pleasure. Box. Two condoms. Lube. Finger massager.

"You used the pleasure box..." *without him?* He didn't add that last part, no matter how much he wanted to.

"No." She laughed as red crawled up her neck and settled in her cheeks.

Damn, he loved that look.

"I was just poking around...not poking. Looking. Just looking." The color on her cheeks was generally saved for ripe tomatoes. She looked about as good to eat.

She selected a small bottle of wine from the mini-fridge. "What can I get you? It's on my father."

He looked at the bottles lining the door. "I'll have a beer."

Chase accepted the bottle Maggie held out to him and followed her onto the bed. She leaned back against the headboard on the right side. He settled next to her on the left, bumping his shoulder against hers.

"So, poking around, huh?" He took a deep drink, and tried to hide a smirk. It probably wasn't working. "What exactly were you poking? And why didn't you wait for me." Okay, he said it. But she'd set herself up for that.

"Stop." She snorted a laugh and covered her mouth. She looked at the closed door with wide eyes.

"Don't worry. I don't think he can hear over his snoring."

She lifted her bottle, a smile playing at her lips. "To poking."

"To poking." He lifted the glass bottle and tapped her bottle with a clink. This was nice. Being here with her. He could see himself doing this every night.

Which put a damper on his desire to be alone, but with her it didn't feel like a sacrifice. She made alone feel lonely—and wasn't that a disaster waiting to happen.

# TEN

MAGGIE'S BARE legs rubbed against the gazillion-thread-count sheets. What an amazing hotel. Way nicer than any place she'd normally stay. Since she'd sunk all her money into Busted, she didn't have anything left over for travel or extras. Which normally wasn't a huge hardship, but she could admit this was nice.

Partner the soft comfy bed with the tiny bottle of wine in her hand—and the gorgeous man sitting next to her—heaven. Heaven? That type of thinking wasn't going to get her anywhere but drunk and regretting her life choices.

She needed a distraction. "So, what's going on with the Lacik case?"

"That's what you want to talk about? We have a fridge full of booze, a handful of your father's cash, and this huge bed and you want to talk about work?"

"Maybe." She did. Work was always a handy diversion from all the other crap.

He tipped his bottle, playing with the condensation falling down the side. His eyes stuck to the label. "How are you holding up?"

"I'm fine."

"Really?" He slanted his eyes toward hers. "Tonight was pretty rough, for anyone. If you want to talk about it—"

"What if I don't?"

"Then we can talk about anything you'd like."

"Lacik case?"

"Anything but that." Chase's lips drew up into a sideways grin. It was sexy and distracting.

She almost forgot what she was trying to talk to him about. Almost. "Why not? I think I've earned some information."

"Good point." He drank deep, finishing off the bottle. "Okay. So, what do you want to know?"

"What is this guy? Dealer? Runner?"

"We thought he was a runner. Hell, he was a runner. Now we're not sure what he is. He had over a key in that backpack he dropped in the alley." Chase got up and threw the bottle into the small trash can. "And the latest...the stuff was probably laced with fentanyl. We have drugs hitting the streets that are literally killing people."

"How are they getting the fentanyl?" she asked, and then put two and two together. "Jillian."

"That's what we think." He took another bottle from

the mini-fridge and twisted off the top. "We visited St. Michael, and Jillian would definitely have access to vials of fentanyl, even with the security measures the hospital has. Lacik and friends would just have to cook down the liquid to a powder. Free fentanyl, and she makes a hell of a profit."

"Hell of a business plan. Sounds like no downside."

"Well, there hasn't been a downside yet, but if we find out she's been selling fentanyl that's been used to kill people, the cell we stuff her in won't be small enough." He nodded and took a pull from the bottle before crossing the room and standing by the window. Chase sighed. "There's a lot of crap that happens here, but at a distance, this is a beautiful city at night."

"It is." She walked up behind and stood next to him. It was a beautiful city. Points of light glittered throughout the darkness—red, green, blue and white. The Ferris wheel slowly turned on Navy Pier, the lights sparkling against the inky black lake.

It was so peaceful up here. No noise. No worries. Miles away from what was going on down below.

"Sometimes I forget how beautiful this city can be." He tipped the bottle back and took another pull.

"Have you thought about doing something else? Getting out of the cop game."

"Nah, I love my job. I could never leave. Sometimes...it's just nice to step away." His body was still, but Maggie could practically see the cogs spinning in his mind.

"It is nice to get away." The cold bottle dripped down her hand. She put her wine on the desk beside the window and rubbed the cold fingers down the gym shorts she was wearing. Chase's shorts. She wasn't sure why she found that so incredibly hot—wearing his clothes on her body. A shirt that had hugged his chest and caressed the ridges of his waist. Shorts that gripped his thighs and cupped his...

That line of thought was not helping.

"How did you walk away?" Chase turned away from the window, frowning a little.

"Walk away?"

"From the force? From the *cop game*?"

She knew that was what he meant, but she wasn't entirely sure how to answer. Walking away from her career, from the long hours and the gracious people of Chicago, had taken everything inside of her. She couldn't have done it without moving onto private investigation. She needed to help others. It was ingrained in her bones. Her skin actually itched when she'd been out of that game for a few weeks. It almost drove her crazy.

"You don't have to talk about it if you don't want." Chase leaned against the window wall and picked at the label on the bottle in his hand.

"It's not that." She expelled all the loss from her lungs in one huge whoosh. "It was the hardest thing I've ever done. But I couldn't stay and listen to the whispers any more. I couldn't stand being held back by outdated policies and bureaucratic bullshit."

"Your father is a bureaucrat."

Wasn't that the truth. "He is. And he knows how to play the game better than anyone. I just didn't want to play political Jenga all the time—worrying about what case might topple everything I built or what comment might get me busted down to patrol."

"Does this have to do with your old partner?"

"Maybe. That was a part of it. I got so sick of watching the good guys lose and there not being a damn thing I could do about it. The old partner didn't help. One minute I'm a detective, planning on going to Staff and Command class, and then I'm busted down to patrol. All based on the word of a shitty cop." And the friend of the shitty cop.

"He was awful. You got screwed." He shook his head and took another drink of his beer. "I never got a chance to tell you I was sorry."

"For?" Ruining her career or walking away from her after they'd kissed?

"For the way they treated you."

"They? Weren't you, like, best friends with him?" She snorted. "I seem to remember watching you walk out of my father's office right before they demoted me." And never talking to her again, but she didn't want to get into that. Her broken heart wasn't the issue. This was about her job—or loss of job.

"Best friends? No. I couldn't stay friends when I didn't respect him." He seemed to get lost in a thought, and then shook his head. "I tried talking to him, getting him to tell the truth."

"No one knows the truth."

"You didn't mishandle the evidence on that case, your partner did. You took the fall for something you didn't do." He didn't ask. He stated it as fact. And it was a fact. "When getting him to admit what happened didn't work, I tried talking to your father—to get him to pull some strings or something to stop the whole demotion."

"Really? You tried to talk to my dad?" That's not what she'd seen. Not that she had been in a great frame of mind back then. Her new partner had lied about her. The precinct was looking for her to fail. And the guy she...*liked*...had talked to her father and disappeared, taking her case with him.

"Yeah. I thought it might help."

"Did it?"

"Obviously not." He laughed but it sounded hollow. "Meetings with your father never seem to go the way I expect them to."

"Hmm. You're lucky. Meetings with my father always go the way I expect them to." And it was usually bad—full of guilt and disappointment.

"Well, I'm sorry about all of it." He took a sip of the beer in his hands and went back to looking out the window.

"Well, I'm done talking about my father." She tapped his shoulder with hers and he rewarded her with one of those uneven grins, a sexy-as-sin smile that really should be registered as a lethal weapon. "Stop looking at me like that."

"Like what?"

"Like, all you have to do is smile and the all the girls' panties just fall to the ground. It might work on the badge-bunnies, but not on me." Which was a good thing, since he was here to protect her—even though she didn't need protection. But it would be unprofessional for her panties or anything else to fall to the ground at this man's feet.

"Are you sure?" He bent over and looked at the floor. He dropped to his knees and checked under the bed.

"What are you doing?"

"I'm looking to see if your panties fell off." The pout on his face when he stood was so damn cute it made the scar on his lip curve. "I must say I'm disappointed."

She wasn't sure why she had the urge to say anything. But it must have had something to do with the ridiculous look on his face. He looked like Ralphie not getting his Red Ryder. How could anyone not feel bad for Ralphie? "They can't fall off if I'm not wearing any."

The disappointment on his face dried up and disappeared. It was replaced by bulging eyes and pure hunger. She loved that look. She'd seen that look so many times when they'd been seeing each other—no matter how temporary. It had been the highlight of her day back then.

And then the highlight was gone. No reason. No explanation.

He licked his lips as his glare practically pierced through the clothes at her hips. That tongue had tasted good, and the way he'd kissed back then, she knew she wanted that tongue to do more than explore her mouth. She'd wanted it to trail slowly along her body, licking her to the core. She had been a Maggie-pop waiting to be licked, and he was the owl looking for the juicy center.

She missed him. She wanted him. She was still the pop and he was still the owl. Not that she trusted him for anything other than a night with her body, but they were here at a hotel. With a big bed. And a juicy core. And a tongue that could lick a lollipop stick clean.

Seeing that look on his face was much more fun than talking about the past or her father or anything. They could play hotel-room-antics tonight, and tomorrow it would all be done. She'd be back home and she could forget about the attack and—no matter if Chase defended her job back then, he'd still walked away from her—how he broke her heart.

But tonight, it didn't matter. Tonight they were being room-antic. Tonight was all they had. And that was more than enough for her. Well, it would be—it would have to be.

CHASE COULDN'T TAKE his eyes off of her. *...I'm not wearing any panties.*

His attention moved to her hips, to his sweat shorts, to where she just admitted to not wearing anything else. He had never been jealous of his clothes before, but dammit if there wasn't a first for everything. His hand itched to be his sweats. His mouth wanted to be his sweats. He wanted to feel her up and down. Taste her.

Her eyes hooded right before her tongue shot out and slowly curved around her lip.

Curved around her lip.

Slowly.

Her lips glistened. His body hardened.

Her breath stuttered. His heart spasmed.

His hand brushed the side of her face. Soft. Warm. Her cheeks flushed from the wine or from his touch. It didn't matter. "You are so beautiful."

"So are you." Her plump lips turned up into a smile as her head dropped. Her hair fell in front of her face. Tragic. "I mean, you're handsome. Not beautiful." She looked up into his eyes.

"I'm disappointed. I've never been called beautiful before." He pushed a piece of hair behind her ear, leaving open skin just waiting to be tasted. He leaned over—

First kiss. Silky skin. It tasted like heaven.

Second kiss. His lips found hers. Her lips were satin under his. She was just as soft as he remembered. He could get lost in her—in this.

His mouth glided against hers, probing deeper while she leaned into him. With every press of every inch of her, his body pulsed. A moan slipped from her lips as he moved his hands lower. He'd waited for this for so long. This kiss sparked a fire in him, heat he couldn't control.

He wanted her. He needed her. She was every dream he'd ever had.

He drew her closer. Feeling her body rock against

the bulge in his cotton pants. He couldn't seem to get close enough.

Stepping backward, he angled toward the edge of the bed and sat down. Maggie straddled him, her ass resting on his lap.

She grabbed his hands and placed them on that ass. Soft mounds that just begged to be kneaded. His fingers dug in. She groaned. "Your hands are so big, so fucking sexy," she whispered against his skin.

Dirty talk. That was so hot. He leaned back, lifting her up and flipping her onto her back next to him. "Bigger makes it easier to do this." His body hung over hers as his hand made its way down the front of her baggy sweats and found bare skin. Lower. Between her legs. She was wet, waiting.

"Chase, yes." Her back arched as her body writhed. "More."

*Shit.* It felt so good, but this wasn't about him. He rolled to the side, out of range for an accidental body rub. His fingers inched inside. Slowly. He pushed in and drew them out, curving his fingers gently. His thumb circled her plump opening. Her hips rocked, pulling at his hand. "Slow down, Magpie."

"Take me," she begged, and fused her lips to his for a dizzying kiss. She arched into him on a sigh. "Fuck me."

He'd follow her anywhere if she just kept talking dirty to him. If he slid on top of her now, he'd go off too fast. Disappoint both of them. He never wanted to disappoint her. He needed to make her feel good.

Ignoring her pleading, he pumped his hand harder.

Faster. Thumb circling, rubbing, pressing. A loud groan spilled from Maggie's lips as her body stiffened, and she paused his hand, stopping his thumb. Pressing down, keeping his fingers deep inside as slick walls contracted and pulsed.

Her eyes closed. Her breathing stopped. And the look of pure bliss made his cotton pants even less roomy as his body responded to everything about her. She was smart and sexy, and if that little show was any indication, her needle was a bit right on the naughty scale.

She smiled, a devilish glint in her eyes. Hell yeah, she was just the right amount on that naughty scale. "You are way too overdressed."

"So are you." His eyes took in the glow on her face and the giant T-shirt and shorts. It should be illegal to cover all that beauty.

She looked down and laughed. "If you can do all that while I'm wearing all these clothes, I'm wondering what you can do when I'm not wearing any."

"Magpie, I got some mad skills." He wrapped his fingers around the waist band of her shorts—and they both jumped when someone banged on the door between the rooms.

Someone? Flores. "There had better be some life-threatening shit going on behind this door." Flores knocked again. "I'm coming in."

*Shit.* Chase rolled off the bed and sprinted for the door. They might both be clothed on this side, but anyone with half a brain could see the well-fucked glow on Maggie's face. And although Chase was pretty damn proud of that look, he wasn't about to share it with anyone. That was his look.

Chase reached out to stop the door as it opened. "Hey, Flores, what's up?" He put his body between his partner and the woman lying on the bed.

"You are. It's two in the morning." Flores and his Einstein-hair didn't make a move to come into the room.

Had Chase mentioned how much he loved his partner? "We were having a nightcap."

"Mmm-hmm." Flores shook his head as he glared. "Is that what the kids are calling it these days?"

Had Chase mentioned how much he hated his partner?

"You should probably go to bed." Flores nodded to their room. "In your own bed."

"All right, give me a minute." Chase went to close the door.

Flores' hand slapped against the wood. "And this stays open." He walked away.

Chase felt like a teen caught feeling a girl up in his room. Which wasn't all that far from reality. The difference was, he was a grown-ass adult in a woman's room. Granted, there had been a lot of feeling up.

"Dad caught us." Chase turned his head and wiggled his eyebrows, hoping that Maggie understood. Hoping for one of her laughs. "I have to go."

She laughed as she crawled to the end of the bed. Crawled? More like stalked. And he wanted to be the prey she was coming for.

His body went from ice cold to red alert in five seconds flat. The woman had a gift.

He walked over to the bed and pressed his mouth to her soft, pliable lips. The kiss lasted forever, but seemed to end too soon at the same time.

She leaned back and licked at the side of her mouth. "Tonight was fun."

His eyes couldn't move from the soft pink tongue molesting her perfect pouty lip. He knew how it tasted. He knew how it felt. And now all he wanted to do was lick her over and over again. "We should do this again."

She dropped back and sat on her heels. "We'll see." The look on her face said *we'll see* meant *no*. "Good night, Detective."

"Good night." Chase wanted to argue. He wanted to make plans to do this again. Make a date. Something. But with *Dad* around there was no way.

Back in the other room, a glaring Flores stood between the two beds. Chase shot him an answering glare. "I'm going to bed. I'm not going back in there."

"You shouldn't have been in there in the first place," Flores said, getting under the covers.

Chase crawled into his bed. Cold sheets met his skin. He knew he shouldn't have gone in there, but her voice was so sweet. And the call of her warmth was a hell of a lot more enticing then lying here in frozen sheets. Alone. He wasn't sure which bothered him more—the loss of her hot body, the loss of her smile, or the fact that him leaving didn't seem to bother Maggie at all.

He was so far out of his league with her. He

wanted her. That wasn't the issue. But watching her. Seeing her. Part of him needed her, and not just for the obvious.

And given her reaction she wasn't affected at all. Not one bit.

He was so fucked.

## ELEVEN

MAGGIE'S EYES cracked open to slivers of sunshine on white walls. She wasn't sure where she was, but she wasn't home. The hotel. She'd come here after Jillian's.

She'd come here with Chase and Flores. The fragments were piecing together. And those pieces weren't all that promising. She'd let Chase touch her—*let* didn't actually cover it—begged was more like it. Not that it hadn't been amazing. But then Flores had come in. Like he didn't know what the two of them had been up to. It had been pretty obvious. How embarrassing.

Even thinking about what went on between her and Chase had her flushed and stupid. *Great.* She slid out of bed and tiptoed over to check the other room.

Snores came from the open doorway, meaning the cop-squad was still asleep. Which was good. Easier. She had no idea what to say to Chase after last night. And Flores? How was she going to be able to ever face

148

him again? She'd need witness protection to avoid the uncomfortable, knowing looks.

And the thought of meeting those knowing looks in Chase's clothes—or worse, in crappy pink scrubs—was too much. She fled into the bathroom before remembering she had nothing—no toothbrush, no change of clothes, not even a hairbrush. She squinted at the mirror, relieved that her hair wasn't too much of a rat's nest, and plucked at the sweat shorts and tee. The fact that they were Chase's still made her feel a little warm and liquid inside. Which was a problem. She didn't have the strength for warm and liquid—not for him. She'd done that before and nearly drowned.

So, forgetting was the goal. She had to get back to her life and clients and chaos. It was her only chance at selective amnesia.

She needed her work, which meant a way to communicate. She needed her phone. That had to be the priority. Getting rid of Chase's clothes would help, too. Removing the smell of him on the clothes would be step one in the forgetting process. Of course, that required her to have clothes to change into. And since hers were currently bagged with the CPD, she needed other options. A store or something. She could have sworn they'd passed a twenty-four-hour discount store or something last night. Across the street. At the corner.

Leaving the bathroom, she slid on the cheap flip-flops from the night before and checked the clock. Six-thirty AM. Early enough to avoid the crowds and avoid being the showcase on the People of Walmart. Did they even put you on that site if you weren't shopping at Walmart? She hoped not.

Quick. That was the word for today. She needed to be quick.

And she could do it. She could walk to the store, pick up clothes and a phone and be back in twenty minutes, half hour tops.

ONE HOUR, one cell phone complete with all her contacts from the cloud, and one seriously cute outfit later, she was back at the hotel carrying her bags. Yes, bags. She found the cutest blue silk top. So she figured she might as well buy the black one, too. It's not like she got out to shop all that often. Plus she'd needed jeans, underwear, a bra, shoes, and socks.

Now she just needed to change and give Chase his clothes back, and then she was going to forget that last night, the orgasm, and the attack at Jillian's ever happened. Super easy.

Even she wasn't buying *that*.

It was never easy to forget an orgasm, especially when there was nearly-screaming involved. No matter how great the shirt was, even perfectly cut silk couldn't perform that miracle.

She walked in through the revolving door as a cop walked out, and made her way past the empty front desk. She hit the button, soft music humming as she rode up to her floor. All was quiet as she walked down the hallway except for the snap of her flip-flops. Until she got closer to her room.

"Thanks, contact me as soon as you find her and try to keep this quiet," a male voice snapped, and a cop walked out into the hallway.

The cop stopped and stared like Maggie was opening Capone's secret vault—there was a spark of interest at first, then she lost interest. "Detectives, I found her," the cop yelled, eyeing Maggie's bags with a scowl. "Were you *shopping*?"

"Uh, yeah." Maggie motioned to her current fashion misstatement of flip-flops, shorts and long T-shirt, but it was hard with her hands full. Would anyone dress like this voluntarily?

"Next time you decide to go on a shopping spree, you should tell the people guarding your life." The cop was still frowning when Chase filled the doorway.

If Maggie thought the female cop had a scowl on her face, Chase's expression defied words. Eyes narrowed. Lips flattened. He looked like a drill sergeant whose platoon overslept.

"Where have you been?" His narrowed eyes somehow squinted further as he took in the bags in Maggie's hands. He had a lot of nerve getting angry at her.

"She needed a shopping spree," the female cop snarled. Way to be bratty. Whatever happened to female solidarity in a male-dominated profession?

"I needed *clothes*." Not a damn shopping spree. Maggie tried to glare little-miss-badge-bitch away, but she kept standing there. "My clothes are currently in evidence bags because they're covered in blood. I needed something to wear."

Chase never took his eyes off Maggie. "Thank you for your help, Officer Poole. I'll take it from here."

Officer Poole and her pinchy-scowly face headed to the elevator, but not before she googly-eyed Chase in his jeans and dress shirt. "Anything for you, Detective."

*Gag.* Maggie actually felt herself throw up a little in her mouth.

Thankfully, Officer Drool didn't turn back around. She went around the corner and disappeared.

"Come inside." Chase stood back, keeping the bedroom door propped open so she could slide past.

Maggie dropped her bags onto the bed, taking out a box of red heels with a crisscross pattern over the toes. They were so adorable. Who would have thought a big-box store would have cute things?

"Why did you leave? Alone? Without telling anyone where you were going?"

"You were asleep. I went a few blocks away to get clothes and a phone." She found her new jeans and tugged at the cardboard tags attached to the back pocket. "I can't exactly go to work looking like this."

"Going to work? Who said anything about going to work?"

She stopped mid yank. "What do you mean?" She had an idea what he meant. And if he did mean that, she had an urge to choke him out with the tags.

"You're not going to work."

That's what she was afraid he meant. "What are you talking about? It's a work day. I'm going to work. You're going to work. We're all going to work. It's what productive members of society do. We perform services for people, who in turn, give us money. That allows us to pay our bills."

"I know how basic economics works. What I don't understand is how you can think you're going to work when the Vipers are after you. They know where you work."

"What's the big deal? I can't hide forever."

"I'm not asking you to hide, but you can lay low for a few days." He ran a hand over the back of his neck. "Think of one of your clients. If they were in this situation, what would you tell them to do?"

"Fine. I won't go to the office today." She tugged out her new cell phone. "I'll tell the girls to work from home today, too. But I have to work. I have a meeting with a few clients. I can do them anywhere. I was thinking Dunkin' Donuts.

"Can't you just take the day off?" His voice rose and got deeper at the same time.

"Can't you?"

His nostrils flared. He looked ready to charge. All he needed was horns. "No, but I have responsibilities..."

"And I don't?" Her own horns were definitely sticking out. She could bet her nostrils were flaring. He was doing everything but waving a red cape.

"You know what I mean. I have bosses."

"I have clients. They don't give me money to watch soaps and eat bonbons." She expected this crap from her father and brother, but not from Chase. "These are real people with real problems, that I help them solve."

"Real problems? You tattle on cheaters."

*Tattle on cheaters?* There was that darn red cape. Anger pulsed in her ears and popped at her temples as her eyesight went fuzzy. Her job was so much more. Only a jackass with asshole tendencies wouldn't be able to see that.

Well, looky-looky. Jackass. With asshole tendies. Six o'clock.

"I'm sorry." Chase almost looked sorry. And he should. She worked hard. She made sure that her team helped the clients make informed decisions or reunited them with their sentimental possessions.

*Tattle on cheaters?* "I don't tattle. I provide evidence for people to make the right choices. I recover property. I do background checks. I do all of the things the cops are too busy to do."

"Are you two done competing for who can annoy me the most?" Perry walked into Maggie's room, his face a mixture of anger and frustration. He pointed at Maggie. "You, get dressed." He pointed at Chase. "You, come in here."

Maggie wanted to hug Perry for getting rid of that annoyance so she could change. She just wanted to put on something besides these baggy Chase-infused clothes. She took off the T-shirt that still seemed to smell like him—spicy and woodsy. If that was even a scent.

But it had to be. It was him. And she couldn't wait to put it and him and his judgey-attitude behind her.

CHASE LEANED against the wall of the hotel room as Flores paced and talked.

"So, once Hendricks wakes, we need to go see her. But who knows when that will happen. Should we try the nursing staff again? Maybe they've seen her with someone other than Lacik."

"Why? We'll just get the same runaround." Chase didn't see the point of bothering the nursing staff, not when they could just go to Jillian Hendricks. *When* they could go to see her. She'd had a hell of a night.

"True, then we can focus on the paperwork that we need to do and finish logging the evidence."

Paperwork. Logging evidence. Sounded like a nightmare. But they'd gotten behind on it from this case. Every time they had a moment to write the reports, something would happen. They'd get a tip or Maggie would cause some sort of calamity. Every tip, every calamity led to more paperwork. It was a vicious cycle.

"Can't I just go to my car?" Maggie walked in the adjoining door and shoved the clothes she'd worn last night at his chest. He wrapped an arm around the items, which was a miracle, because he swore time just stopped. His mouth dried.

The clothes covering her body should be illegal, or at least a misdemeanor. Tight black jeans clung to her curves like evidence tape. Tight blue top, with fluttery little short sleeves. If she raised her arms, that shirt would gratuitously show a toned stomach. And it was toned. He could still remember the feel of it under his palm.

"Why do you need your car?" Chase picked up his bag and shoved the clothes inside. He stared at the zipper on the bag, focusing his eyes anywhere but on her. His mind was going back to bad places. Last night was a mistake.

He knew it the minute she'd practically dismissed him after Flores walked into the room. He'd suggested they do it again. Together. Screaming orgasm. Sounded amazing, right? And she'd just looked at him and said, "We'll see." *We'll see.* Really. How she could have turned off everything they'd done together, so quickly—he had no idea. But she had, without a backwards glance.

And then this morning he'd been scared shitless something had happened to her. But she just walked through the door like nothing was wrong. Didn't mention last night. It was like the whole thing never existed. Like he never existed.

"I was talking to Perry." Plastic bags crinkled in her hands as she repositioned them. "I need to get my car so I can work...not at the office. I'm heading to the double D."

Flores shook his head, but didn't speak.

Chase took over. He was going to prove he existed if it killed him. "You can't go alone."

"Why not? I know how to handle myself. We're talking about a coffee shop in Lincoln Park. Are you afraid Trixie and Chad are going to jump out of their BMW and hit me with their Kate Spade bags?"

Was it wrong that he suddenly wanted Trixie and

Chad, whoever they were, to hit her with their Kate Spade bags? "I'm sure you can handle yourself."

"Right." Flores finally found his voice. "But we've been given strict orders to keep you with us."

"With you? Where?"

"We're going to the precinct to work on reports." Chase couldn't believe they were having this argument. The woman had been covered in blood less than twenty-four hours ago. She had to know what danger they were up against—what danger probably wanted to find her.

"You can't write reports at Dunkin' Donuts? From what I hear, your kind love donuts—and bacon."

Really? "Resorting to the cops are pigs joke?"

She laughed, but not in a cute, funny way. It was hyena laced with evil cyborg. He half expected her to tie him to train tracks and play with her mustache. "Not all cops. Just you."

Naturally. He was the bad guy because he worried about her. The fact that he worried about her as much as he did was a concern for another day. "You know, I'm not that bad just because I want to keep you safe."

"If you think you're a pig because you're trying to keep me safe, you're dumber than you look."

"I can't argue that." Flores laughed. "I'm going to check us out. Let's get out of here."

Maggie stood guard at the front door, not letting either of them pass. "To my car?"

"Look, you can't go alone." Flores shook his head. "How about I'll head back to the station and work on logging the evidence. Montgomery, here, will take you to your coffee."

Maggie protested, "Do I really need a babysitter?" at the same time Chase said, "Don't we both need to work on that evidence?"

"Look. We all have things to do. Get them done." Flores shuffled past Maggie and out the door.

She gave Chase one glare-infused look before turning and following Flores. If this was how she was going to act—this was going to be one long day.

## TWELVE

TWO HOURS LATER, Maggie sat in a brown vinyl booth, surrounded by white walls covered in pictures of donuts and coffee cups, interspersed with the occasional coffee bean photo. Two donuts in a bag and a half full large coffee sat in front of her.

"Is anyone going to show up or are we just going to sit here all morning?" Chase grated from behind her. They were apparently stuck at the hip today. Which wouldn't be so bad if his mouth had an off switch.

His voice grew a fraction louder. "If you wanted coffee, we could've stopped on the way to the precinct. You didn't have to pretend you had a meeting."

First off—really—why didn't his mouth come with an off switch? Second—she couldn't see his smug face or body, but she could hear the implied quotations around that last word.

"Maybe you should try having a cup of coffee," she said, trying not to clench her teeth. "You might not be as cranky." She could feel his breath on the back of her neck, which meant he was close. Really close.

He laughed, a deep sound. *Sexy. Hot.* Not that she thought it was sexy or hot. It was more like someone else might find it that way. Not her. Not now.

She was way too mad to enjoy having him that close. Although last night had been amazing, it had been one huge mistake. Any action that could lead to another one of those mistakes, although tempting—*okay very tempting*—any action that would lead to her trusting him with her body was bad.

Not that he couldn't be trusted with her body. It was her heart. It was her feelings and her hopes. She loved her job and he thought it was a joke. He thought she was a joke. He'd made that clear. Why would she want to be with someone who thought she was a punchline?

If she wanted that kind of punishment, she could go visit her family. They were always good for knocking her self-esteem down a few notches.

She flipped open a random file in front of her and stared at the words till they blended together in psychedelic waves. They'd stopped by the office to pick up the files she needed, but there was nothing for her ten o'clock appointment. She always had a file. Even on new cases. And she was supposed to meet one of her lawyer contacts on this one, which made the lack of file even weirder.

The lawyers she dealt with from this firm rarely met her in person; they always offered some information through email or over the phone. But for some reason, this time they wouldn't give her anything. Not even a clue. Sometimes Maggie got some weird cases, and she had a feeling this was one of them.

"I got your message to meet here." Enzo Borelli set his briefcase on the table.

Maggie had been so busy analyzing the lack of folder, she missed the man walking in the door. And that was saying something—at least with this particular man.

Enzo was ovary-sighing gorgeous. His black suit fit nicely over broad shoulders. Big hands rested on top of the briefcase. And it wasn't just a hot body. He was good-looking—for a lawyer—strong Italian features, light brown hair that made his olive skin stand out, and warm chocolate eyes. Okay, the guy would be good-looking no matter what he did for a living.

He gave her a small smirk. Somehow, it didn't piss her off. It just looked damned cute. "This feels very surreptitious. I almost feel an urge to sneak an envelope under the table and talk in code." And he was funny. Goodness, she swore she feel her ovaries pant.

"Not necessary." Maggie took a sip of coffee. Cute or not, this whole thing felt off. She wasn't sure why they were meeting in person to begin with.

"Why aren't we meeting in your office?" He scanned the room.

"Office complications."

His attention focused on her. "Is this not going to work out?"

Will what not work out? She still had no idea why

they were there. "My complications will not affect your case." Hopefully. "What exactly is the case?"

Enzo settled himself on the other side of the booth and opened the leather attaché.

Maggie raised her eyebrows. "No coffee?"

"No time." He dropped a file—a two-fister, an epic novels' worth of data—onto the table. Wow. If that was the file, it begged the question of why they needed her small firm.

He slid the two-fister across the table and pulled out a smaller file. "This is privileged information. It must be dealt with delicately."

"Absolutely."

"One of my partners, Stanley Welford, has created an exploratory committee. He's thinking of running for mayor. Before we invest time and money into this endeavor, we need to find the skeletons. What will people find if they dig far enough?"

She eyed both folders. "Can't you ask him?"

"We have." He handed over the slimmer folder. "Here's what he's identified as potential issues. But we both know the reality—no one ever divulges all their secrets. I want you to find them. See if any of these issues he's identified run deeper than he's admitting, and make sure that nothing can be found that would surprise us."

"How long do I have?"

"Three months." He closed his briefcase. "Then we announce he's running." He handed her a check. A very large check—not Publishers Clearing House large, but an extra zero kind of large. "That's the first half.

There's more, if by the end of the campaign, we have no surprises."

"I'll get Danni and Jessi on this right away."

"Good." He stood to his full height, all six feet of gorgeousness. "How *is* Jessi doing?" He sounded really strange. Like he shouldn't be asking but had to anyway.

Maggie eyed him, curious. What was up between him and Jessi? "She's fine. You should stop by the office and say hi sometime. You haven't been by the office in ages."

"To be fair, I had planned on seeing her today." A smile played on his lips but his eyes were sad. Why would he be upset about Jessi—why would he have any feelings at all?

Guilt pecked at the back of her neck. This was her fault that they weren't meeting in the office this morning. "Yeah, sorry about that."

He blinked and stared at the wall. "Did she ask about me?"

Whoa. Enzo and Jessi? "Do you want me to pass her a note in homeroom and find out?" Maggie wanted to laugh, but the pained look on Enzo's face smothered the impulse.

He shrugged. "It doesn't matter. I don't think she wants to see me very much anyway."

"Why?" Maggie knew that Enzo and Jessi had a run-in with the Mayor last year, but Jessi had only gone to that party because Maggie was unavailable. Nothing had happened between them. They had barely met at that point. Come to think of it, Jessi did go all weird any time Enzo came up in conversation. And now Enzo was acting all weird. Huh. Maybe they liked each other. How did she never notice that before? She was a PI, for goodness sake. Although to be fair, he'd been in New York for the past year. "What happened?"

"Nothing worth talking about." He glanced at something behind her shoulder. Probably the man who was here to protect and stomp her nerves. "Are you okay?"

She wanted to see what Chase was up to, but she wasn't sure she wanted to know. "Yeah, everything's fine."

"Fine?" Enzo leaned down. "Fine enough that you're being watched?"

When in doubt, play dumb. "Watched?"

"The guy behind you is staring at you."

"Maybe he's watching you." She was turning into a five year old. *He's not my stalker, he's your stalker.*

"Excuse me? Excuse me!" Enzo went around the end of the booth just as Chase slid out and stood up.

Maggie didn't want to watch the testosterone fest. But she couldn't let this get out of hand. Although... Enzo was a big, muscular guy. He might be able kick the crap out of Chase. Now that would be fun to see. Especially if they stripped down and slathered themselves in oil.

"Can I do something for you?" Enzo eased closer to Chase and turned into an Italian pufferfish.

Chase tilted his head to the side. "Nope."

They were the same height. Both big. Strong. Good-looking. Although between the scar on his lip and the lines across his forehead, she'd have to say

Chase's face had more character—he'd obviously seen some shit over the years. And that knowledge, that strength, made him hotter somehow. Better looking. Not that she'd ever admit that to anyone.

"Why are you watching me?" Enzo growled.

"I'm not. Should I be watching you?" Chase showed his badge.

Enzo's chest deflated a notch as he stared at the shield. "CPD."

"Yes."

"Is there a reason you're staring at us, Officer—" he looked closer at Chase's wallet— "Detective Montgomery?"

"Staring is a bit of an exaggeration. Just paying attention." Chase stuffed his wallet back of his jeans.

Maggie took pity on Enzo. "He's with me. My father might be a bit overprotective over a case I'm working." She smiled as she wrestled the giant file folder into her purse. "It's precautionary."

"Did you hear what we were talking about?" Enzo asked Chase.

"Nope." Chase shook his head. "Don't care what you were talking about."

Enzo looked from Chase to Maggie and nodded. "Okay. I look forward to hearing from you, Maggie."

"Thanks." Maggie watched him walk out the door.

"So that was the all-important meeting you needed to keep?" Chase sat in the seat Enzo had left open. "Finding dirt on potential politicians."

"I thought you didn't hear what we talked about."

"A bit of an exaggeration, but I wasn't lying when I

said I don't care." Chase tapped the table. "So, you ready to go?"

Go? "That was only my first meeting. If you have somewhere to be, please feel free to leave."

"I wouldn't dream of leaving you here alone." Chase leaned back, sliding his feet under the table and bumping Maggie's ankle.

"Excuse me? Are you Maggie Lane?" A young girl stood over the table. Her voice was low. Her head hung low.

"Yes. Brandi Katsaros?"

"Yeah." She nodded and turned to Chase, but she didn't look him in the eye.

"Mr. Montgomery was just leaving." Maggie nodded to the bench across from her as Chase slid out. "Please, have a seat."

"Thanks." Brandi was young. Timid. Her shoulders slumped. Her head was down. This poor woman looked like she was perpetually scared. There was only one reason for a woman to look that scared—something or someone had done that to her.

Maggie wanted to find the son of a bitch and beat some manners into him. "Can I get you a drink? Coffee. Tea. Donut."

"No, thanks."

Brandi plopped a crocheted purse to the table. It was dirty, but there were bright colors visible underneath. She hugged the bag close to her chest and played with a loose string hanging from the side.

Sometimes it was best to let the client start the conversation. But sometimes clients needed a bit of coaxing. Especially those that looked ready to bolt. "So, why did you need to see me today?"

"I was hoping you could help me." The long sleeve on Brandi's right arm slid up, revealing dark bruising. "I think my dad is doing something illegal."

"Did he do that to you?" Maggie nodded to the deep blue fingerprints lining her forearm.

Brandi nodded and turned away.

"Have you thought about going to the police?"

"I can't go to the police." Fear swirled in her wide-open eyes as she leaned forward. "He said he'd kill her."

Her? There was someone else. "Who will he kill?"

"My sister, Brianna." A tear pooled in her eye. "Last time I called the cops, he was back home in a few days and he swore he'd kill her if I ever called them again."

"Why are you here today?"

That tear slid down her cheek. "He hit her. He never hit her before. She's so young. But he did. She didn't finish the dishes. I can't let him touch her again." The girl stared at the table and played with the string.

"How old is she?" Maggie heart wrenched, watching her.

"Eight." This girl was broken and trying to take her life back. Taking her life back for her eight-year-old sister.

"This is all I've got." The girl handed over an envelope. There was probably about five hundred bucks in there. The poor kid. She couldn't have been more than twenty years old, and her life savings consisted of five hundred bucks and a sister she wanted to rescue from abuse. "I want you to look into my father. He owns the car dealership over on Ogden. I sometimes work the books and he's laundering money." Brandi drew out a handful of paperwork with Kut Price Cars on the header. "This is all the information I have, but I don't know what to do with it."

"Why don't you take this money and just run?"

"He'd do anything to find us. We're his property. I need help."

Property? Maggie didn't care what it took, she was helping this girl. She sifted through the pages, thinking these looked like originals. "Are these copies?"

"No. I took everything I could and came here."

*Crap.* If she took all the originals, he might notice they were missing at some point. And given his obvious control issues, it was probably going to be sooner rather than later. "Is there anyone else who helps with the books?"

"Just me and Dad."

"Okay." Maggie tried to keep a smile on her face, but this girl and her sister were in danger.

She wasn't the finance guru, that was Leti. But even she could see large amounts of money being transferred between accounts. Okay, large amounts was an understatement. More like holy-shit amounts. Something shady was definitely going on here. Five-hundred-thousand-dollars shady. Enough money for a greedy SOB to be willing to kill for.

And if it wasn't, Maggie would send Danni rummaging around in his history. They'd find something to put this guy away for a long time. This was the reason she did this job—to help people like Brandi and Brianna.

And she'd do whatever it took to make sure they were safe.

---

CHASE DIDN'T GIVE a crap about the lawyer and his exploratory garbage, but listening to Maggie ease this young girl's mind was a whole other issue.

This young woman was obviously abused. He could tell the moment she'd approached the table. The eyes that wouldn't look up, the way her body seemed to curl into itself. How could anyone do that to another person? And it was her father? How?

A father protected their little girl from the atrocities of the world—they weren't supposed to be the atrocity.

"Do you have somewhere to go?" Maggie asked, pulling out her phone as she sifted through the paperwork in front of her.

"Not really." The woman played with a string of her purse. "We have no other family and we're not allowed to have friends."

"Where's your sister?"

"School."

"Where's your father?" The wheels in Maggie's head were turning. He could practically hear the whine of the gears.

"Work."

Maggie paused to take a picture of a document with her cell. "My family has a cabin in the dunes."

The girl frowned. "Are there dunes in Chicago?"

"No, Michigan."

"Oh." Brandi's smile slid down at the edges. "That's nice, but I don't have a way to get there."

"You let me worry about that." Maggie pointed at one of the spreadsheets, taking another picture. "Is this your home address?"

The girl nodded and actually looked at Maggie with lit eyes. Any disappointment was gone. "Are you really going to help us?"

"I'm going to do everything I can, but you need to do your part. Go home and grab what you can for you and your sister without getting caught. Money. Clothing. Keep it light. I'll send someone to the house in one hour to pick you up. Gray Crown Vic."

The way Maggie talked—the passion—she could talk a snowman into believing a space heater was in his best interest.

Thank God she was on the good side.

"You did a good job of getting us information." Maggie patted the girl's hand before slipping the papers back across the table. "I want you to keep the paperwork. He might notice these are missing. And keep the money. You'll need this for your sister."

Brandi took the envelope back. "Are you sure?"

"Yes. I'm sending someone to pick you up as soon as you leave, so make sure you move discretely and fast."

"But what if my dad comes home for lunch?"

Maggie stopped. Blinked. "Does he do that often?"

"Sometimes."

"Okay." Maggie nodded, eyes narrowed. "I'll make sure he doesn't leave the car lot."

"Thank you so much." Brandi brushed away a tear sliding down her cheek. She stood up from the table at the same time Maggie did.

Maggie smiled at her. "You're welcome."

Brandi jumped at Maggie and engulfed her in a hug before heading out the front door.

After Brandi was gone, Maggie pulled out her cell phone and dialed. There was no hello, no pleasantries. "Are you all together? Good. Put me on speaker. We have an emergency. I need you to drop what you're doing." Her eyebrows arched and her voice got louder, sharper. "I don't care, drop it all. I'm going to send you some documents. I need you to find *everything* on this guy. We need to get him in Federal custody ASAP. So we need to work fast, and Danni? Make it as admissible as possible. Leti, can you text me a timeframe when you'll have a complete makeup? Jessi, you take my car and the keys to my dad's beach house in Michigan. Take some money from petty cash. You'll need to stop at the grocery store."

Her shoulders slumped at something one of them said. "Yeah, go to the office if you have to. I'll explain everything later. Thanks, ladies."

She disconnected the call and immediately started swiping at the screen, tapping the pictures of the paperwork. Chase heard the familiar swoosh of a sent text.

Finally, Maggie looked up at Chase. "Did you hear all that?"

"Yeah, I did." He leaned forward in the booth, trying to see the spreadsheets she just sent. "That was nice of you to give her the money back."

"She's going to need it to start over."

Chase nodded. Yes, she needed to start over, but— she was a kid. And her little sister was only eight. What was happening to them was wrong, but— "Shouldn't we call DCFS?"

Maggie raised her eyebrows. "DCFS? How long till they act on this? Days? Weeks? We know there's a problem. We need to get them out of there now, before he does something horrific to those girls. So, no, we shouldn't call the Department of Children and Family Services. Are you okay with that?"

Was he okay with that? Part of him wanted to say no. There were rules for a reason. The thought of those girls in harm's way one more minute had him on the verge of finding their asshole father and beating the shit out of him, which wouldn't help the situation. Getting them out was the primary goal. Making him suffer was secondary.

He nodded. They'd get them out and work on arresting Daddy-dearest later. "Money laundering, huh? Do you have an FBI agent you can call to get this investigation going?"

"I might." She shook her head and her face fell. "I would call my dad and get his help, but I don't want to explain all of this. He won't understand."

Chase took a deep breath. "Um, I graduated with a

guy who's working in the Organized Crime Division. I could see if he can get this fast-tracked."

Her slow smile heated something in his chest. "That would be amazing." Her phone beeped with an incoming text, and she swiped at the screen. "Can you contact him now? Danni and Leti should have the financial information in about three hours."

"Three hours?" He'd done enough research over the years to know it took time—a lot of time—to get that type of data, between finding the correct banks and getting the warrants.

"We have our ways."

"But are they legal?"

Maggie shrugged one shoulder. "They'll stay as close to the right side of the law as they can, flag whatever's inadmissible and identify where to get the data so the FBI can get it through the proper channels. Leti has a gift for finding probable cause. I'm sure the FBI will need that to start the investigation." She hooked her bag over her shoulder. "Are you ready?"

"Ready?"

"Yeah, wherever I go, you go, right?"

"That's the rumor." He picked up his empty coffee cup and followed her to the front door, lifting the lid to the garbage can and waited while she dumped her trash. "Where are we going?"

"Kut Price Cars on Ogden. I want to make sure this guy doesn't try to head home."

He held the front door for her and followed her to his car. "Should you be snooping around this guy while you're dealing with Lacik? If he's laundering cash, he could be mob? Gang? Aren't you already in enough trouble?"

She turned on her heel, fire in her eyes. "Nothing has happened with that whole gang thing. Everyone's working out of Leti's house, and no bad guys have gone near the office. Have you talked to the cops staked out at my house? Has anyone even tried to approach it?"

Apparently, he wasn't really part of this conversation, just a sounding-board with a face, because she didn't wait for an answer. "No. No one's approached my house, either, right? So, I could go back home and get back to my life. Not that that matters right now. Right now, I need to find information on this dirt bag who uses his daughters as punching bags. I need to get him out of their life before they forget to flush the toilet or they accidentally look at him sideways and he decides that today is the day he's going to kill them."

Chase held up his hands in surrender. "All right. All right." There was no way he could talk her out of this excursion, and he wasn't sure he wanted to. He agreed with everything she said. "We need to get to the dealership and fast."

"See." She smiled, her teeth all white and shiny. It matched the happiness dancing in her eyes. "I knew you could be smart enough to see things my way."

THIRTY MINUTES of Chicago bumper-to-bumper traffic later, Chase followed Maggie into the small dealership. Dealership was a bit of a stretch. It was a small building—maybe twenty by twenty feet—with the front three walls covered in windows. Two desks, and a door that led to who-knew where. But no showroom, and the lot outside consisted of ten to fifteen cars. All used. Most looking like they'd survived a road trip to hell and back. But the signs clogging up the space—*cash only, bad credit, no credit, no problem*—said the staff was just waiting to take advantage of those down on their FICO.

"Can I help you?" A skinny man with red suspenders came out of the back room, his eyes bouncing from Chase to Maggie. "Are you a cop?"

"No. I'm not a cop." Maggie eyed a rusted bucket of steel outside on the lot. At one time the thing looked to have been red, and the car looked old enough to actually be made of steel. "I need to talk to Peter Katsaros. My friend told me to deal with him directly."

"I assure you, young lady; I can sell you a car just as well as Mr. Katsaros."

"Yes, I'm sure you can. But my friend..."

"He's a busy man."

"Is he here? I really need to see him. He should be expecting me."

The man looked her up and down before turning and heading to the back room. Maggie whipped out her phone and typed a quick text.

"What are you doing?" Chase nearly hissed. "He's going to know something is up when he comes out and he's not expecting you." What was she thinking?

"I've got it under control." Her phone dinged, and she smiled as she read the text.

"This better be God-dammed important." A short,

balding man stormed through the door, his face an alarming shade of red. Chase really didn't want to call 911 if this guy keeled over—he'd never live this down.

Maggie's smile was blinding. "Mr. Katsaros. I'm so glad to finally meet you. A friend of mine, Toni Barnett, said I should talk to you about getting a car. She said her neighbor offered *aamaazing* deals." She sounded... chirpy. Maggie was a lot of things, but chirpy was not one of them.

"The Barnetts?" Katsaros' dark eyebrows merged together.

"Yes, Toni said she'd call you. Did she not call you?" Maggie look of confusion had Chase practically believing her story.

"No."

Maggie slowly shook her head and sighed. "She can be so scattered sometimes, with the kids and her husband. I'm so sorry to interrupt. We can come back."

"No. You're here now."

"Well anyway, my brother—" she nodded at Chase. Her brother? Oh, hell no. "—and I were talking to Toni and we mentioned how we needed to buy a car for our little sister. It's a graduation present. You know, before she runs off to college. Do you have kids in college?"

"No."

"Be thankful. My parents are going broke." She walked past a few clunkers and rested her hand on that wannabe-red rust bucket that was probably held together with duct tape. She ran her hand along the flaking paint and hummed—a low guttural hum that rocked Chase to the core.

If they weren't standing out in public— Oh, right. He was her *brother*.

Katsaros seemed to be enjoying the groan as well. A little too much. "You like this one." He put his hand next to hers. His cold, clipped tone changed to a soft growl. "It's sexy."

"It is." She nodded as she sucked her bottom lip into her mouth. "But should I get my sister such a *sexy* car?"

"Does she look like you?" Katsaros touched her hand. His eyes were glued to her mouth and that lip.

Chase could understand.

"She looks like me, just younger."

"Then you can definitely get her this car. Your beauty will make any car pale in comparison."

Maggie tilted her head and looked up at Katsaros through her long lashes. The only thing missing was a blush. Apparently the blush was not part of the acting package. "You are so sweet."

Mr. Red Suspenders came outside and stood next to the car. "Mr. Katsaros, don't you have to leave?"

"Oh, no." Maggie puffed out her bottom lip and stomped her foot. "I really was hoping to get this car today."

"I have a few minutes." Katsaros smiled at Maggie. It was really more like a leer. "Did you want to test drive?"

"I would love a test drive." She did everything but clap and jump up and down. Although even without jumping up and down, her chest seemed to bounce with happiness.

Katsaros seemed to be pretty happy about the bouncing, too. His eyes were fixed on her chest.

"Ahem." Suspender guy was not falling for the jiggle.

"I'll go get the keys." Katsaros disappeared into the building, with red suspenders on his heels mumbling about some meeting.

"Are you really going to buy this piece of crap?"

"No, but Jessi is at the house. I need to keep him busy until they're packed and at the school."

"How did you know about the Barnett's"

"Danni. I needed a referral. She got me a name."

"You are seriously dangerous."

Her phone chirped and a smile lit her face. "They're a block away from picking up the sister."

"Good."

The front door of the dealership flew open, and Katsaros walked out jingling keys around his finger. He looked Maggie up and down. His Jabba-the-Hut tongue slid along his pale crusty lips. "The car's a little small, so I was thinking we should probably go for the first ride, just you and me."

"My brother and I decided we should just go for it. Get the car."

The little man didn't seem to know if he should be disappointed he wasn't going to get to drive and feel up Maggie, or if he should be happy he was selling the shit car. "Sounds like a great idea. You're a good sister."

"I try." She unzipped her monster-sized purse and removed a small wallet. She grabbed a credit card and handed it Katsaros. "You take Visa, right?"

Chase studied the card in Maggie's hand. Penelope Ward was stamped in silver text along the bottom. Unless she'd changed her name, that card was someone else's. Or at the very least—fake.

"Cash only," Katsaros said.

Penelope—also known as Maggie—sifted through her big purse and produced twenty bucks. "Do you have cash?" She turned to Chase.

"Nope."

"Oh dear." Maggie sucked on that bottom lip again as her brow furrowed. "Is there a cash machine close by? I can get you the money and come right back."

Katsaros nodded. "Around the corner at First National Bank."

Between what his daughter had said earlier, and the initial less-than-warm welcome, Katsaros struck Chase as a no-bullshit kind of guy. And Maggie, with her no cash, credit card only—in a place where the signs outnumbered the people and quite a few said cash only—was all bullshit. Yet, this guy didn't get mad. He couldn't seem to drag his eyes from her bottom lip. The lip she was currently molesting again. Molesting.

No wonder the guy couldn't remember he should be mad.

"I'll be right back." She turned, putting some serious sway to her hips as she walked across the lot toward where Katsaros had indicated a bank might be.

"I'll be right here." Katsaros leaned against the car, that damn leer still on his lips.

Maggie turned and gave a three finger wave as she

disappeared around the corner, Chase following along like a lost puppy.

"Now was that so hard?" The sway was gone. The sweet was gone. The molesting of her lip—*you guessed it*–gone.

That last one made Chase sad. He didn't like watching Maggie be anything but herself, but if she wanted to suck on her lips, or his lips for that matter, he wasn't going to complain. "Watching you eye-hump him? It wasn't the most fun I've had all day."

Maggie rolled her eyes. "It wasn't that bad." She checked her phone. "They have the sister. We need to get to Busted."

"Your agency?"

"Yeah. Leti has some information." She peeked around the building. "Coast is clear. Let's go."

The problem was they had to walk right past the dealership to get to his car, but if they moved fast... "Nope." He snared her arm and yanked her back. "That guy is like a Chihuahua in heat. The minute he sees you, he'll be trying to climb you like a tree."

"Well, we have to leave."

"Stay here." He pulled out his keys. "I'll get the car and pick you up in front of the bank."

"Fine." She took the five steps to the bank and leaned against the glass.

"Don't move."

She rolled her eyes. Again. And mimed planting her feet into the ground. If only her feet really worked that way, they could've avoided so many problems.

He ducked down and ran to his truck, parked off to

the side of the car dealer's lot. He slid behind the wheel and merged into traffic. They didn't have long before the mini-horndog noticed she wasn't coming back.

He whipped around the corner and parked in front of the bank.

No one leaned against the glass. Maggie wasn't pacing out front. *Son of a bitch.*

He never should have left her alone, not even for thirty seconds. He should have glued those feet to the ground when he'd had a chance. Katsaros or suspenders couldn't have gotten to her, not without Chase seeing them. No back alley. Nothing. A string of shops lined both sides of the street, and that was it. Where—

Movement on the other side of the street caught his attention as Maggie walked out a door carrying two cups. Dunkin' Donuts. Really?

He probably should've noticed the giant pink letters right away. He probably should've specified *don't go to the donut shop* while he got the car. But when you tell someone don't move, you assume they won't move.

Of course, this was Maggie. She always moved.

She ran across the street and knocked on his window. "I figured we're going to need this." She handed him a cup through the slowly lowering window before running around to the passenger side.

Whipping open the door, she put her cup in the holder and jumped in.

"What part of 'don't move' was confusing?"

"I just figured we have a long afternoon ahead, we'd

need some caffeine." Maggie took a sip. "I was gone two seconds."

"You were gone the two seconds when I was looking for you. The two seconds it took for me to wonder where the hell you'd gone or who the hell had gotten to you. Those two seconds stunted my life by at least a year."

"I'm sorry." She actually did look sorry. "I didn't mean to scare you." She glanced out the passenger side window. "We should probably go, before my new friend realizes I'm not buying his car."

"Yeah, we should." He threw the truck in gear and headed toward the detective agency. He wasn't sure going there was the best idea, but she was right. No one had seen or heard from the lowlife she'd met in Jillian's house. Maybe Lacik had decided he didn't care about Maggie. Maybe he cared more about his drugs.

It's the only way Chase could keep going on their current path. So that was the story he was sticking to. Whether he believed it or not.

# THIRTEEN

CHASE DROVE his truck into the alley and angled into one of the spaces behind the big red-brick converted warehouse. There were two doors facing the alley. The one on the far left of the building said "Busted" in big purple letters. The other one, toward the center, said, "Sal's".

"Shit." Maggie stared at the pot-bellied man standing on the back porch, yelling into a cell phone. From what Chase could see, he took the phrase *spitting mad* seriously. At least he looked pretty pissed.

"Problem?"

"Usually." She pushed open the passenger door and slid out. Walking around the back of the car, she dropped her head and slid her hand up to cover her face. If that was her idea of hiding, she was sadly mistaken. Most men would notice that blonde hair anywhere.

Or maybe that was just Chase.

"Gotta go," the angry guy said into the phone before shoving it into his pocket. He pointed at Maggie, his eyes narrowed into sharp daggers. "You. I told you, talk to those *girls* about parking in front of garage doors."

"I've talked to them. I'm sure they didn't—."

"Those girls don't drive good. They park in front of doors all night. My men can't put truck back and couldn't get to tools."

"I'm sure my *girls* wouldn't park in front of your sacred doors. They wouldn't want to listen to your condescending, misogynist attitude." Maggie stomped up the porch stairs, her finger wagging.

"If they didn't park in front of my doors, who did?"

"I have no idea. I left my Magic 8-Ball back at my house," she snapped.

"Did you leave broomstick there, too?"

Maggie stepped forward. "You should be thankful I did or I'd stick it up your—"

"All right." Chase made it up the stairs and stepped between them. He had no desire to stick a pair of handcuffs on her and haul her down to the precinct. Well, he didn't want to haul her down to the precinct, anyway.

He also didn't want to have to kick this guy's ass.

"You are worst landlord I ever have. You're crazy." Phone guy was dangerously close to that ass kicking. "I'm going to find new place."

"Find another building. I dare you," she called over Chase's shoulder as he herded her backward toward the door to Busted.

She turned around and whipped the door open, almost clocking Chase in the face. "That guy drives me crazy."

"I hadn't noticed."

"He threatens to move every month. He never does." She leaned out the door one more time before committing to the inside. "Why don't you ever leave?" she yelled, and then huffed. "No one's out there."

"Maybe he's looking for a new place."

Maggie laughed. Really laughed. "I don't think I'm that lucky."

The door clicked closed behind her as she led him past a set of stairs leading to the second floor and what appeared to be a small bathroom. The office was small, but not suffocating. There was enough room for two desks, and a wall of bookshelves filled with file folders separated this area from the front. Little slivers of sunlight came from a set of rectangular windows up near the ceiling.

"It's about time." A tall woman with long black hair and sun-soaked skin snapped her hands to her hips. She had to be at least six feet tall, but that could have been the insanely high heels. "What did you bring me? There is some crazy shit in these accounts."

"Crazy shit we can give to the FBI?"

"Crazy shit that could get him thirty years or more." The woman stood over her desk and pointed a manicured nail at the spreadsheets before running a hand through the long curves of her hair. "Following the money was like a back-alley scavenger hunt. The money goes from his bank here, to Switzerland, and then to Cyprus. We almost lost the trail after that—there was another name on the account in the Cayman Islands. And that account? There are so many accounts funneling to that one it isn't funny." She shook her head. "For a dive with crappy cars, they pull down a lot of money. And that money takes one hell of a world tour. It looks legit, but no matter how hard they try, they can't create VIN numbers out of thin air."

A redhead with her hair in a ponytail came down the stairs. Chase recognized her from CPD. Or at least she used to be with CPD. "That's where we got them." Her slippers didn't make a sound as she shuffled across the room.

The dark-haired woman looked up from the spreadsheets and sighed. "Could you at least put on some real shoes?"

The redhead stopped short. "What's wrong with these? This is Rick and Morty."

"Shoes shouldn't have faces."

The redhead looked confused. "Whatever. I cross-referenced valid VIN numbers and the cars they've sold. Not all of their sales have valid numbers."

"Who are you?" the dark-haired one asked Chase, and then ignored him to shuffle the pile of paperwork.

"Chase Montgomery."

Her head snapped up. "Wait. *The* Chase?" Her brown eyes roamed up and down his body. And not in an *I want to do you* kind of way. More of an *I want to skin you alive* kind of way.

The redhead—what was her name? Chase couldn't seem to remember—nodded, eyes narrowed. She apparently knew who he was too. He had a feeling it was good thing there weren't any weapons nearby. These women did not appear to like him. And he had no idea why.

"Do I know you?" he asked the dark-haired one. Maybe she was another former cop. It would make sense. Maggie and the redhead were both ex-CPD.

She laughed. "No."

"Did I pull you over when I was patrolling back in the day?" He had to have done something to earn that look of contempt cross her face.

Her laugh deepened. "No."

Maggie held out a folder. "Don't mind Leti. She obviously hasn't had her daily dose of caffeine." Maggie gave Leti some sort of look. "She's a pain in the ass without it."

Leti grasped the file and shot her hip out to the side. "At least we can pinpoint why I'm a pain in the ass. What's your excuse?"

"I was born this way." Maggie walked across the small room to a second desk, covered in paperwork and surrounded by filing cabinets and bookshelves. If she could find anything in that mess it would be a miracle.

The redhead sat behind the computer at the other desk. "Okay, Lady Gaga."

"Do you remember Danni Stein?" Maggie waved at the redhead with one hand, at the same time she sat down and opened the drawer of her desk, producing a big bottle. The insides rumbled like maracas as she opened the cap and tipped two small pills into her hand. "Tylenol?"

"I'm good." Now he remembered the redhead. "Danni. You worked in the cyber division."

"Yep." Danni was the computer guru who would get him and his team intel on the job. Not that he'd had all that much one-on-one time with her. But she seemed nice. At the least she wasn't eyeing him like she was going to yank out his spleen and eat it.

And sometimes, that's all you could ask for.

---

MAGGIE WATCHED her friends as they stared at Chase. Well, Danni didn't stare, but Leti did. Leti had never met the man. Which had been a good thing. Maggie could see the wheels turning in her head already. How could any red-blooded woman not see how hot he was?

All the pining and drinking Maggie had done was probably starting to make sense. She'd been stupid for love. It hadn't been Maggie's finest hour, and she hated to think about it, but it was hard when your mistake stood in the middle of your detective agency. *Mocking you.*

And his presence did somehow mock her. She wasn't sure quite how, but it was there like a black cloud raining on her parade.

"Since he's here, does that mean you still need a babysitter?" Danni let out a giggle. Like needing a babysitter was somehow funny. Although Maggie would bet it wasn't the need for a babysitter, but who the babysitter was that Danni found hilarious.

Let the mocking commence.

"Apparently." Maggie couldn't help but eye her captor up and down. She wanted to complain about his hovering—about the fact that she supposedly needed someone to keep her safe like she was a toddler whose parents were on an extended vacation. But really, if one was going to be forced into being chaperoned, there were worse captors she could have.

Thoughts like that were the reason Chase was her strongest weakness.

"Sometimes I swear your dad is as bad as a Jewish mom." Danni laughed. Apparently, she found this funny. When her mom went all helicopter, she wasn't wearing that goofy smile.

"I was going to say Mexican mom." Leti took the chair next to Maggie's desk. "I'm surprised you don't have black steel bars on the windows." She leaned over and eyed Maggie's feet. "Although a plastic bubble might go better with those shoes."

Maggie held up one foot. Those shoes were cute. "What's wrong with my shoes?"

"They're like jellies. Like those shoes we'd wear to the beach when we were seven."

"Yes!" Danni slapped her desk and wheeled over to Maggie. "That's exactly what they look like. I was trying to figure it out. Plastic crisscrosses. I had a pair just like that, but it had a plastic flower in the center."

"We have two young women on the run for their life. Maybe we should focus on that and not on my shoes." Maggie looked at the crisscrossed pattern. It did look rather jelly-ish. Not that she'd admit that to them.

"I think we can make fun of your shoes and put

Katsaros in jail at the same time." Danni poked at Maggie's shoe, running an index finger along the puffy pattern. Like Danni could talk while she wore cartoon slippers on her feet.

"We are excellent multitaskers." Leti leaned down. "How does it feel?"

Maggie shoved back until the chair bumped into the wall, and slipped her feet behind the legs before Leti could start fingering her feet.

*Fingering her feet.* That just sounded wrong.

"Get to work. Multitask on the cases you have." Maggie knew they were great at multitasking. It was a requirement of the job, working more than one angle at a time. They had to keep each job spinning as they followed them through to the end.

Usually their multitasking superpowers came in handy. But today it was more annoying than anything else. Speaking of annoying... "And stop parking your car in front of the garage door. The testy tenant couldn't get into his garage all night."

"We didn't park here last night. You called and told us to go home. This is the first time we've been back." Leti sighed as she stood up.

Maggie hadn't even thought of that. She'd told them to work from home until they could sort the Jillian mess out, or until they had to find an intense amount of dirt on a dirtbag. Of course, her friends rarely ever did what she told them to do, so one could understand her confusion. "So, who was parked in front of the garage?"

"I don't know. I left my tarot cards at home." Leti sat on the edge of her desk.

Danni laughed. "You totally took my line. I was going to say crystal ball."

That Maggie had basically said the same thing to the testy tenant was probably why the three of them got along as well as they did. Tarot cards, crystal ball, Magic 8-Ball—similar, but still different. It was what made them good at their job. No. It made them great at their job.

"You could go next door and ask him." Chase had somehow wandered over and was leaning against the wall by Maggie's desk. She'd forgotten he was still here.

Cue the laughter from Danni and Leti.

"That is so funny."

"Ask testy-tenant."

The two women doubled over in fits of laughter. Like testy would give them any information.

"I'll go." Chase stepped away from the wall and reached for his badge on the way to the back door.

"Are you going to let him go alone?" Danni stuck a file under her arm and headed for the stairs.

Maggie shrugged. "Why not? He's a big boy."

"Hike up your big girl panties and go deal with the testy-tenant before Chase ends up giving away our parking spots and offering to fix all of his make-believe problems." Leti straightened a stack of papers and sat at her desk. She was right.

The tenant had a habit of making up issues to get new stuff. It had taken a bathroom remodel and kitchenette rehab to figure that out, and Maggie didn't have the money to renovate the whole office. Chase didn't know about any of that. The little tenant could be persuasive when he wanted something.

She had to stop him. It was her job. And since this was her building—her responsibility.

CHASE BANGED on the back door of Sal's Delivery Service just as Maggie came outside.

"He's not going to answer." Her scent crept around him and slapped him in the nose.

That smell. It was hard to forget that smell. He'd actually dreamed about the scent. It reminded him of her. Of happiness.

"He'll answer." He had no idea if the guy was even there, but the look on her face after he'd said it was worth the risk of being wrong. Chase knocked again and tried the knob. No luck. "You have a question. We need an answer. If you're afraid to talk to him, I can take care of it."

"I'm not afraid. I just don't want to deal with his bullshit. But if you're a masochist, I won't argue."

"Not argue? Then what will you do during the interview?"

The door flew open and the little man who'd yelled

at Maggie earlier stood in the frame. "What the hell you want?"

Chase turned to Maggie and caught the shock in her eyes. Yep, Chase was right. He gave her a smile as he flipped open his wallet, showing his badge. He had it waiting, since the piece of tin generally got him a minute or two of Q and A.

"You call cops?" The little man glared at Maggie and waved Chase inside. The large warehouse held a fleet of vans with the words Sal's Delivery Service painted on the sides. Chase had a feeling he was about to talk to Sal.

Sal pointed at a window near the ceiling. "She tell you that she's slum-lord? Look at this place. Broken window hasn't been fixed in three months."

"It's a double pane window. The inside glass is cracked, not broken. The outside is fine." Maggie shook her head. "And he hasn't even told you how it broke. A soccer game. Inside. Who plays soccer inside a building?"

With every word Maggie said, little guy's face notched up a shade of red. These two together were the opposite of productive.

"It was company picnic—"

Chase stepped in front of the little man, waving his badge. It was shiny and would hopefully draw his attention away from Maggie—and maybe help tone down the pulsing vein in the old guy's neck.

"She didn't call the cops. I need to talk to you about the car parked in front of your garage."

"Her car?"

"I'm sure you've seen her car before. Was it Maggie's car?"

"No." Sal's eyebrows slashed in confusion. Or frustration. "One of the others."

"Do you know which one of the others? Which one of her staff?"

"I don't know."

"Then how do you know it was one of my staff?" Maggie was not helping. Chase glared, but her mouth kept moving. "Did you know there are like a million cars in the city of Chicago?"

Chase switched his attention back to Sal. "Did you see the color, or the model of the car? Did you get a license plate?"

A license plate would be ideal, but Chase had a feeling this guy didn't notice it at all. Especially since he was so convinced it was one Maggie's employees.

"A black piece of shit, like hers."

"Mine's gray." She didn't argue the piece of shit reference. Smart.

"Yeah. The girl—small one, black hair—took it today with the other car."

"So there were two cars," Chase said. "And Jessi drove away with them both?"

Sal threw his hands up. "No, she can't drive both. The Jessi girl took gray one."

"Did the two cars leave at the same time?" If they left at the same time, it could mean nothing. But it could also mean someone was following Jessi—some douchebag looking for Jillian who'd be willing to attack anyone to get to her.

"Maybe, but I don't think so." Sal ran a hand over his bald head. "Girl left, then the car. Or maybe the car left, then the girl."

So basically, they had nothing. He turned to Maggie. "Can you try to call her?"

She pulled out her phone and dialed. Her eyes lit up as she held the phone to her ear, but slowly dimmed. "She's not answering."

"Wasn't she driving? She might not be able to answer."

Maggie stared at her phone, almost like she was willing it to ring. "Yeah, there's no hands-free in my car, so there's the whole safety thing." She hit a button and brought the phone to her ear again.

Apparently, she wasn't that worried about the safety thing.

Cymbals jingled from the cell phone in his pocket. He looked at Maggie. Their eyes met. Horror erupted in his chest and was reflected in her stare. The screen lit with an unknown number.

He accepted the call and brought the phone to his ear. "Montgomery."

"This is Officer Poole. I'm assigned to the City Hospital, watching Jillian Hendricks."

He'd almost forgot about Jillian and the fact that she was lying in that hospital bed after the attack. "Is everything okay?"

"Yes. She's awake."

"Thanks. We'll be there in thirty." He ended the call and slid the phone in his back pocket.

Maggie's eyes narrowed. At least she'd stopped trying to call Jessi. Temporarily.

"Jillian is awake."

"Oh." She looked down, almost disappointed. "I'm glad she's okay." The look on her face said she might be glad Jillian was okay, but her mind was stuck on Jessi.

"So, we done here?" Sal walked to the door and pushed it open.

"Sure." Chase lifted his hand and rested it on Maggie's lower back—guiding her out. There was no way he'd walk out until she was out of the building. Maggie and Sal together were like toddlers fighting for Mommy's attention. And Chase had no desire to referee who needed a time-out.

Chase's hand slid along her back as she walked over the threshold and into the sunshine. Her skin was warm, but he could feel the worry seep from every bunched muscle. He just wanted to rub his hand along each and every one, getting them all to relax.

They stood in front of his car. He didn't move his hand. He couldn't. Not when she was so concerned. Not when one of her own was in potential danger. He understood. She wouldn't relax until she knew where Jessi was.

"Do you have access to the GPS on Jessi's phone?"

"No...wait." She tipped her new phone to see the screen. "My brother bought me this app for Christmas— well, his wife did. She was worried about me in bad neighborhoods." She swiped and clicked with the intensity of a Chihuahua with a bone. "I have to download it...

damn password… There." She stared at the screen before turning it so Chase could see. A blue dot blinked on I-90, slowly moving toward the lakeshore in Michigan. "Thank God. They're still on their way to the cabin."

"Good." He watched the dot move. "The other car must have left before she came back for yours."

"Yes." She smiled, and some of the rigid tension melted out of her back.

And yes, he hadn't moved his hand. There was a chance he'd never move his hand again. She was warm and soft, and honestly? The thought of leaving made him jittery. The implication of that might have worried him, if he actually took a minute to think about it. Which he didn't plan on doing.

As it was, having her this close quieted any thoughts or implication of those thoughts. Not that he was complaining. He liked having her close. He missed having her close.

Maggie turned to him and smiled. Her body inches from his. So close he could feel her soft to his hard. So close he could feel her breath. And did he mention that scent? Vanilla and flowers. It was all her, and it took everything inside him to not lean in and breathe deep.

He had missed this. Her.

"Thank you." She leaned in and rested her lips on his. Soft lips. Sweet and languid. No demands, just a gentle kiss that stole his breath and made his chest thump.

He'd forgotten how much he liked her. And being with her was making him remember. Which wasn't a good thing. He'd barely survived the first time.

Her hands roamed slowly up his chest. Even through a shirt, he could feel the electricity of her fingers against his body. Every part of him lit. He could probably run a potato clock for months just from one touch.

And this wasn't one touch. One hand wrapped around his waist as she pushed deeper. Her tongue slowly traced his lips. Wet, hot circles arrowing straight through him. Her mouth took everything. His breath. His thoughts.

He had to stop this. They were in the middle of a parking lot. And this wouldn't end well. It never did. There were people around. And perps. And those bad guys wanted Maggie.

He leaned away, little gasps tightening his lungs. "We should go."

Maggie nodded, and a piece of hair dropped in front of her face.

He tucked the lock behind her ear, her head tilting as she looked up at him under long lashes. She was so fucking beautiful—and distracting. But he couldn't get distracted. Not now. "I hate to say this, but you know, Brandi and Brianna—their case just fell into our laps, today. If someone was sitting on your agency for the past week or so, they wouldn't be waiting for them. They were waiting for you. We need to get everyone out of here before they come back. At least until we know what's going on."

"You're right." She nodded. "Let's get them out and then head to the hospital. Jillian needs to start giving me some answers. And I have every intention of getting answers to every single question, before one of my friends gets hurt."

Chase wanted to argue that he needed the answers, but the determination in her eyes—this had gotten personal. Her friends were in danger. She was in danger.

He just had to keep an eye on her—make sure she didn't make any mistakes. Or worse, get herself hurt.

***

MAGGIE WALKED in the front door of the hospital, behind Chase. They'd gotten Danni and Leti out of the office before heading over to question Jillian about her criminal ways. Criminal ways? Maggie's somewhat sunny attitude toward Jillian was long gone. She wasn't just some cheater. She was a drug-stealing gang abettor who didn't care who she hurt. And somehow Maggie and her crew were caught in the crosshairs.

The five minutes of not knowing if Jessi was all right had been like an anvil to the head. It knocked some sense into her. These people were dangerous, and Maggie wasn't about to let her friends get in the middle of it.

Although, knocking some sense might have been an overstatement, since the first thing she did once she realized Jessi was safe was to lock lips with Chase. So maybe that anvil had knocked some of the sense *out* of her head. Because that had been a mistake. It had felt amazing at the time, but the look on Chase's face told her all he felt was regret.

And to be honest, regret was like chickenpox. It spread rapidly, scabbed over, and took forever to heal. And no matter what happened, she just kept picking at the scab.

"She's in room 2331." A nurse behind the counter batted her eyes after Chase showed his badge. Although she might have batted her lashes beforehand, too. Chase had that effect. And the nurse was obviously affected.

The antiseptic smell tickled Maggie's nose as they left the nurses desk and walked past a waiting room.

"Montgomery." Perry poked his head out from the waiting room. His eyes roamed from Maggie to Chase before settling on the watch on Chase's wrist. "Get lost?"

"Some of us were working," Chase said.

"Uh-huh." Perry poked Chase's chest with a file. "This is called working."

Chase opened the manila folder, and Maggie peered over his shoulder. The top sheet was a DMV printout with Jillian's picture and a name. Jolene Simpkins.

Maggie frowned. "Who's Jolene Simpkins?"

Chase turned his head. He was so close she could taste the mint of his toothpaste. Or maybe that was just her remembering the taste of his toothpaste. Minty and oh-so-addictive.

She eased back, waiting for the yelling. It wasn't her business. She should wait in the hall, but he didn't say a word to her. He turned to Perry. "Name change?"

"Name change. Life change." Perry pointed at the folder. "Look at the CQH."

Maggie never understand why they called a Criminal History Inquiry a CQH. Shouldn't it be CHI or at the very least a CHQ? These were the things that kept her up at night. Okay. Maybe not this specific example kept her up at night, but stupid questions tended to keep her up at night. And this was probably going to be one for the rankle bank.

Chase flipped past the DMV record and skipped down to the criminal history.

Identity Theft...

Drug Possession...

Misdemeanor Theft...

The list kept going. "Jillian, or Jolene has been a very bad girl." Maggie leaned over Chase and turned the next page and the next. "Very bad."

Chase cocked his head to the side and stared at the file.

"We should go ask her a few questions." Perry took the folder back from Chase and started down the corridor.

Chase followed, but stopped to give Maggie a pointed look. "Let us handle this. Don't speak."

"Ruff. Ruff." Maggie stuck her tongue out and panted, bending her arms and letting her hands flop. "Too bad for you, I haven't quite learned to roll over."

Officer Poole sat in a chair outside the room. For the love of all that was holy, weren't there like, thousands of cops in Chicago? Why did Maggie keep bumping into Officer Drool?

Drool's face lit up when her eyes found Chase. Of course she lit up. Just his presence turned her into a pinball machine—all loud noises and glaring light. Maggie usually liked pinball machines. This one, not so much.

"You can take a break." Chase smiled. No wonder the girl was all googly-eyed. That smile was dangerous. "We'll take things from here."

"I could use a cup of coffee. Can I grab you one?" She batted those eyelashes as she eye-banged him.

"No thanks." Chase turned to Maggie and Flores. "You ready?"

"Only cops inside." Drool was really starting to piss Maggie off.

"No problem. She'll wait here." Chase nodded at Maggie, like she was supposed to stay. Heel.

Like hell.

Chase smiled. "You know what. I could use that coffee, Officer Drool." Okay, Chase didn't say Drool, but wouldn't it have been hilarious if he actually had said that?

Maggie tried to hide the chuckle building in her throat, but the cops surrounding her just looked at her like she was crazy. She was used to that.

"Do you want sugar or cream or..." Officer Pool of Drool apparently didn't know how he liked his coffee. Good to know. She didn't know the man as well as she thought she did.

Maggie sighed. She was being a brat. She shouldn't be so judgmental of Drool— Poole. It wasn't the woman's fault he was hot in a Han Solo scoundrel kind-of way.

The scoundrel gave Poole directions for his coffee and watched her walk away.

"Let's go in." He nodded to Maggie. "But keep quiet."

Now that Poole was out of eyesight, Maggie bared her teeth at him. "Ruff."

Perry sighed. "Just let us do our cop thing. Okay, Maggie?"

Like she could say no to him. "Sure."

"Come in," someone said from inside the room.

Chase opened the door and walked into the hospital room, followed by Perry. "Good morning, Miss Hendricks." Maggie lingered in the hall after the door swung closed. She hated to say it, but maybe Poole was right. Maybe she should stay outside. If she went in, Jillian might have questions. Then again, if Maggie stayed out, *she'd* have questions.

Maggie opened the door just wide enough to slide through, and stood against the wall—out of the way. She didn't like having questions.

"More police." Steve sat in a chair next to Jillian's bed. He readjusted his glasses and fingered the collar of his light pink IZOD polo shirt as he stood. "Have you found the monsters that did this to..." Steve's eyes rounded as he got a good look at Maggie.

She attempted a smile, but she was pretty sure it fell flat. She'd completely forgotten about Jillian's boyfriend—the client. Well, she didn't forget about him per se, she just forgot he'd probably be here.

Chase took a step closer to the bed. "Miss Hendricks, we're here about the break in."

"Are you the cop that saved me?" Jillian's half-closed eyes, ringed by vivid bruises, were on Maggie. Lacik had screamed that she was a cop when he'd taken Jillian hostage at the sushi joint...when Jillian was on a date with Lacik, not Steve. It was only natural Jillian was a bit confused.

"I'm not a cop," Maggie said.

"But—you saved me right? How come you were at my house?" Jillian-Jolene winced. The girl was covered in so many shades of bruise, she was practically a Smurf.

"Yes, I saved you. I was watching you." Maggie tried to puff up her smile—make it more believable.

"Why were you watching me?"

"We should probably get back to the police's questions so they can leave." Steve gave one of those flat grins to his girlfriend. "You need your rest."

Jillian tried what looked like a pout. "But why was she watching me?"

Silence. No one said a word. Chase and Perry looked at Maggie, maybe waiting for her to answer. Sorry, but this wasn't her secret to share. Steve stared at Jillian with no animosity, just concern. Jillian looked around the room like a tourist seeing the big city for the first time—all bobbly neck and wide eyes.

"She's watching you because I hired her." Steve finally said.

Jillian stared at him. "You. Why?"

"I thought you were cheating." Steve inched his

hand away from hers. "I didn't want to ask you to marry me if you were seeing someone else."

"So, you hire someone to watch me? You could have asked."

"Are you cheating on me?" The words were a whisper. Maggie figured he had to know the answer, but he got points for asking.

Jillian's eyes narrowed, then relaxed. "She's going to tell you anyway. Yes."

"Why?"

"Why not? You fold your socks. You iron your underwear."

"So that's a good reason to cheat?" Steve's voice cracked before he reined it in. "I love you."

Jillian sighed, and something that might have been sympathy curved her lips. "I told you. I don't do relationships. I don't want to sit at home watching sitcoms. I don't want to eat pot roast every Thursday."

"All of the sudden I'm the bad guy because I won't eat raw fish and I don't want to shake my body on a dance floor." Steve poked the bridge of his glasses, pushing them back up his nose.

"No, it's because you won't even try." Jillian lowered her eyes to her lap. She looked so worn. So sad. Maggie could almost feel a tiny pebble of sympathy for her...if Jillian wasn't a drug-stealing liar.

Steve cleared his throat. "I didn't think it was that important to you."

Jillian shook her head and glared at Maggie and Chase. "Whatever. Are you done here?"

"I have a few questions about the attack." Chase managed a glare at Maggie before turning to Jillian.

Somehow this was her fault? Maggie had nothing to do with Jillian's addiction to dancing and sushi. Maggie hadn't forced Jillian to sleep around on her boyfriend. Maggie also hadn't coerced Jillian's boyfriend into throwing all of his cards on the table. Chase needed to keep his glary eyes to himself. This was not the time to deal with all that. There were more pressing matters.

"Jillian, I love you. We need to work this out." Steve kept trying. He was a tenacious guy, even if not the sharpest tack. Jillian was obviously bad news.

"Steve, I need to talk to you." Maggie stepped away from her ineffective hiding spot against the wall. Maybe he needed more of an explanation to fully understand that.

"Right now?" he asked, looking like a kicked puppy.

"Yes." Maggie opened the door to the hallway and waited for him to follow before leading him down the corridor. Beeping, clicking, and machines that mimicked the sound of Darth Vader breathing were all added to the noise of various soap operas. She checked every open door until she found an empty room.

"Here." She walked inside and Steve followed.

"Why do you need to talk to me? I already know she cheated on me, but we'll work it out." His face was drawn. His eyes were rimmed with dark circles from lack of sleep...or the knowledge that his girlfriend had been playing hide the maki roll with another man. But that was just the tip of the sashimi.

How was she supposed to tell this guy that the woman he loved was not only cheating, but stealing drugs from the hospital where she worked? And, oh yeah, Jillian wasn't even her real name.

Maggie felt like she was about to tell a three-year-old there was no Santa Claus, or a drug addict there was never just one more fix. She was going to implode his world, and when it was done he wouldn't want to "work it out."

At least she hoped not. For his sake.

## FIFTEEN

CHASE WATCHED Maggie leave with anti-sushi-man. The poor guy was seriously thinking they'd work it out. Hopefully Maggie could talk some sense into him. At the rate Jillian was going, she'd be doing five to ten at Logan, so unless the boyfriend was looking for a long-term pen pal, he should cut his losses and run.

"So, Miss Hendricks, do you know who attacked you?" Chase smiled. He hadn't used her real name. Yet. He didn't want her to shut down before he got the information he needed.

"No."

"Do you know why they attacked you?"

"How would I know why, if I don't know who?"

"Let's try this again, Jolene." Perry moved closer to the bed. "What were you and John Lacik doing together?"

Jillian's eyes popped open at the mention of her real name. "Lawyer."

This was why Chase hadn't wanted to throw her real name out yet. "So, you're the victim here, and you want to wait for your lawyer to answer questions? You know that whatever this guy is looking for, he won't stop till he finds it. Even if that means he has to come back here. He will."

"He hasn't been back yet."

"You've been unconscious. Once he figures out you're awake, he'll be banging down your door."

With perfect timing, someone banged on the door, and Jillian's body nearly went airborne. White knuckles clutched the bedding as her eyes widened to cartoonish proportions.

A nurse stepped into the room. "Good evening, Jillian. I'm sorry to interrupt, but you need your rest."

"Are visiting hours over?" Chase didn't want to piss off the hospital staff, but he needed these questions answered—now. No matter when visiting hours were over. Although, if the nurse told him to leave, he would. He wasn't a monster.

Although, maybe Jillian needed to deal with this issue on her own.

"No, but with a trauma like this, we want the patient to get as much rest and relaxation as possible." The nurse checked the machinery and wrote down some information in the chart.

"We can leave. The Vipers aren't coming after us." Chase turned toward the door, but his eyes stayed on Jillian. If her reaction a minute ago was any indication, she wouldn't want them leaving anytime soon.

"No, please stay."

The nurse finished her paperwork and eyed Chase and Flores up and down. "Don't stay too long. She needs her rest." She left the room.

Once the door was closed, Chase started—or continued, depending how he looked at it. "What were you and John Lacik doing together?"

"Dating."

"We should leave." Chase didn't have time for this. If she wanted to be the bait, so be it. He glanced at Flores and jerked his head toward the door.

"No. No." She sat up straight. "I don't want you to go, but John and I are dating."

"And..." Chase waited.

"And?" She sighed and leaned back against the pillows on her bed. "And we've been in business together. The drugs are leftovers. It's not like anyone was going to use it. All we do is waste it. Almost full vials, so I took the leftover medication for his business."

For his business? It sounded so innocent—like he was an entrepreneur, not a drug selling dick-wad. "What medication?"

Jillian worried the bedspread, smoothing out the edge. "Fentanyl."

"To make a more addictive and lethal form of heroin?" Flores sat in a chair in the corner of the room.

"No. Not like that. I mean, yeah, it is more addictive. But we talked about the dosage to use so that people wouldn't overdose."

"He must have lost the memo." Perry turned to Chase. "Are we at four dead?"

"Five."

"I told him to keep it under twenty micrograms. Twenty micrograms." Tears pooled in Jillian's eyes. "That's what I told him."

"The guy who stormed into your house. What was he looking for?" Like there was any doubt in Chase's mind what the deadbeat was looking for.

"We had a few bottles of medication."

*Bottles? Medication?* Chase was positive he hadn't said the word out loud, but his face must have had it written all over it because Jillian flinched.

"Okay, bottles of fentanyl."

"How many is a few?"

"Ten."

His definition of *a few* was very different from her definition. "And how big are these bottles?"

"I don't know. Eight ounces?"

"Full?" Eight once bottles of Fentanyl. Not one, but ten.

"Yeah. I've been working a lot of overtime, and it only takes me a few weeks to fill a bottle."

"How did you steal that much without anyone noticing?"

"How could you steal pain medication from patients who needed it?" Flores' face showed the disgust that Chase felt.

Jillian stared out the window. She seemed to be struggling with something. Maybe the truth. Maybe she wanted to answer with that one word that drove him crazy. *Lawyer.*

But instead she gave another sigh. "It's not like that.

I didn't take medication from patients. Just the stuff that would have been wasted."

"So you took the wasted meds—the stuff the hospital was going to throw out."

"It's ridiculous." Her hands fluttered. "It *is* such a waste. The hospital buys five milliliter vials because that's less expensive than buying the two milliliter single-dose ones. And some patients take lower doses, so there's always going to be stuff left over. The hospital buys the bigger vials knowing it'll get thrown out. It's all so wasteful. Everyone's trying to make a buck, so I figured why not put it to good use. Maybe make a few bucks myself."

"Your good use has a body count," Flores growled.

Chase forced himself to sound calm. "How did you do it? I know you have to have someone watch you throw out any medication."

Jillian shrugged. "I would give the patient their dose and hold onto the vial until break. Everyone is so busy, we wait till the end to waste meds. I'd squirt the leftover fentanyl into an empty bottle of hand sanitizer and replace it with water before I grabbed another nurse to waste the medication." She shook her head. "The other nurses can vouch that I've wasted medication, but all I'm doing is wasting water. And I get to keep what the hospital was just going to throw out. It's like when you take old produce out of the garbage at the grocery store."

Flores snorted. "Yeah, normal people don't do that."

"But you could. It's garbage." She leaned forward,

her voice strengthening with every word. "They're not going to use it, so we do."

"It's illegal."

Jillian eased back against the pillows and all that strength drained out of her. "It should be illegal for these companies to overcharge for medication that's never going to be used. Where are the cops busting these greedy conglomerates?"

Chase wished he could argue, but he couldn't. That didn't make selling it on the streets all right, though. "So, where are the *few* bottles now?" Few. He still didn't see ten bottles of this crap as a few.

Her eyelids drooped, and he reminded himself that she was in the hospital and recovering. "They're in a red b...ag. Under my...my bed. Hide-a-key under the blue pot with yellow..." Her head rolled to the side as her words slurred to a stop.

That nurse had been right about Jillian needing to rest. And if they didn't wrap this up soon, that nurse would be up his ass like a hemorrhoid.

"Thank you." Chase watched her nod off. "We'll be in touch." He opened the door and walked out.

Perry followed him out into the hallway, looking left and right. "Where do you think Maggie went? Have you thought about putting a bell around her neck?"

"The thought has crossed my mind." He headed toward the elevator. There wasn't much the other way, and she'd be looking for a room or place to hide away and talk. Hopefully, she was talking some sense into that guy, although how much could she really say with an active investigation going on?

---

Maggie hated this part. She hated having to tell clients the truth about the people they loved and trusted. But she had a responsibility to him.

"Look, I know she cheated. I get it." Steve reached for his back pocket. "I can give you cash for the balance of what I owe you."

"It's not about that." She cringed. She hated that money was even mentioned when she was about to shatter his word. But her damn fish liked to eat, and liked a roof and walls. All things that took money. "I can send you a bill."

"Okay. Well, thank you." He slid his wallet back into his pocket. "I should get back to her."

"Wait. You don't know everything." She blocked the door, scrambling to find the right words. He needed to understand. Maybe she'd been looking at this all wrong. Maybe she should skip the whole police *and* PI thing and find work as a barista. They were always giving good news and caffeine. Everyone loved baristas.

"What more could there be to know? I'm going to propose to her."

Propose? She needed to work fast. "Look, I found out some more information about Jillian. It's not just that she was cheating on you, although that's pretty awful. I would guess that would be pretty awful...especially if you were going to marry her."

"What else could there be? Is she a stripper or something?"

"No, not a stripper." Although being a stripper would probably be good news in comparison. She reeled in the overwhelming desire to ramble and sucked in a deep breath. "Look, while I was watching her, we ran into the police following her boyfriend." Literally ran into the police, or the police ran into her, but who was counting. "She's been stealing drugs from the hospital where she works. Have you watched the news lately? The heroin laced with fentanyl is coming from the stuff she's been stealing."

Steve took a step backward and sat down hard on the empty bed. "Drugs?" His eyes were wide.

"Yes. People have died."

"She's stealing it from the hospital and patients. Is she selling it?"

"I don't know how she's getting it from the hospital, but she is stealing the medication and yes, she's selling it."

He made a strangled noise. "That would explain the new flat screen and the cappuccino maker." He rubbed his face with both hands. "What am I supposed to do now?"

"Steve." Maggie walked over to the side of the bed and rested a hand on his shoulder. "I can't tell you what to do, but I can tell you that she's going to jail. If you stay with her, you'll be looking at years alone. And then maybe one day she gets out. Will you be able to trust her in your house with patient information? Would she try to order medication using your credentials, or try to get it from someone on your staff?" She gave his shoulder a pat. "I'm sorry. It's just something you have to think about." If there really was anything to think about. True, she'd had more time to come to grips with Jillian's lies—oh, and she wasn't planning on proposing to her.

"I thought she was the one. I love her. I do, but I'm just a dentist." Steve's hands fell to his lap and he stared at Maggie. "I don't want to have to watch my back. I want someone I can grow old with and have kids. How could I trust her around kids? Is that wrong?"

Faced with the bleak look in his eyes, Maggie felt like crap saying anything else, but maybe knowing all of it would be for the best. "I'd love to tell you that she'll change, that she'll come out reformed. But she's already been in jail. You're thirty-one, right?"

He nodded, frowning a little, and Maggie leaned her hip against the footrail of the bed and continued. "If she's lucky, she'll only get ten years, and maybe she'll get parole earlier than that. I know you love her. But do you want to put your life on hold while she pays her debt to society? Is it fair for you to have to pay for something you've never done?"

"But—I love her."

"Does she love you? If she does, why would she put you and your life in jeopardy—with another guy." Maggie bumped his shoulder. "You deserve better."

"I know. I just can't believe this." He stood up and paced. "I just wanted to make sure she wasn't cheating, not...this."

"Then walk away. Clean break. Let her deal with

the mess she's made. Distance yourself. And move on. There are plenty of woman out there—who don't commit felonies."

"That's a pretty low bar." Steve offered her an anemic smile. The poor guy's world was crumbling around him. But this was for the best. "I should probably move all my stuff out of her place then."

"Probably."

"Clean break, right?"

"Excuse me." Chase and his broad shoulders took up the doorframe. "We should head out."

"We're done here." Steve exhaled a long, loud stream of air and headed toward the door. "Thanks, Maggie."

Chase moved to the side to let him through, then came in the room. "That was nice."

"How much did you hear?" Maggie shook her head. "Breaking a guy's heart is nice?"

"I heard enough. And yes, nice. Telling that guy what he needed to hear is nice. Maybe he can move on and find what he's looking for. He won't waste his time."

"I guess." She wanted to believe that. She had believed it as the words left her lips. "What if she was his soulmate? What if he'll never find what he's looking for, because Jillian was the one? And I opened my big mouth and talked him into walking away."

How many times had she thought she'd missed out on the one when Chase had walked away? And here she was telling Steve to walk away. She hated giving the bad news, but she knew it was a necessary part of the job. And every once in a while she would get hired to watch someone not cheating, not stealing, and not selling drugs. Although, the selling drugs things was a new one.

Chase shook his head. "Do you think God would play such a cruel joke on this guy and have his *one*—out of millions of people, mind you—be a drug-dealing tramp?"

"Drug-dealing tramp?" Maggie raised her eyebrows.

"Tell me she's not." Chase wasn't as attractive when he was right. Correction, he wasn't as attractive when *she* wasn't right.

Maggie couldn't exactly disagree. The woman did have a history of stealing, drug trafficking, and cheating. Then there was also the lying. There were so many words that could be used to describe Jillian, and none of them were good.

Chase tipped his head to the side and shrugged one shoulder. "I see why you love your job. I couldn't have told him half of what you'd said. You weren't held back. You were able to tell him everything. And you were right." Why did he look more attractive again when he was telling her she was right? The sincerity in his eyes and the way his lips wrapped around the words, *you were right*. So damn sexy.

"Where's Perry?" She had to change the topic before she jumped him right here in the hospital.

"He went back to the precinct. Don't you want to know what Jillian had to say?"

Jillian's interrogation. She forgot all about that when she'd left with Steve. "Yes, I want to know."

"Then let's go. We need to stop at Jillian's. I'll give you a breakdown on the way."

"Really?"

"We're in this together. Wherever I go, you go, right?" He went to the door and held it open.

She shot him a smile as she slid out the door. "That's the rumor."

# SIXTEEN

WHEN CHASE PULLED up to Jillian's house the sun
was already down, and he could barely tell the outside
was covered in ugly popcorn stucco. The lights were all
out. No movement. Exactly what he'd hoped to find.

"At least she wasn't stealing pain medication away
from patients," Maggie said.

He'd told her everything Jillian had said during the
interview, and she was pretty hung up on that fact. He
didn't get it. "Does it somehow make it better? She was
stealing drugs to sell to kids—drugs that killed people."

"Not better..." She stared at her hands, apparently
lost in thought. "But at least the patients didn't have to
suffer. When my mom was in the hospital...watching
her? She couldn't talk. Her eyes didn't open. I always
hoped she wasn't in pain—that the nurses gave her all
the meds she needed."

He reached across the console, bumping a pair of
Flores' sunglasses, and wrapped her hand in his. "I'm

sure she didn't suffer." Of course, he couldn't be sure. But actually, admitting that out loud wouldn't help anyone. He'd learned that when he'd watched his grandmother drift away. He didn't want the truth. He wanted to know she was moving on to something better —that all her pain was over. Belief was a powerful healer.

Maggie gave a half smile and turned away. She picked up the sunglasses, a pair of gold wire-rimmed aviators. "Are these yours?" *And insert subject change.*

Which wasn't all that upsetting to Chase. Things had been starting to get a bit heavy. "No. Flores bought those thinking it was still the eighties."

"He has sunglasses in your car." She slid them on.

The smile on Chase's mouth had nothing to do with the woman across from him wearing ridiculous sunglasses that engulfed her face. He just knew what was coming. "He does, and I have sunglasses in his car."

"Does he have a drawer, too?" She poked at the random pens and breath mint boxes stuffed in the center console.

"No." Chase lifted a box of Mentos from the clutter. "But these are his favorite."

"Awww. How sweet. Does Raquel know you two have gotten this serious?"

"She doesn't mind sharing him with me. In fact, she's constantly trying to get me to take him."

She laughed as she put the sunglasses back. "That's probably why Perry is constantly trying to stay on her good side. He's afraid he'll get stuck with you."

"Probably." Chase laughed and looked over the

darkened street. No cars. No traffic. He opened his door to the cool evening air. Crisp and moist. The lawns were still matted and brown from the winter's snow. All the trees were tall brown stumps sprouting sticks. "Although, let me tell you, he is no picnic."

"Is any man a picnic?" Maggie opened her door and stepped out.

Chase stopped in the middle of the street and stared. Really? That's where she took the conversation?

She flipped a hand at him. "I didn't mean it like that. I mean, really, is any man or woman a picnic? Is life just one big picnic? Ant free. Rain free. No weird crust forming on the fermenting potato salad. No! Mayonnaise-based salads should not sit out, and rain happens. So do ants, for that matter. Everyone needs a break." She smirked and turned on her heels. "Some of you just inspire longer and more elaborate breaks."

Who could argue with that logic? Chase sighed and walked across the street and around the corner. In front of Jillian's house, he found the blue flower pot with a yellow stripe and slid the spare key from underneath. Up the cement stairs he stomped, trying to keep his annoyance in check. A hidden key for a house filled with illegal drugs. Dumbest thing ever.

"Hide-a-Key, huh?"

"Don't get me started." He yanked down the police tape and used the key to open the front door.

The house was still. Quiet. The smell of blood—metal and funk—swished around his nose.

"What are we looking for again?"

"Red bag under the bed." He walked through the

living room, giving a wide berth to the evidence hardening on the floor. "Don't touch anything."

"But I wanted to complete my Hummel collection." She pointed at the remaining baby-faced porcelain figurines lining the shelves around the room. Most took a nosedive in the battle last night, but there were still a few left.

"Don't touch." His footsteps echoed in the silence as he made his way through the living room and kitchen to a bedroom. Clothes and various crap lined the hallway. And the bedroom—so much worse. There was a knee-high shrine-pile to the shoe gods propped in the corner. Clothes hung from a workout bike that looked like it hadn't seen a workout in years. Wherever there weren't clothes, there were inches of dust. No dust on the floor though, if there was a floor. All he could see was mounds of fabric.

Maggie kicked a path to the bed and kneeled down. "I can't see with this bed skirt in the way. Am I allowed to touch it?"

"Yes."

"So, there are some things I can touch and some I can't. Will you be providing a list of acceptable touching items?"

"Look under the bed, before I give you something to touch." He knelt and lifted his side of the bed skirt.

Nothing. The room was covered in crap, but all he saw under the bed was Maggie staring back from the other side. And, apparently, the bedroom floor was hardwood. "Check the closet." He stood up and lifted the mattress. Nothing. He moved the clothes on the floor, dumping what appeared to be a wicker clothes hamper. No red bag.

"Anything?" He slammed open dresser drawers. Empty. Finally, he scattered the tower of shoes. "Son of a bitch."

"It's not here."

He really wanted to say something about her stating the obvious, but she looked just as upset as he did. He didn't want to be a total dick.

She pulled out her phone and checked it for the millionth time that night.

"Still no word?" *Now who was stating the obvious?*

If she'd heard anything from Jessi, she wouldn't look like a robbery victim. "Nothing. The car made it to the cabin, though."

"It was a long trip. They might have had something to eat and fallen into bed."

"Maybe."

"If we don't hear from them by noon tomorrow, we'll call the local PD." He motioned to the door. "Why don't we head back to the hotel?"

She slid the phone into her pocket and stepped toward the door. A crackle came from the underfoot. Maggie bent and unearthed a mangled picture frame. Clearing away the glass fragments, she stared at the picture of Steve and Jillian laughing in each other's arms. Something was obviously churning through her head.

"Are you okay?"

"Yeah. It's just..." She angled out one large piece of glass and set it on the pile of shards she'd created on the dresser. Her finger traced the edges of the frame. "How did they go from this—so happy—to hiring a PI and cheating?"

Chase didn't know how to answer. So many things could happen in a relationship. He'd been there. It was probably one of the reasons he'd given up on the concept a few years back. It wasn't that no one measured up to Maggie. Well, maybe it was a little of that, but he didn't think anyone would ever stick around.

Not that he'd wanted anyone to stick around. Except for Maggie. And here she was standing in front of him.

He moved across the room and leaned in. His lips brushed her temple, feeling wisps of soft hair and the warmth of her skin. The picture was obviously bothering her. He couldn't bear to see her hurting. He might not have an answer, but he could be here for her.

She turned away. "I'm sorry."

Unless she didn't want him to be there for her.

He waited to see why she'd pulled away—why she was sorry. But she didn't say anything for a good minute as she stared at the photo. "I just don't think we should get this confused. Maybe we should back off on the kissing."

"Why? I like kissing you."

She laughed, but it had lost its jingle. "I like kissing you, too. But we need to step back so we can find Jessi and locate the drugs. I don't want start something we have to finish."

"Why would we have to finish?"

She shook her head as she put the frame on Jillian's dresser. "Maybe I should go home."

"You can't go home. How about a compromise? No more kissing, and we'll head back to the hotel and order some food."

"Okay. I could use food." She walked out of the bedroom.

He followed, locking the door once they were both outside. The key slid nicely in his jeans pocket. There was no way it was going back to a Hide-A-Key—drugs or no drugs. "How does a couple of dogs and a beer sound?"

"A couple of beers and a dog sounds better."

"You're right. That sounds much better." A woman after his own heart.

If only that were true.


Two hours later, Maggie said, "This might be the beer talking, but—best hot dog ever."

Chase's teeth bit through the crisp casing of the Chicago-style hot dog. "Yeah, this was a good idea." He sat across from her on the bed in the hotel room, open Portillo's wrappers in front of them both.

Mustard dripped down her hand. "Shit." She put her hotdog down as the yellow carnage extended further and further. Her tongue drifted out of her mouth, slowly sliding along the arch of her palm. Painfully slow. Her tongue twirled, lapping along her skin like a cat with a salt lick.

He should turn away. But how the hell was he

supposed to take his eyes off the tip of her tongue trailing down her index finger. Every part of his body exploded as she slid that finger in her mouth and wrapped her lips around the base. Sucking. Her cheeks hollowed as she pushed her finger in and out. He shifted on the mattress, unable to keep still. *For fuck's sake.*

She lifted her head and stared at him. "What?"

*What? Really?* "How's that mustard?"

"Messy." She pushed another finger in her mouth. At least this time it was quick.

"I see that." How the hell could he have missed it?

"Too bad Perry had to go home to his wife." She picked up her hot dog. "He's missing out."

"Yeah." Missing out, all right. Maggie eating a hot dog was practically X-rated. No one else needed to see that.

She picked up the hot dog and took another bite, her tongue flicking along her lips.

He honestly could not be expected watch this and do nothing. Could he? His jeans were uncomfortable and his mouth felt dryer than a cotton farm.

*I don't want start something we have to finish.*

He'd almost told her how he felt—how he didn't want to finish something they had to start. But given her frame of mind, he didn't think she'd find any amusement in turning her words around. Or find the good in the fact that he wanted to make something out of what they had.

"Mmmm..." She groaned as her eyes closed.

This had to stop.

Chase finished his hot dog—one, two bites. He inhaled it. It was rude, but he didn't care. This sham of a meal needed to be over with already. Crunching the Portillo's paper into a ball and tossing it into the bag, he snatched his beer and tipped it down. The liquid cooled his insides but not much else. "I should go to my room."

"Why?" She grabbed a fry and dipped it in ketchup. Predictably, ketchup dripped on her lip.

He knew what came next. Her tongue. He had to get out. He jumped off the bed. "Ice cream. They have an ice cream bar downstairs. Want some?" He focused on tossing the bag in the garbage can. By the time he looked back at Maggie, her lip was ketchup-free. Thank God.

"I'm still eating." A gob of mustard dropped onto the center of her shirt. Her finger rubbed against the material at the bottom of the spot, scooping up the bulk of the yellow goop and sliding it into her mouth.

For cripes sake, couldn't she eat a hotdog without licking on every part of her body? He'd love to lick every part of her body—from her crisscross-covered feet to the soft, demanding lips—and everywhere in between.

The between was what made his body absolutely throb.

"Okay." He turned. "I'll improvise."

He ran out the door. Ran. Like a skittish deer. But it was either that, or stare until she ran him down. He'd choose skittish deer over roadkill any day of the week.

Maggie sat on the bed watching TV and listening to the noise coming from the next room. Or more importantly, the lack of noise. Chase had gone to get ice cream and brought her a cup over an hour ago. Then he disappeared.

He hadn't come back. Not to talk to her or see her. Nothing. What did she expect? She told him she wanted to step back. Which wasn't exactly true. She didn't *want* to step back. She needed to.

She couldn't live through another disappearing act. The only thing that got her through the last one was copious amounts of wine, a block of chocolate the size of her head, and crying on her best friends' shoulders.

It was the reason her friends weren't all that excited to have him back in her life. And they were right. Standing in Jillian's house and seeing that picture? They had been happy once. And then what? Now Steve was trying to pick up the pieces of his life, not even knowing if he should walk away. He'd hesitated when she told him to leave. Honest to god hesitation. He was actually considering giving her a chance. And Maggie knew why.

That picture.

That picture of them when they were happy. And he probably wanted it back. Sounded familiar.

She and Chase had been happy once, and deep down she knew she'd do anything to get that back. But she also knew he'd walked away. If he walked away again, then she'd be stuck trying to figure out what was wrong with her. Why couldn't he love her?

There might not be enough chocolate and wine in the world if that happened.

But heart or not, she couldn't understand why it was so quiet over there. Maybe if there was something more interesting on TV she wouldn't care. Or maybe if she hadn't played all the games on her phone till she ran out of lives, she could focus on something else. But right now, all she could think about was Chase.

It had to be boredom. Why else would she be so invested in what he was doing? And honestly, the door was open. What would it hurt to go see how he's doing?

Before she could argue with that logic, her feet hit the plush carpet and she walked to the open door and rapped her knuckles on the jamb. "Knock-knock."

"You're still up." Chase sat on one of the two beds and poked at his cell phone. He must not have run out of lives. Lucky guy.

"So are you." She leaned against the frame.

"I just finished a few of the reports and figured I'd answer a few emails." He poked the phone one final time and tossed it on the nightstand between the beds. The tight T-shirt he had on gave her a front-row view of strong arms and a chest that screamed to have whipped cream licked from every crevice. The track pants, which should have been baggy, seemed to hug all his boy-parts in snug, delicious ways. "Is everything okay next door?"

She wanted to tell him no, that he should come check it out. Clothing optional. But she managed to ignore the fire burning in her belly as she said, "Everything is fine."

"Okay good." He ran his hands along his thighs. Thick thighs that would look amazing slathered in chocolate—or without chocolate. "Do you need anything?"

*You.* She thought the word, but thankfully didn't say it out loud. Because honestly, his chest might be whipped cream worthy and his thighs chocolate worthy—his body, though? It would look amazing with her slathered all over it. Using any of those words would lead to hot and sweaty bad decisions. "I think I'm okay."

"Okay then." He looked around the room, like he didn't want to be there. There was an intensity between them she'd never experienced with him before. It wasn't the usual sexual tension. It was a quiet, stilted pressure that made her skin twitch.

She didn't know what tomorrow would hold. If they caught Lacik, she'd never see Chase again. She couldn't leave things like this. She wouldn't. She sat on the edge of the bed—inches from Chase. Her hand found his. Strong, weathered hands—hands that had seen work. Hands that had read her body like a braille hymnal.

Why were they keeping their distance? What was the harm of taking one more night and hopefully getting each other out of their systems? Why sit here in nervous silence?

She traced a path along each of his fingers, playing an internal game of eeny meeny miney moe. When she brought the lucky winner to her mouth and kissed the tip, Chase held his breath.

"Maggie." He said her name like a prayer. His eyes rolled back and he bumped his head against the headboard.

"Chase." She dipped the finger between her lips and sucked.

"I thought we were keeping our distance."

"Screw distance." She drew his finger from her mouth in a painfully slow release. Turning to the bed, she knelt in front of him, arching her leg over his. Straddling his lap, she inched forward till her thighs rested on his.

His hands shot out and pulled her closer. "Is this close enough?"

"I want you closer." She melded her hips to his, friction making her core throb. The reverence in his eyes made her body clench.

Her mouth dropped to his. All the want and need in her body and in his eyes pounded in the meeting of their mouths. It was hot tongues and clashing teeth.

Chase's hands pushed at her shoulders. His breath raged. "Wait." He closed his eyes and shook his head. "I'm going to hate myself for asking this, but are you sure this is what you want?"

She moved his hand from her shoulder to her breast and arched back. "Yes."

"Say it." Chase moved his hand, massaging with steady strokes, but he didn't lean in. He kept his body back against the headboard.

"I want this, Chase. I want you inside me." She rotated her hips as he pulled her tight.

His mouth devoured her as he lifted her off his lap and set her on the bed. Apparently, all she had to do was ask, and now she was going to receive.

SEVENTEEN

VIBRATING. Maggie woke up the next morning with her vibrator buzzing. Her eyes peeled open. The buzzing stopped. Damn batteries must be dead. That's what happened when you left the thing running all night.

Vibrating. Damn thing started again.

"I think that's yours." A male voice broke through the vibrations. Not any male. Chase.

Why would Chase be here with her vibrator? Maggie looked around the room. Not her room. The hotel. She turned toward the buzzing. Her cell phone vibrated on the side table. Cell phone. That made much more sense than a vibrator.

After the first session of *screwing distance* they'd made their way back to Maggie's room. It was amazing how much area they could cover during a nighttime marathon of *sticking it* to distance.

And it was amazing. She'd never felt so close to

anyone. Ever. He knew every button to push. He was like a Maggie-whisperer.

Her phone skittered some more, and she picked it up. Her father's name glared back from the tiny screen. It was way too early to deal with him. Not to mention she'd never been disappointed that her phone wasn't her vibrator before. First time for everything.

"Jessi?" Chase turned on his side and wrapped an arm around Maggie's waist.

*Jessi.* Maggie was officially the worst friend and boss. She'd completely forgotten about Jessi. Although it wasn't necessarily her fault. Chase had top-notch distraction techniques. "Nope. I'm worried about her." She ignored her father's call and swiped to the contacts on her phone. After clicking on Jessi's name, her picture popped up on the screen as the phone rang and rang.

No answer.

Chase leaned over her shoulder. "Nothing?"

"No."

"I'll get local PD to do a wellness check." Chase tilted his head and brushed her lips with his. "We'll find out what's going on."

"Thanks." She attempted a smile. She just didn't feel it.

"Don't worry. I'm sure it's fine," he said, weaving his fingers through hers. "Why don't we get ready? I need to get to the office."

He kissed her palm. Soft lips. Her chest hummed with every searing stroke of his mouth against her skin. His hard body rested against hers—his front moving in rhythm with his breathing—her back molding to him. She could stay like this forever.

Way too soon, he rolled over and left the bed. Apparently, forever was over.

She groaned.

"Sorry, babe." He slapped at her blanket-covered ass, but still managed to find it. "We've got to find Jessi."

Grabbing briefs and jeans, he quickly dressed. "I'm ordering breakfast while you get ready. What do you want?"

Her stomach kicked at just the thought of food. Jessi and those girls were still out there. "Just coffee."

"You sure?"

"Yeah." She pulled the blankets over her head. The sheets covering her were warm and smooth. It was comfort. And safe. And she didn't want to leave the room. Right now, they still had hope. What if something had happened to them? She didn't even want to think about it. She wanted to stay in her quiet cocoon just a little bit longer.

A dial tone filled the air. *Beep. Beep.* "I'll have an egg and cheese bagel and two coffees. Can I get those to go?" Chase asked. The phone clicked when he hung up.

"Ready to go?" The blanket jerked, and Maggie snatched for it.

No. "Yes."

"Good." A quick tug, and the blankets slid down her body.

Cold air nipped along her skin as the blanket

slowly disappeared. "No." She held onto the edge, but Chase gave one more yank and the blanket was down and gone.

She shivered. "It's cold out here." She was naked. And uncovered. And her nipples were hard enough to cut glass—if that was something that was necessary in life.

"Get up, Magpie. We got things to do."

She left the warm, wonderful bed and found her clothes strewn all over the room. There might have been some grumbling—maybe a dash of glaring, and definitely a smidge or two of stomping.

Pants. She found her pants sprawled in the corner of Chase's room. Of course, no shirt.

"Remind me to never plan a morning date." Chase stood over the side table poking at his cell phone—fully clothed. How had his clothes landed in one pile last night? She tossed a bed pillow onto the floor and found a sock.

Morning date. Like there'd ever be a morning date. Or an evening date. This wasn't a *dare to date* opportunity. This was a— *we have a free hotel room and some free time, so let's practice some free sex—* opportunity.

No matter how enjoyable the opportunity was. She rescued her underwear from the top of the lampshade as Chase watched, a huge grin scrawled across his face. She'd thought the hike of shame she'd taken yesterday was embarrassing. This was so much worse.

"Lose this?" Chase held out her shirt—with the mustard stain.

So. Much. Worse. That canary-eating grin still stuck on his stupidly smug face did not help.

"Thanks." She yanked it from his hands and bolted for the bathroom. Dropping the clothes on the counter, she leaned over and turned on the shower.

Her reflection was the stuff of bad mug shots. Not that there were ever good mug shots. Hair stuck out in Medusa spikes. A red line crossed her cheek from sleeping on her hand or something. Her eyes carried an entire set of matched bags. Thankfully, the steam built fast and the reflection in the mirror disappeared.

A much-needed shower later, Maggie was dressed and wearing the clothes from last night—minus the mustard-stained shirt. She really should have bought a whole other wardrobe yesterday morning, but she never thought she'd be here another night. Steam rolled out of the bathroom as she walked into the cool air of the hotel room and found the other shirt she'd bought, still in the department store bag.

Chase stood near the bed holding a cup of coffee. Offering it to her like an angel coming with heavenly gifts.

"Thank God." She brought the small cup to her mouth and tipped it back. Hot liquid burned as it passed down her throat. Slowly sliding down and warming her stomach. "Where's the rest?"

"That's all there is. We'll pick up something on the way."

"On the way?"

"To the precinct."

"I guess that means I have to tell my father about

the beach house." The thought of that sat on her chest like a stone.

"I could tell him."

"Nah, I want to." *Want* was a bit of an overstatement. "It's my story to tell."

Half a bagel sandwich sat on a tray on the dresser. It looked good—fluffy eggs and cheese stuffed between a head-sized bagel. Half the head was sitting in Chase's hand, and her stomach growled as the scent of butter and eggs hit her like a wheel of cheddar. She needed to eat. She couldn't go all day and not have anything to eat —not if she wanted to be useful.

She picked up the half sandwich and raised it to her mouth. Warm gooey cheese strung down as she took her first bite. Heaven.

"You said you weren't hungry."

"It's your fault. It smells so good." She wrapped a string of cheese around her finger and popped it in her mouth as Chase stared. And he wasn't staring in his *I want to eat you* kind of way. No this was different. "Stop looking at me like I stole your bike."

"This is worse than stealing my bike. I can get my bike back. You stole my breakfast." Chase swiped a hand at her food. "Once you eat it, you can't give it back."

"I can give it back, but I don't think you'll want to eat it after I have." She took another bite. Every mouthful forced the nerves in her stomach to calm a bit. That could have been the coffee, though. Coffee was magic.

"You're buying me breakfast." Chase grabbed his keys.

She bit into the bagel and groaned. They must have used extra butter on the bagel and extra cheese. It was a heart attack waiting to happen, but it tasted so damn good. "I thought this was breakfast."

"It was my breakfast. You said you didn't want anything but coffee." He leaned over, his mouth hovering close to hers. "But now you owe me."

"I owe you and you want breakfast?" Her body gravitated toward his—traitorous body. She had things to do and didn't have time for his body anywhere near hers.

But the thought was really tempting.

"Yep." His hand slid slowly down the side of her face. "Breakfast, for now."

"And for later?" Little flickers of electricity spun around her stomach at the thought of later. Later held so much promise.

"And later—I'm going to lick and taste until you groan that way again." He turned and walked out the door.

Two hours later, Chase sat at his desk in the precinct trying to keep his eyes from drifting across the bullpen of cops and detectives to the woman in the conference room. The precinct was busy, phones rang and keys on computers clicked as people typed up reports. Chase's phone had rung on and off all morning, but nothing could take his mind off Maggie.

If he was smart he would have put her in a conference room with no windows—or at least on the other side of the building. But no. In his infinite wisdom, he thought it would be a good idea to keep an eye on her. Well, it worked. His eyes were on her, sitting at the conference table twirling the pen in her hand, and nowhere else.

She still looked worried, but the email from the Spring Harbor Police Department saying they were on their way to do a wellness check at the cabin seemed to have lifted some of the stress from her shoulders.

Not that he could blame her. If one of his guys wasn't answering his cell phone, he'd be worried too.

"Montgomery." Chief Lane came from Snake Row —the curved hallway that lined all of the big-wig offices. He took one step, passed the conference room at the end of that hall where Maggie sat, and shook his head. The old man walked toward Chase, that scowl somehow deeper. "We need to talk."

That was never good—no matter who said the words. Chase followed the chief through the bullpen and out into the cool spring day.

"I got a disturbing call this morning. I have a friend in the FBI, and they mentioned a collaboration between our office and the FBI task force. You can imagine my surprise, since I knew nothing about this."

Shit. He never thought the FBI would reach out to the chief. Miscalculation. "I came across some information to solidify a case against Peter Katsaros. It didn't fall under our jurisdiction, so I contacted a friend in the FBI. I provided information on money laundering and criminal activity."

"And where did you get this information? You are working three cases—the Johnson case, keeping my daughter safe, and getting John Lacik off the street so you don't need to keep her safe. Do any of those cases leads to Katsaros?"

"We were able to close the Johnson case." Chase wasn't lying. Maybe misdirecting slightly. He hated to hide things from his boss. Lane had been there for him so many times over the years. The old man put Chase on the fast track to Lieutenant and had treated him like a son.

The chief sighed. "Is there something I don't know?"

So much. But what was Chase supposed to do? Maggie didn't want her dad to know...or maybe she had just said she didn't want to tell him. That was it. She'd said he wouldn't understand. Easy enough. Chase would just need to make him understand.

"Sir, I received information that Katsaros' daughters needed help to get away from their abusive father." Removing children from abuse was always easy to understand. "We removed them from the home and..."

"How exactly did you remove them from the home? Did you contact DCFS?"

Had he thought this would be easy? Maybe if they had followed the legally-accepted procedure to get them out of the house. He knew it. Hell, he'd known it then. "We didn't have time to get them and the bureaucracy involved."

"Bureaucracy? This doesn't sound like you." The chief shook his head. "It sounds like Maggie, and what she calls bureaucracy is actually rules. Rules that keep people safe and ensure that agencies don't act outside of their jurisdiction. Rules that keep us from succumbing to chaos. Rules that enforce the law."

Bureaucracy. That *was* her word, not that Chase would admit that to her father.

"I don't like you encouraging this nonsense, and I sure as hell don't like her influence over you. My daughter needs to come back to CPD, and she won't if everyone keeps coddling this obsession of hers."

"This has nothing to do with CPD. This was Maggie helping two abused girls get out of an abusive home."

Chief Lane pinched the bridge of his nose. The universal indication that he was not happy. "I don't like you getting mixed up with her. She's destroyed her career, and I don't want to see her destroy yours too."

"I don't think—"

"You're right. You're not thinking. How did those children get out of the house?"

"Maggie's coworker picked them up."

"So they've been abducted?"

Abducted? Chase thought about that. The removal of a child from their home without consent of the parent or legal guardian... Shit. "Technically, yes, but..."

"There's no but. Either you've aided and abetted an abduction or you haven't."

"I don't know what to tell you." Chase knew the answer, but he had no idea what the chief wanted him to do about it. It was done.

Chief Lane moved his hand back and forth over his forehead. That was a new one. He'd never seen the man this pissed before. Of course, Chase had never told the chief he'd broken the law before.

What the hell had he been thinking? Easy. He wasn't thinking. That was the problem. He was following Maggie and doing things he would never do—going against his best judgement.

"This is done. We need to move forward." Chief Lane nodded his head, almost like he was trying to convince himself he believed it. "Let's get back to work. We need to bring those children back immediately. See to it that it gets done. What's the status on Lacik and his crew?"

"We still have people posted at Maggie's, and we have some feelers out to determine which one of his cohorts made that visit."

"Keep me posted. I want to know the minute we have this guy in custody." The chief turned and walked back into the building.

Chase leaned against the building and took in a deep breath. He loved being with Maggie. He loved everything about her—except who he became when she was around.

Which was a distracted law-breaking idiot. This wasn't him. He upheld the law. He did what was right because no one was above the law. And yet, he had completely ignored all of that and let Jessi drive those girls over the border and into Michigan. *Abducted.*

Jessi took them from their father. The ends didn't justify the means—no matter how much he'd wanted to believe that getting them away from their father was the right choice. Taking the law into his own hands was never acceptable.

***

MAGGIE STARED at the texting app on her phone as she leaned back in the chair. The conference room was cold, but she wasn't complaining. The cold kept her mind alert. Her focus was way off and nothing could change that, but the cold at least prevented her from staring at the wall and not getting anything done.

Not that she'd gotten a whole lot done. She'd gotten an invoice together for a previous job, and she'd reached out to someone who'd asked for assistance via their website. So that was something.

What she really wanted was word on Jessi and the girls. Anything. So far, they'd gotten nothing. The cops were supposed to be checking on her father's beach house, but they hadn't checked in yet.

If that wasn't bad enough, she couldn't seem to keep her eyes off the man across the room. Well, she couldn't when he'd been sitting across that room. Now she was forced to stare at an empty chair after her father came in and stole her eye candy. It was amazing. Her father was not only trying to take away the job that she loved, now he was taking away her enter-tainment.

Her father walked back in through the side door of the precinct, his usual scowl firmly in place. Either Chase did something to piss him off, or he was mad at her.

His glare found her as he walked toward the conference room.

*Oh, goodie.* He was mad at her.

Her father stepped inside the conference room and shut the door. This was not shaping up to be a good interaction. He sat across the table and folded his hands. He didn't say a word. His thumb tapped the side of his hand. He was either trying to figure out what to say or he'd officially run out of words. Her vote was for word famine.

"It's taken me a while to come to terms with your choices."

He'd come to terms with them? When did that happen?

His thumb kept tapping. "For some reason, you don't want to be a police officer. *I* will have to live with that."

Emphasis on the "I". Like this was something she chose just to punish him. Like it had anything to do with him.

He stood up from the table and stalked over to the window. "What you do with your life is your business, but you're starting to take down good cops with this —this path."

What path? And what good cop was she bringing

down? She wasn't doing anything but her job. She didn't want to bring down anyone. She wasn't even sure if she had that kind of power.

He sighed and ran a hand over his forehead. "I heard about the Katsaros children."

Ah, that. Dammit. She wanted to be the one to tell him. She wanted to frame it just right. Not that there was a good way to frame that she'd given the keys to the beach house to Jessi and two strangers. No wonder he was on the warpath.

But she could fix this. Maybe. "Don't worry. I have the police checking the house and they'll only be at the beach house for a few days. Jessi has the keys. So, it's someone we trust. Once the FBI can build a case…"

"The beach house?" He looked so confused.

"The Michigan house in Spring Harbor."

"My house? What about it?"

The realization that her father might not have known about the whole plan with the Katsaros kids was hitting her square in the jaw. Hopefully, his figurative anger wouldn't hit her next. "I let the two girls we're helping use the beach house. Jessi is with them."

"So the children you abducted are in my house." His voice raised to an ungodly roar that swung straight into her chest like a battering ram.

"They're not *abducted*. We helped them get away from an abusive parent."

"Was DCFS involved?" He seemed to be tempering his voice—which was good, since she could tell he wasn't voicing his temper. His eyes held fire that seemed to be causing his skin to glow red.

This conversation was not going in the direction she'd hoped. "No."

"Then it's child abduction." He slapped the table and leaned over toward her. "You kidnapped those children and took them across state lines. Then you brought them to my house. My. House. You've brought this family, my name into this.

"Dammit, Maggie. I have watched you swirl your life down the drain. I have tried to talk to you. But this —this is too much for even me. You're not only trying to destroy my career, but Chase's as well."

"It's not like that."

"I don't care what it's like. I want them out of my house and back in the state of Illinois by the end of the day. I'd ask for the keys back, but it's safe to say I'll be changing the locks tonight." His skin flamed brighter with anger. The vein in his neck pulsed.

"Dad—"

"I know you don't respect me or the things I stand for. Honor. Service. Law. But you need to respect the fact that you are ruining those of us that do. I'm asking you to stay away from Chase. He has a career. He has a future. And all you'll do is destroy that. Like you've destroyed everything else in your life."

"Dad, I can't." It was more she didn't want to.

"That's the difference between you and him. When given the option of continuing a relationship with you or letting you go, he chose to let you go."

"What?" When was he given the option?

"Why do you think he stopped talking to you all those years ago? He was smart enough to know that he held you back. If you care about him, you'll see that too."

A bullet would have hurt less. The words cut and twisted a gash in her chest. Her father had told him to leave. It made sense.

She'd thought her and Chase had chemistry back then. She'd thought he liked her. Apparently, he had. But he'd been too busy listening to her father. How could Chase? How could he just walk away? How could he just jump when her father said, "save yourself." Probably because he was trying to save himself.

"Have those girls out tonight." Her father walked out, leaving the door open behind him. And that was it. He was gone. He didn't give her a chance to explain.

She didn't get to give her side of the story at all. The anger in his eyes had nearly killed her. She hated letting her dad down. She hated hurting him. That could not have gone worse.

And what about Chase. What was she supposed to do? She didn't want to ruin his career. She had known getting involved with him was a mistake. It was all a mistake. Her father was right. She needed to get away from him. Fast.

If she could just get word on Jessi. She picked up her phone and shook it. It didn't ring. Not that she thought shaking the damn thing would make the thing buzz.

*Buzz.*

Or maybe it would. She answered the phone before it could buzz again.

"Ms. Lane. This is Officer McKenzie with Spring

Harbor Police Department. We did a wellness check on fifty-seven Waterway Lane. A gray Crown Victoria was in the driveway, but it appeared no one was home."

"Did you break down the door?" Maggie would've broken down the damn door.

"No. The lights were out and the doors were secure.. No appearance of foul play. They're probably out."

"Out where?"

"Shopping? To the beach?" The cop on the other end sighed. "Look, I'm sorry but we have real problems to deal with. We can't look for your friends on their vacation."

"They're not on vacation."

"We can't do anything for forty-eight hours. Then you can file a missing person's report."

"Thanks." She wanted to say that with the sarcasm it deserved, but she knew he was just doing his job. It wasn't his fault. And they probably had more important things to do than find every person who hadn't returned a call. If the cops had that kind of time, her brother Kevin would have been tracked down every day of his teenage career. "Can you please check the shed on the beach? Please."

"Sure. I'll call you right back." The line went dead.

Jessi and the girls wouldn't all fit in that tiny shed, but she needed to feel like something was being done to find them.

Maggie stared out the open conference room door. It was up to her. She just needed a car to get to Jessi. The man with the car had moved back to his desk. And if what her father had said was correct, she was ruining his career.

That was not on her agenda for today or any other day. She could do this on her own, even if she'd given Jessi her car.

She texted Danni for a ride. It was time to take control and stop waiting. This was her mess. She was going to fix it.

## EIGHTEEN

CHASE LOOKED up from his paperwork. Maggie still wasn't back in the conference room. She'd left a few minutes ago to go who knew where. Probably the bathroom.

He looked at his phone. Not a few minutes ago. Fifteen minutes ago. He was rethinking keeping an eye on her. He not only needed to keep an eye on her, he apparently needed to tie a bell around her neck.

He got up and checked the conference room. No computer. No paperwork. Who took that stuff to the bathroom?

Unless she hadn't gone to the bathroom. But where else would she have gone? Out of the building? Shit. The chief had reminded him that Chase was the one keeping her safe. Or more like he was supposed to keep her safe.

His phone vibrated in his pocket. He pulled it out and brought the thing to his ear. "Montgomery."

"This is Officer McKenzie with Spring Harbor Police Department, calling back. I checked that shed and there's no way anyone could fit into that little space."

"Calling back?" When had he called first?

"Yeah, I spoke to some woman using the other number. I couldn't get a hold of anyone on this line earlier."

"Of course." That was when Chase was in the middle of getting an ass-chewing from the chief.

"I told her to file a missing person's report in forty-eight hours. The car is here, but no one is answering the door."

"Can't you go in?"

"Not without a warrant. They're probably sunning themselves at the beach right now. It's a nice beach. Give them time, and they'll probably call you tonight."

"Thanks." The line went dead and he shoved his phone back in his pocket.

This phone call and the missing woman from the conference room wasn't feeling like a coincidence. She wouldn't leave, would she?

Of course she would.

And if he was in the same situation, he'd be halfway down the highway by now. Shit.

Chase strode out the front door, past the cops, past the people standing on the sidewalk waiting for the bus. Maggie wasn't mixed in with any of those groups.

He walked around the building and there she was, standing on the sidewalk next to the side of the building. The side without a door. Without windows. The side of the building where someone who was trying to get away with something sneaky would hide. "Leaving so soon?"

Her shoulders bunched and he could practically hear her eyes slam shut as her head dropped forward. *Yes.* Busted. Too bad he couldn't see her face. He'd bet there was a whole hell of a lot of guilt squinching up her eyes.

She straightened her spine and hiked her bag up higher on her shoulder. "They couldn't find Jessi."

"But they found the car. They think she went to the beach."

"She wouldn't just go to the beach when she's sitting on witnesses."

"I hear it's a nice beach."

She spun around. "It's a nice beach, but she sure as hell wouldn't ignore my calls."

"Is this the one that stole your car and then hung up on you?"

Red crept up her neck and splashed across her face. She looked like a cartoon thermometer waiting to explode. One deep breath later, color drained. "She didn't steal my car. I lent it to her. To get her away from you."

"So you knowingly obstructed justice and removed a witness from a crime scene."

She painted a scary attempt of a smile on her face. "No. She was hiding in the back and hadn't seen anything. She took my car and went to sleep. Like normal people do."

"She didn't hang up?" He didn't know why he was

poking at this. But it was fun. She was getting so worked up, which was a nice change of pace. He was usually the one worked up—worried about her.

Let her squirm a bit.

"She did, but she was asleep."

"Maybe she's asleep now." There was no way she'd been asleep for the past eighteen hours—but again—seeing Maggie squirm...

"Maybe you're an asshole now."

"That's a given." He smiled. He was finally getting to her. "So, what is your plan? Are you going to stand here and wait for a smoke signals? Hire a PI?"

"Danni's coming."

He should have seen that coming. He should have known she'd reach out to her coworkers—her friends—to get to Jessi. He couldn't say he liked it all that much, though. "Why?"

"I need to get to Jessi."

"I get that, but I can take you." He laughed. "Unless you're afraid to be alone in the car with me."

He'd meant it as a joke. World's crappiest joke. The indecision dancing around those troubled eyes told him what he didn't want to hear. She didn't want to go with him. She might not be afraid, but she was...something. Something that made her want to avoid him.

Which put a huge damper on his plans to recreate last night over and over again.

He took a breath. "I saw your father talking to you. What did he have to say?" Like he needed to ask. But he had to get this out in the open.

"Not much." Unless there was an invsibile crime

scene on the sidewalk in front of her, she was avoiding his gaze.

He leaned down and angled his face closer to hers —caught her eyes with his. "I don't care about what the chief said. I'm all in."

"Okay."

Okay? That's all she could offer. Not, *I'm in, too*—ideal. Not a *screw you*—less than ideal. But *okay* was pretty darn close. "Okay what?"

"What do you want, Chase?"

A red Mercedes SUV rolled up to the curb in front of Maggie. She turned, lightning bolts practically spitting from her heels as she bolted for the car door.

Chase wrapped a hand around her arm and held on tight. If she did get a chance to bolt, he was pretty sure he'd never see her again.

"Let go, Chase."

"No."

"Don't we have laws against this?" Holding a person against their will—yeah.

He let go. "Don't run." He was so tired of her running.

"I'm not running." She sucked in a deep breath and sighed it out. "I have to go to them. Jessi is my family and those girls—those girls are my responsibility. I can't let anything happen to them."

Tingling chimes came from Maggie's pocket. "Is that mine?" She pulled the phone out and went pale. "Jessi."

"Put it on speaker." Danni said. Apparently she'd

gotten out of the SUV at some point. Not that Chase had noticed. Or cared.

Maggie jabbed at the screen. "Where are you? Are you okay?"

"I'm fine," a definitely male voice grumbled. "But your three friends are not fine. They want to go home."

"Who are you?" Maggie's eyes narrowed at the innocent phone in her hand, like she was going to singe the thing with X-ray eyes. Good thing she didn't have those or their only connection to Jessi would be ash.

"It doesn't matter. What matters is I want what you stole from me. Jill owes me something, and you have it."

"What are you talking about?" She hit mute as the voice on the other end shouted obscenties and frowned at Chase. "Who has the drugs? We couldn't find them at Jillian's house."

Chase shrugged. "Well, If he's looking for us to bring them to him, someone else must have taken them."

"Who?" Maggie asked, still scowling.

Chase looked from Maggie to Danni. They all probably had the same look of confusion in their eyes.

Maggie unmuted the phone. "Just to make sure, you're looking for the fentanyl."

"Yes."

"Fine. We'll get your stuff, but we want the women unharmed."

"As long as you do as I say, yes."

More assurance would be nice, but she'd take what she could get right now. "Okay. How do you want to do this?"

"Bring me the bottles. We're at this beach house in Michigan. Your friend says you know where it is."

"We'll bring them."

Danni mouthed, *What are you doing?* Maggie shook her head. Despite his misgivings, Chase knew she was doing the right thing. Never show them all your cards. As long as this dirtbag thought they had the drugs, they had leverage to get the women back. Without that leverage, they had nothing.

"And don't try to bring me garbage," the dirt bag growled. "I have a fentanyl test kit. No trade until all the bottles are tested."

Well, there went their leverage. They couldn't very well give him a bunch of fake fentanyl if he was going to test it. They also didn't have a bag full of fentanyl lying around.

"You have five hours."

"It takes five and a half hours to drive up there," Maggie protested as the line went dead. She jammed the phone in her pocket.

"And we don't have the drugs." Danni leaned against her car.

"I know. I know." Maggie's tone said what Chase was thinking.

No drugs and no time to get them. Hell, they barely had time to get to the drop empty-handed.

"You checked Jillian's place?"

"We checked her room and under the bed where she said it would be."

"If this dirtbag doesn't have it, who does?" Danni fiddled with her keys.

Wasn't that the question of the day. Chase looked from Danni to Maggie. "Who had access to Jillian's house?"

"Shit." An almost angelic look illuminated Maggie's face. "Steve."

"Steve?" Chase wasn't sure what Steve had to do with it. Didn't they break up?

It was like Maggie read his mind. "After I talked to him at the hospital, Steve was going to pack up his stuff."

Shit. Steve must have taken the damn bag. "Do you know how to get in touch with him?"

Danni grabbed her cell phone and tapped a few buttons. "He's home."

"Why are we tracking the guy that hired us?" Maggie looked over Danni's shoulder.

"I like to know all sides of the equation." Danni walked over to the driver's side door and whipped it open. "Are you coming?"

Chase stood next to the car and stared as Maggie opened her door. "Come on."

He wanted to go with them. Well, he wanted to get to Steve, but he'd rather be the one doing the driving. "I can drive, if you want to park this thing."

"Why?" Maggie dumped her computer bag on the passenger seat and Danni tossed it onto the back seat behind the driver's side. "Do you have something against Mercedes?"

"No." The door lock popped.

"Then get in."

He opened the door and slid in the back. In. The.

Back. Seat. He hadn't ridden in the back seat of a car since he was picked up by the cops in high school for loitering. He hadn't liked it back then, and he didn't like it now. Call it a control issue. Call it carsickness. In his world, it was all the same.

The car jerked forward, stopping suddenly next to a sign at the exit of the lot. A slide left, pressing him into the doorframe, a jerk back, and they were heading down a rundown side street. Right into the pothole that ate Chicago.

His body flew up, and the ceiling of the car met his head. Hard. Lights flashed in front of his eyes as he grabbed the seatbelt and wrapped it around his body. He jammed it in with a click, fighting the urge to hold onto the belt for dear life and cry like a baby.

"Damn potholes." Danni's red hair bounced in spikes as she hit every divot in the road.

Maggie's hand slapped the dashboard as she tried to hold on. "You could try not hitting all the potholes in the city."

"This street is holier than Swiss cheese." Danni made a hard right, and the car bucked to the side and up.

He was pretty damn sure she'd aimed for that one. His hand hovered over the seatbelt, prayers lingering on his lips.

Maggie braced her hand on the ceiling as they hit another round of bumps. "Why did I let you drive? I know better than trusting you with any life in a car." She winced and tugged at the seat belt. "Especially my life."

That was a fantastic question. Why the hell had he gotten in a stranger's car? Hadn't his teachers stressed the importance of stranger-danger? Apparently, he hadn't been listening.

Of course—lately—most of his decisions went against the basics he'd been taught in school.

*Don't take rides from strangers.*

*Learn from your mistakes.*

*Clean up your own mess...*

That last one seemed to be the biggest issue he had these days. He needed to clean up two messes—his career, and whatever had gone wrong with Maggie. He just didn't know how he was going to go about doing that.

***

MAGGIE WANTED to jump out of the car and kiss the ground after they jarred to a stop in front of a gray brick row house. They were alive. A half hour in the car with Danni and she hadn't run over any man, woman or child. Overall, a success.

The north side neighborhood was relatively quiet. Trees swished along with the hum of the wind blowing down the narrow street. Rush hour was on the verge of starting, but hadn't quite taken hold of the roads.

"This is it." Danni poked and prodded her cell phone. She could control the world from that one device. And her face was usually buried in that thing. Probably why her driving sucked.

Maggie opened the door. "You coming?" she asked Danni.

"Nah, you got this." Danni kept typing and swiping. She wasn't big on the "action" part of the job. She was more the brains behind the computer.

Closing the door, Maggie followed Chase up the front steps of the narrow house and waited while he knocked on the black front door.

Noises came from inside before the door flew open. Steve stood in the doorway wearing a "kiss the chef" apron. "Umm. Hi." He waved a spatula at them.

"Hey, Steve." Maggie stepped around Chase. "Did you go to Jillian's and pack up your stuff?"

"Yeah, you told me to move on." His eyes shifted from her and Chase to something behind him.

"I did. But we think you might have taken something of Jillian's."

"Oh."

"May we come in?" Chase pushed the door open a bit. He must have seen the shifty eyes as well.

"Sure." Steve opened the door wide, still blocking the way. "I have a date here."

"A date?" Already? Not that she'd say that out loud —anything to get him away from the drug-stealing train wreck.

"Sort of. It's one of the hygienists from my office."

Did this guy look for the worst possible person to date? Or was he just clueless? Moving from drug dealer to sexual harassment wasn't the best choice.

She stepped inside, and—wow. The place was gorgeous. A bit plain, but still wow. Bare white walls and white furniture. The only color came from a large black and white geometric painting above the fireplace. "Nice place."

"Thanks. Follow me." Steve walked through the living room and into the large dining room, which wasn't any less color-starved. Black chairs and a black table sat in the center of the space. More white walls. Another painting, a gray clown with a wide white frown. Varying shades of gray finished off the depressingly creepy masterpiece.

Maggie started to feel a smidge of sympathy for Jillian. If this guy's life was as exciting as his decorating —he either inspired naptime, or a nightmare based on Sorrow the Clown.

"Here's everything I grabbed from her place." From the floor, Steve picked up a plastic container about the size of a mini-fridge and set it on the table. Clothes stuck out and hung over the side. No wonder the lid didn't fit.

Chase stuck his hand inside, and dropped a pair of satin boxers on the table. His lip curled, and he swiped his hand on his thigh.

"I hope those are clean." Maggie didn't mean to say that out loud, but it just fell out. Given the glare from Chase, he didn't find it all that amusing. She thought it was pretty funny, but pushed the laughter deep down where it wouldn't bubble up and get her in trouble.

Chase reached inside the plastic box of surprises. Socks—most definitely not clean. A tan T-shirt with the words *Dentists do it in Your Mouth*. Pervy. Steve was losing points by the minute.

"It's not here." Chase pushed what clothes were left to the side.

"What's not here?" Steve said with that mouth as he looked over Chase and Maggie's shoulders, ignoring personal space.

Now all Maggie could seem to do was picture what he did with that mouth. Disgusting.

"We thought you might have taken a red bag."

"My duffel?"

"Your duffel? Jillian didn't mention it was yours." Chase's voice held an edge.

"Of course not. She always took my stuff." Steve pulled the bag out from where it sat on one of the chairs, and put it on the table. It sloshed, and Maggie's heart did a tap dance. Steve huffed. "That should have been my first indication she was a thief."

Chase tugged the zipper open. "Do you know what's in here?"

"Clothes."

"Clothes?" Chase shook the bag and it sloshed again.

Steve frowned at the bag. "Well, my toiletry kit should be in there."

Reaching inside, Chase removed all the clothes and found a big aluminum makeup case. He shook his head as he flipped up the clasp and opened the lid. Ten plastic bottles were nestled inside. Full of clear liquid. Enough to do a lot of damage to a lot of lives.

"What the hell is that?" Steve tried to look into the box.

"Is this box yours?"

"No. Never seen it before."

"So, you won't have a problem if we take it?"

"What is it?" Steve kept trying to eye the contents.

Chase turned the box to him. "Drugs."

"All yours." Steve stepped back like Chase had slapped him. He actually looked afraid.

"Thanks. We're taking the bag." Chase clicked the latch and zipped the red bag. He pointed to Maggie. "I'm driving."

Maggie waved at Steve. "Thanks." Then she followed Chase outside. As she shut the front door, she noticed a small camera angled toward the front stoop. A camera. She'd forgotten about the camera at the beach house.

She practically ran to the car and whipped open the driver's side door. "A camera. My dad's house at the beach has a camera. Can you do your magic and access the feed? Keep an eye on the girls."

"Sure, but we have to hurry if you're going to get there in time." Danni tapped on her phone without looking up. "You were in there for about a half hour. You now have four hours to get to the cabin."

"Isn't it five and a half hours away?" Maggie leaned against the door, waiting for Danni to step away from the vehicle. She might be excited about Danni getting eyes on Jessi and the girls, but there was no way she was letting her drive again. There were limits to friendship.

"Exactly. I was able to find you a boat to take you to Traverse City. Should get there in half the time."

"But we're not heading to Traverse City." Chase

stood behind the driver's side door, and a look Maggie had never seen before crossed his face.

"Right. You'll take the boat to Traverse City." Danni started the car and locked her seatbelt into place. She still hadn't looked up from her phone. "There'll be a car waiting for you there."

"Danni."

Danni looked up from her phone. Finally. "What?"

"Chase is driving."

"Oh." Danni looked from Maggie to Chase and shrugged before undoing her seatbelt and getting out. She opened the back door and slid into the back seat. "Okay."

Maggie stepped around the car and got in the passenger side.

"Hurry up, everyone." Danni's eyes were back on the phone. "Your captain's waiting for us."

Chase got in, handed Maggie the bag, and put his seatbelt on. "Which dock, and why is my captain waiting for us?"

"Diversey Harbor. And your captain isn't waiting for anyone. The captain of the boat is waiting."

Chase drove toward Lake Shore Drive and stopped. Brake lights. Rows and rows of brake lights. Rush hour was in full swing, which meant this trip was going to take a lot longer than planned. "Whose boat are we meeting?"

Danni huffed, actually huffed, like giving information was some type of hardship. "Enzo's."

"You called Enzo." Maggie could huff, too.

"Do you know anyone else who might have a boat we can borrow?"

"Can we get there in time?" She didn't actually care how they got there, where they got the boat, or any of the other information. She needed to get to Jessi and the girls in time.

This was her fault. She sent them all away. Defenseless. And now they were being held by some lunatic. She couldn't let anything happen. Not on her watch.

# NINETEEN

CHASE HATED BOATS. Hated everything about them. The bobbing. The engine noise. The biggest issue was the water. He hated water. Or more importantly, drowning in the water. Panic swam in his gut.

At least the panic knew how to swim. His grandmother had sent him to the YMCA when he was a kid. For swimming lessons. He'd lasted five minutes, they'd switched his swim lessons for basketball, and he'd never regretted it. Till now.

He kept his eyes on the road as he headed toward the pier. They only had four hours to get up north or he'd just drive. But there was no way he'd make it up there without breaking multiple traffic laws. And the way the cars were moving—or not moving—he'd not only have to speed, but plow through the other cars like a Transformer on a mission.

Of course, that would probably lead to a ticket or worse, a night in jail.

Making the call to the chief to tell him he'd been arrested was not something Chase wanted to do. So he kept driving toward the pier, trying to figure another way. Any other way.

"Wouldn't a helicopter be faster?" Flying. He could do flying. People didn't generally fall overboard into the water when flying.

"Do you know of anyone with a helicopter?" Danni looked up from her phone and stuck her face between the front seats. She looked excited. He could tell, since it was one of the first times she'd taken her eyes off the phone in her hands.

"No."

She leaned back with a frown. "Oh. Then flying is out the question. Unless you know someone with a plane."

"No." Avoiding this voyage at sea was becoming less and less of an option. And traffic was not cooperating.

Red light. Crawl through the intersection. Brake lights. At this rate, they'd be lucky to get to the pier before Thanksgiving.

"Why did we have to figure all of this out at rush hour?" Maggie played with her fingers. She was obviously nervous. Not that he blamed her.

Three and a half hours till the meet.

"Turn right here." Danni leaned forward again, invading the front seat.

"We can't park along there." Chase stopped but didn't turn.

"We don't have time to get to the lot. Turn right

and I'll drop you at the harbor." Danni had moved back against the back seat and was now tapping at her phone. "Enzo's going to meet us at the head of dock H."

Enzo? Why the hell was Enzo meeting them anywhere? They were meeting a captain. A boat captain. Someone who was paid to keep the boat from tipping over. Not some schmuck lawyer who thought he was god of the sea because his company owned some fancy-ass party boat.

"Why is Enzo meeting us there?" Maggie opened the glove box of the car, asking the question Chase was about to ask out loud.

"He has access to a boat. We need a boat. Turn right."

Chase did what he was told, and at the same time he saw Maggie produce a .45 from the open glove box. "I'm taking this," she said.

Taking this? As in going with? "Maybe you should stay back with Danni." The words came out before he could stop them. It's not like he didn't know how she'd respond.

"Maybe you should stay back with Danni." Maggie drew a keychain attached to what looked like a can of mace from her purse and slipped it in her shirt. Probably her bra.

Was it wrong he found that incredibly hot?

Danni pointed between the seats. "Park along here."

Chase slid over next to the curb and stopped. Stepping out of the car onto the cracked sidewalk, he inhaled a deep breath of lakeside Chicago. The air was cooler and moister at the lake than the rest of the city. The liquid A/C stretched out before him, blue water beating against the jetty and spitting pellets into the air.

The lake was angry. And they were going to jump willingly into a plastic bowl and float on it. Float. Ideally they'd float.

"I'm going to hack into the cameras at the house. See you on the other side." Danni was back in the front seat and already pulling away from the curb. There went his ride.

"Let's go!" Enzo Borelli jogged toward them, wearing jeans and a T-shirt. The guy had made a complete turnaround from the first time Chase had seen him. Then he had been a slick lawyer in a suit, all put together. Now, not so much. His hair stuck out all over the place and his stare was wide and intense.

Really? Crazy-eyes couldn't be the captain.

"Boat's ready. We can shove off anytime." Crazy-eyes shooed them both toward the docks, a key jiggling in his hand.

Chase wanted to ask if Enzo should be driving. He wanted to ask if there was another captain that maybe didn't look like Dr. Brown from Back to the Future. But the docks were empty, and barring knocking on every mega-yacht two piers over, he didn't see a way to get someone right here, right now.

Enzo stopped and looked at Chase and Maggie. "Is this it? Where's the rest of the team?"

"We're the team."

Enzo's face fell.

"Hey, Enzo." Maggie put her arm around his shoulder. "We're going to get her. We just need to leave now."

He didn't say a word. Just kept his head low. Maybe knocking on every door wasn't such a bad idea.

Maggie tightened her arm around him and leaned in. "Jessi's going to be okay. But she needs you. You got this?"

Enzo's eyes slowly opened as his head lifted. "I do."

*He's got this.* At least that's what he'd said. Chase followed the guy along wooden slats that squeaked and wobbled as he walked. There was no handrail, so Chase walked slowly. Deliberately. Stopping when Enzo climbed on board a sleek powerboat.

It was more than twice as long as Chase's truck, so it had to be at least forty-five feet. Bigger was better, right? Shiny blue and white paint. And it had two big ass propellers on the back.

It looked like it cost a fortune. Which actually made Chase feel a bit safer. No one threw down this much coin on something and didn't learn how to use it. Right?

"This is gorgeous." Maggie whistled as Enzo opened a small door and stepped inside. "You never told me you owned a boat."

"It's not my boat. It's the firm's." He held his hand out to Maggie, who took it and stepped onto the shiny floating deathtrap. If crazy-eyes didn't own the boat, there was no motivation to keep it floating—well, except for the whole drowning thing.

Enzo didn't look like he wanted to drown, but that didn't mean he didn't want cops to drown. Dammit.

Chase was losing his shit. *Stop acting like a little bitch.* Nobody wanted to drown. They were all here for one purpose, to save those women.

"You coming?" Enzo had moved to the steering wheel and was flipping switches and turning the key.

"Yeah." Chase said the words, but his feet were planted on the dock. He didn't have a lot of memories of his dad, but the *teaching young Chase to swim* episode had been burned into his brain. Drunk Dad picks up kid and tosses him in deep end of Grandma's pool. Flailing. Gasping. Lungs filling. Silence. Grandma pulls kid from the water. Yelling. Coughing. Gasping. Kid vows to never go near bodies of water ever again.

And Chase had kept that vow. With the exception of a brief stint at the YMCA, he'd managed to avoid large bodies of water. Hell, he wasn't particular on size. He avoided small bodies of water. He even refused to bob for apples.

"Hey, man we have to go." Enzo was on the dock again, his hand hovering over a rope knotted around a metal piece on the dock.

Chase nodded and forced his feet to move. The boat barely rocked as he made it to the center of the deck. He could do this.

Maggie walked over to Chase and Enzo jumped back on board. The movement shifted the boat away from shore. "Are you okay?" She looked at him with such concern. It would have made him feel good, but he was too busy keeping his lunch down to get the warm fuzzies.

"Fine." He said the words without giving her a second glimpse of the breakfast sandwich he ate this morning. Surprisingly. He could almost feel the green around his gills warming his face as the air grew stale and thick.

She pointed at the bench behind him. "Have a seat."

"Sure." He sat. What else could he do?

Enzo revved the engine and eased away from the pier, easily navigating the packed harbor and the other boats that stuck out from the slips.

Chase closed his eyes, willing the green to go away.

The engine noise went from a low grumble to a gurgling roar as the boat sped up, the ride smoothing out as it shot over the water. Air. Glorious air infested his lungs.

He was in the center of the boat, feet away from either edge. He could do this. He just had to stay right here. Not move. And maybe he'd make it to Michigan without losing the contents of his stomach or his mind.

***

Two hours later, Maggie shivered as she leaned back in the padded white chair next to the center console. The sun dropped down below the horizon, leaving the dark lake cold. Wind whipped across her cheeks. She thought wearing her cropped leather jacket was a good idea—and it had been when the sun shone— but now it barely kept the wind from slicing through her core.

Enzo pushed at the throttle. He'd been growling at it for the past two hours. He was in a hurry. Maggie got it. She wanted to get there as quickly as possible, too.

Chase groaned. "Sonuva..."

"Are you okay?" She didn't know why she was even asking the question. He was not okay. Far from it. His face was greener than a leprechaun's hat. She never should have let him get on the damn boat.

"Fine." Chase leaned forward, holding his head.

Yeah, he looked fine, if fine meant looking like a teenager after a dozen shots of Jägermeister.

"We'll be in Traverse City in about ten minutes." Enzo didn't turn around. Thankfully. The speed this boat was whipping across the lake, he shouldn't have been looking anywhere but the water.

The boat angled hard right.

Maggie's hands clamped on the arms of her chair. The boat righted, snapping back and sliding hard left before righting again.

Another groan. Chase closed his eyes. He shouldn't be here. He should be at home, eating pizza and watching sports. It was bad enough he was heading toward the shitstorm she'd created. And it was a shitstorm.

Brandi and Brianna had trusted Maggie to get them away from their abusive father, not deliver them into the hands of some crazy asshole—okay, another crazy asshole they weren't related to by blood.

And Jessi... she'd trusted Maggie to teach her the business, not get sucked into some hostage-slash-kidnapping escapade. Maggie had to get Jessi home.

There wasn't another option. She had a son. Jessi had a son she had to get home to. The kid wasn't going to grow up without two parents. He'd already lost his father. Well, Maggie assumed his father was lost. Jessi was uncharacteristically silent when it came to Matty's father.

The boat slowed as they approached the dock. The dock itself was smaller, fewer bays. But Enzo was able to slide into a space with little more than a turn of the wheel. Or maybe Enzo just made it look easy. The moment the boat bumped the dock, Enzo swung over the side and used a rope to tie the boat to a metal thing. Once he finished with that, he got back on board, cut the engine, and dug through a cabinet under the console.

He pulled out the duffel bag with the wooden box. "Are you both ready?"

Chase nodded, but his head still hung down, nearly touching his chest.

"Look." Maggie sat on the seat next to him. This was her chance to fix her most recent mistake. "I think you should stay here."

"I can't..." He started to stand up, but she pulled him back down.

"You look like hell."

"Thanks." Chase grabbed his head and leaned his elbows on his knees. He wasn't arguing with what she'd said, though.

"I can tell you don't feel well." She ran a hand down his arm. She wanted to run her hands over so much more, but that would be counterproductive to what she had to say. "And this is not your fight. This is my mistake. I have to fix it."

"I can help." Chase shook his head and stood up. It was a little too dark to see if the green was still coloring his face, but his voice wobbled like it was coming through fog. He was still standing up, so that was a good sign. *If* she wanted him to come with her.

But she didn't.

"I don't want your help." She stood so she could meet his eyes. She hoped he would see how serious she was without having to say the words. She didn't want to make this a thing.

"I don't care what you want." His voice got stronger.

"No, Chase." She pushed him back down. "It was a mistake letting you come with. There's too much that can go wrong. We're giving a known drug dealer a supply of drugs. This won't just get you fired. This will get you time in jail."

Chase popped up onto his feet and rested his hand on her arm. "It's the same thing that will happen to you if you get caught."

"Yeah, but I'm not a cop."

"No offense, Magpie, but I've just endured over two hours of pure torture on this floating raft of misery. I didn't do it for nothing." Chase swayed, but he managed to jump onto the dock. "Do you need help?" he asked Enzo, who was tying another rope from the boat to the dock.

Enzo shook his head. "I have this. Are you two ready?"

"This is illegal. I think I should go alone." Maggie tried to get them both to stay. This was their careers. Her career was already shit.

Enzo rubbed his hands as he stood up, and his stare moved to Maggie. She'd never seen that look on his face before—not aimed at her anyway. Eyes narrowed. Head tilted. Anger practically smoking from his ears. "That's not happening." Enzo clicked open his gun and tilted it in the light before closing it and sliding it in the back of his jeans. "Car's up here if you want to come," he said, hiking the duffel bag over his shoulder.

"Does he have the fentanyl?" Chase didn't bother waiting for an answer, he shook his head and followed Enzo to the darkened parking lot.

There wasn't much Maggie could do but follow. She wasn't thrilled with getting everyone else involved, but it was a little late to do it without them.

She'd tried to get them to turn around. She tried to get them to leave this to her. But honestly, she wasn't sure what to expect from the guy who'd taken Jessi and the girls. All she knew was she needed to make it right, and if these two were willing to go in there with her, she wasn't about to look a gift horse in the muzzle.

# TWENTY

THE WOODEN BOARDS whined and creaked as Maggie walked the plank toward the parking lot. Well, she could only assume it was a parking lot. The sun had completely disappeared, leaving the sky full of sparkling tea lights. It was beautiful, and something she'd never see back in Chicago with the crashing glare of the city lights.

Of course, the darkness meant she couldn't see the ground five feet in front of her. The only indications there was a lot at all were the dual headlights on a car and a flickering bulb in the street lamp at the end of the lot—On. Off. On. Off—casting an eerie glow worthy of a haunted warehouse.

Perfect. She'd somehow entered a slasher flick. And she was on her way to meet a guy with a gun. Well, at a minimum he probably had a gun. He might have brought associates with rocket launchers, for all she knew.

"Mr. Borelli." A driver in a suit and tie stood in front of a black Mercedes.

How they'd found a formally-dressed driver in the middle of nowhere, she'd never guess. She didn't care all that much either, as long as suit-boy could get her to Jessi.

"Yes." Enzo aimed straight for the front passenger door. "We're going to Spring Harbor. Fifty-seven Waterway Lane."

"Yes, sir." Suit guy shut the door behind Enzo as he opened the rear passenger door for Maggie. "Ma'am." He nodded and pressed the door shut. Chase was already in the backseat, behind the driver.

Maggie leaned forward. "We can't just show up at the house together. He said no cops." She kept her voice low as the driver walked around the outside of the car. She didn't think suit-guy was a hazard to the operation, but why chance it.

"I'm not a cop," Enzo said.

"Yes, but you're also not me."

"Do you have a suggestion?" Chase asked her, and rolled his eyes at Enzo. Getting these two together was such a bad idea. Too much testosterone in one place.

"I do." Maggie had spent every summer at this house growing up. Sometimes with her dad. Sometimes with just her mom. Later, with her aunts. No one knew the house and that land better than she did. Now she just needed to give these guys a crash course.

The driver's door opened and suit-guy slid in.

"Do you have paper and a pen?" She asked him, assuming the guys didn't have anything to write with.

The three of them had the clothes on their backs and maybe a gun or two. Hopefully, more like two.

"Sorry. I do not." The driver started the car, heading across the lot and out onto the narrow streets.

Darn it. She needed something to show the layout. Something to set the stage and get them thinking how they were going to sneak up on the drug-dealing thug. She pulled out her phone. "Okay, look here." She opened a drawing app she'd downloaded for her niece and closed the stick figure with fiery red hair holding hands with a shorter stick figure holding a doll. Her niece was so damn adorable.

"The house is a one-story in an L shape." Using her finger, she drew a sideways L on the screen. "The inside is open concept, so if he's smart" —she had no idea if the guy had half a brain cell in his head— "he'll stick to the rooms where there's only one way in. That leaves one bedroom and the sewing room."

"Sewing room?"

The sewing room. It hadn't held a mannequin in years, and the sewing machine and fabrics were long gone, but no one in her family could bring themselves to change the name of the room. "It was my mom's space."

Chase reached out and rested his hand on her knee. Not in a naughty exploration kind of way, but in a nice, supportive way. She almost turned away, but it felt good. So good. She didn't get a chance to talk a lot about her mom—not with a houseful of men who avoided feelings like they avoided cleaning the toilet. And heaven forbid she brought up her mother, and showed a few tears—you'd think she'd told them to clean the toilet with their toothbrush in between swipes of their teeth.

"Which room do you think he'd go with?" Enzo asked, peering at the screen.

"Probably the sewing room. It has windows on three walls, so he can see pretty much the whole house and yard." She pointed at the entrances, windows and various places they could hide.

The car fell into silence, the only sound the soft whirring of the heater. Streetlights blasted the interior with light as Chase's fingers slowly found Maggie's hand.

She didn't want to slip her fingers through his. But she did. She didn't want the electricity buzzing up and down her arm with each caress of his fingertips. But it did. She didn't want him to keep holding her hand, making her body feel comforted and alive. But he did.

She couldn't seem to stop the *didn't-wants* any more than she could stop her heart from beating double-time when he leaned over. "Are you okay?"

No. She wasn't okay. All the *didn't-wants* were pressing on her chest. Because—she did want—really badly. But her father's words haunted her. The reality of this situation terrified her.

They were negotiating with terrorists. They were handing over enough illegal drugs to kill a small village. And Chase was a cop. He could lose his promotion, his job, his livelihood. And all because she'd made a mistake.

She was dragging him down. There was no other

explanation. And she refused to hurt him. She turned away and plastered herself against her door.

The air was frosty and the lack of his hand took away any comfort she might have felt. The cold from the door seeped into every pore, chilling her entire body.

The look on his face as she pulled further and further away was pure torture. She could almost see his heart break. And she almost reached out to comfort him—but wouldn't that be the dumbest idea ever—because she could feel her heart break, as well.

The ache in her chest swelled and burned along the edges. She wanted him close. She wanted to tell him she loved him...

*I love him.*

She always knew. But she'd hoped it was indigestion. Instead, it was love. And that was why she had to get as far as she could from the man, before she managed to ruin every good thing he had built. She loved him enough to let him go. There had to be some honor in that?

Too bad she didn't feel all that honorable.

"Should we all show up to the house in this car? Aren't you supposed to be alone? Maybe we should get out before the house." Thank God for Enzo and his ability to get back on topic.

Alone. She was supposed to be alone, but somehow, she ended up with half the Village People—a lawyer and a cop. Was there a lawyer in the Village People? Not that it mattered.

All that mattered was Chase and Enzo shouldn't be

a part of this. They were both sworn to uphold the law, and the whole situation went against everything they stood for.

Enzo turned to the driver. "Can you drop us off a block before the address I gave you?" He glanced at Maggie. "Is that far enough away?"

"Stop at Overbrook Drive and Millside." She nodded to the driver, who made eye contact with her in the rearview mirror. That was more than far enough away. That would give her a good ten minutes or so to make the swap. It would keep both men out of the whole illegal drug trade.

She turned to the guys. "I'll give you ten minutes to walk to the house, then I'll go in."

The pained look was still there on Chase's face. Better to hurt him now, rather than drag it out and hurt him later. At least that was her story.

She didn't have time to think about any of this. The driver hit the headlights as he slowly drove up to the right corner, bathing the street in darkness until Maggie opened the back door and the interior light spilled onto the sidewalk. She slid out of the car and waited for Chase and Enzo.

"Head down toward the beach," she told them, pointing. "Follow along the beach and around the curve. The house is at the end, before the condominiums." Most of the home owners were at their non-vacation homes—back to their real lives, in their real towns, leaving the homes here dark and lifeless.

"Be careful." Chase grabbed her hand and held it

just a tad too long. He was just close enough for her to see the intensity in his eyes.

The situation was dangerous. And they might not make it out of this alive. This could be the last time she saw him or touched him. This could be the last time she felt him.

Her body leaned into him of its own accord. Seriously. She had nothing to do with the fact that her body slid up against his. And she couldn't control when her mouth lingered ever so slightly in front of his. "I will."

"Good." His breath was hot against her skin. His lips plump and inviting, just begging for her to rub against them. Gentle fingertips slowly found her face and tilted her head up to look into his eyes.

Those eyes. They held all the questions. All the worry. Everything she was trying to escape. She couldn't look into those eyes any longer.

She leaned in and closed the gap so her mouth could move against his, fast and furious. Her knees buckled as a bolt of longing shot down her core. His arms found her and wrapped around her waist.

And somewhere inside her, she prayed he would never let her go.

But deep down, she knew she could never stay.

***

CHASE COULD TASTE her and feel her. The press of her mouth to his was like a drug, dragging him deeper and deeper. Her lips were strong and sure. And every kiss felt like she owned him. And she did.

He didn't want it to stop, but it had to. Her tongue swept along his bottom lip. A groan lodged in his throat. Why did it have to stop, again?

"Are you two about done?" the annoying third-wheel nagged from the side of the car.

Maggie pulled her lips away. "Um, yeah. I'll give you ten minutes." She turned around and slid back into the car, but not before she licked her lips. Licked her lips.

That kiss they'd just shared had been combustible. Desire. Passion. Want. Desperation was all wrapped up in the kiss. Almost like she poured everything she had into that one final kiss. Like she was saying good-bye.

Maggie closed the car door. He and Enzo had ten minutes to get to her father's beach house. Ten minutes, and she'd be there to confront this guy. And she couldn't do it alone. He wouldn't let her.

Chase nodded at Enzo, and led him down a cracked sidewalk. When it ended, he stepped around a stockpile of firewood and past a grouping of trees. Open air. The wind off the lake rushed past him, bringing the musty scent of sand and rotting wood.

The darkness almost swallowed him. Everything was blacked out. The houses. The sky. The sliver of a moon and multitude of stars couldn't slice through the black night.

Enzo followed behind. At least Chase assumed he was following behind. He could hear a slight scuff of soles on the sand-covered sidewalk. *Snap.* How did he find the only branch?

"*Shhh...*" Chase kept his voice low as they walked around another clump of trees and hit soft sand. His shoes sank, and sand jumped and spit at his ankles, slowly trying to climb up the leg of his jeans.

One house. Two houses. The walk seemed never-ending. He just wanted to get to Maggie. He counted each one they passed till he hit the one-story cottage. All the lights were on inside. Inside. Outside. Almost like whoever was in there was worried about someone surprising him.

Good. He should be worried.

Chase stopped behind a row of trees along the edge of the beach and checked his watch. They still had time. His arm flew out to stop Enzo from walking any further. "This is the house. We have to wait for Maggie."

"But she's in the house." Enzo pointed to a large picture window.

Un-fucking-believable. Maggie stood in plain view, hands on her hips, watching Lacik rip open the duffel bag. She'd gone in without them—without backup. What the hell had she been thinking?

She nodded and talked, acting like it was no big deal. She'd jumped into the lion's den without him.

Lacik leered up at Maggie, his eyes glued to the area between her neck and stomach. *Eyes up, asshole.* She couldn't enjoy having him ogle her chest like that. And he wouldn't be if Chase was in that room. Why the hell hadn't she waited?

"We need to get in there." Chase unholstered his gun and crept to the door like Yosemite Sam. He turned to Enzo. "Keep quiet and do as I say." He slowly twisted the door handle. It clicked.

*Shit.*

He listened for a sound. Anything indicating somebody inside had heard him. But all he heard was low voices and the soft hum of music.

He might still have a chance to save the situation. He just had to get Maggie and her friends to safety, take down Lacik, and get the drugs off the street. All without injuring anyone in that room or himself—oh, and preferably without firing his weapon. Any discharge would require a report. A report would have to be signed off on by his boss, which would get back to the chief.

If something bad happened to Enzo the cock-blocker—well...

Okay. He couldn't let anything happen to him either.

So. Take down Lacik, drugs off street, everyone safe, no weapon discharged... That about covered it. That's all.

Yep. He was pretty much fucked.

## TWENTY-ONE

MAGGIE STOOD in the sewing room of her child-hood home and waited for Lacik to move his eyes from her chest. Gross. He was barely out of high school and she was...halfway to being a full-fledged member of AARP.

He drew the aluminum case from the bowels of the red bag. Snapping the lid open, he smiled. She thought the leering, nice-tits smile was gross. Not even close. The I'm-rich-and-who-cares-who-dies smile was so much worse.

"Is that it?" The other guy in the room, Jillian's attacker from the other night, shook a gun toward Jessi, Brianna, and Brandi, who were perched on the edge of a floral couch looking absolutely terrified. The women's hands were tied behind their back and all three of them had multiple pieces of duct tape angled over their mouths.

Hopefully, Danni had gotten that camera up and

running. When Maggie brought these guys down—and she would—she wanted these idiots to sit and spin for a long time behind bars.

Maggie needed to get them out of here. This room, with its girlie touches, was one hundred percent her mother, and hands down Maggie's favorite room in the house. However, it also didn't have anything she could use as a weapon, or any way to get the girls out of the house. No door. Huge windows, but she'd have a hell of a time opening them up.

Something shifted outside the room. Cop eyes. Very angry cop eyes, staring back at her from behind the wall leading to the kitchen. *Not yet.* She pressed her hand down ever so slightly and gave him a look that said wait. She had this.

He stood back, watching, his eyes still angry. But at least he wasn't coming in guns smoking.

Lacik slid a bottle out of the case and poured a dot of the clear liquid into a test tube. He pushed a paper strip into the liquid and watched as the liquid travelled up the strip.

"What's it say?" Creepy-stache, now officially the kidnapper, craned his head to look at the strip.

Lacik grunted. "Nothing yet. It takes a few minutes."

Brianna squirmed on the couch, and creepy kidnapper guy aimed the gun her way.

"Hold on." Maggie stepped forward, throwing her hands up in the air when Creepy aimed the gun at her. "She probably can't breathe with the tape over her nose."

He ignored her and leaned over Brianna. "What's the problem?"

Maggie couldn't help but roll her eyes. These were the brilliant minds orchestrating this enterprise.

"She's probably not answering 'cause of the tape over her mouth." Lacik slid the bottle back in the case. At least someone understood the laws of speaking—you needed your mouth.

Creepy-stache yanked the tape off Brianna's mouth. She howled. "I couldn't breathe."

"Well, that's the problem when you talk too much." Creepy picked up the roll of tape. "Keep quiet, or more tape is going over your scream-hole.

"You're in trouble. My daddy is going to get you."

"Yeah, kid." Creepy's mustache shook as he laughed. "And who's your daddy?" He smirked.

"Peter Katsaros."

The shudder of fear that passed through Lacik and his other half was almost comical. Almost.

"Why the fuck you hanging out with Katsaros' kids?" Lacik stared at Maggie.

She didn't know what to say. She couldn't tell them the truth. But why the hell would a thirty-year-old woman be *hanging out* with kids? "Shopping. They came down here to go shopping."

"Shit." Lacik slammed his fist onto the desk.

"Did they bring fake drugs?" Creepy asked Lacik, keeping his gun aimed at Maggie.

"No. It's real." Lacik paced back and forth. "What are we supposed to do?"

"Let's get the hell out of here," Creepy said. Finally, something intelligent.

Lacik ran a hand through his hair, blond daggers sticking up in jagged spikes. "They know who we are. Her father cut out a man's spleen for stealing his chair. We stole his kids. What the hell is he going to cut out for that?"

"We kill them then." Creepy cocked the gun.

The muzzle of the gun was aimed at Brianna. Right at her head.

"No." Maggie stepped forward. "I lied. We kidnapped them."

"What?"

"Ask Brandi. They came to me for help, so I took them away from Katsaros. He's probably looking for them right now." Maggie hoped that was a big fat lie. Their father better be in lockup by now. "If you kill them, you'll never be able to go back to Chicago. But if you bring them back to their father—you'll be a hero."

Lacik turned to Brandi, and she nodded her head. He carefully pulled the tape off her mouth. "Why did you go to her for help?"

Maggie gave her a look, wishing for telepathic powers. *Don't tell him the truth. Make something up.* If the guys figured out Maggie was trying to put Katsaros away, they'd lose any leverage of getting the girls back home alive.

"I stole some money and ran away." Brandi looked down at the floor. She'd really missed her calling. She should be on stage. "I was tired of him controlling me."

"How do we know you won't snitch?" Lacik asked her.

Brandi's face hardened. "I'm not a snitch."

"Just a thief."

"It was my money." She huffed. "He just wouldn't give it to me. So I took it."

Lacik seemed impressed, or the very least he bought her explanation. He grabbed the duffel bag and hiked it over his shoulder. "Let's get them to the car."

"What about these two?" Creepy-stache snarled. Why was he all pissy? She brought their drugs. She handed them a way to escape the wrath of Katsaros. What else did he want?

Lacik shrugged. "We'll leave them here."

"But they know who we are."

"So?" Lacik pulled a cigarette from his pocket and lit up, exhaling in a gush of smoke. So much for her father never knowing they had been here.

"So? They can ID us." Creepy was whining now.

"I ran her over in an alley. You got your ass kicked by her at Jillian's." Lacik giggled. Actually giggled. What man giggles? Granted, he was all of probably twenty-two. But still. "She could always ID us."

"Then we have to get rid of her."

The fact that he was referring to *Maggie* finally hit her She had a gun in her sock, but she'd never be able to reach it in time. The pepper spray in her bra, though? "Why would I ID you? I just want to go home and watch soap operas." She ran a hand along her neck and held it steady. Two inches to the spray.

"My grandma likes her stories, too. Which ones do you watch?"

His grandma? She was now being compared to the elderly. She inched her fingers under the collar of her shirt.

"Who the hell cares what she watches on TV?" Creepy stomped his foot. Another person against soap operas. Who would've thought he'd have something in common with her father? "Get them out here. I'll take care of these two."

Chase's eyes met hers. He looked ready to strike. She shook her head, which turned into her stretching her neck from side to side. She needed the element of surprise. And if he jumped out like a 5-o jack in the box, they'd lose that element.

Separating these two morons came first. She swore they both were sharing one brain, but they managed to each have a gun. Inconvenient. Lacik's was currently sticking out of ratty track pants, so he wasn't exactly cocked and ready, though.

Lacik looked from Maggie to Jessi and shrugged. "Get up." He pointed to the sisters.

She'd noticed a beat-up jalopy parked on the street in front of the house. Figures it would be theirs. Maybe she'd get lucky and the thing would fall apart as they drove away—of course, she had to live through Creepy's attempt at execution first.

Brianna and Brandy stood up and Lacik stepped behind them. He yanked at the tape wrapped around their wrists and guided them toward the door. "Don't try anything stupid, and you'll both get home nice and safe."

Maggie looked out into the living room, and as Lacik turned to go out the front door, Chase's face angled out from behind the kitchen wall. She nodded to the front door with her mouth.

He stepped out of the kitchen. Darn it.

He wasn't going to go after the girls. Didn't he know she could take care of herself? Of course he didn't. Her father didn't trust her to handle herself. Why would the man she loved?

Chase stood behind the wall in the kitchen, watching everything unfold. Well, it was more like itching to join the action across the room. He stayed where he was and waited for Lacik to pass.

The sound of Lacik coaxing the girls across the living room and then the sound of the front door screeching open told Chase it was time to scratch his itch. The guy holding Maggie and Jessi hostage was talking, but he had his back to Chase. Stepping into the main room, Chase go a clear look at Maggie's face.

Her eyes widened and she tilted her chin toward the front door. She wanted him to walk away. She wanted to handle this herself and for him to follow the girls.

Like hell. The one with the gun was making Chase twitchy. He didn't like the gun aimed at Maggie or Jessi. The creep was going to hurt them, or worse. He couldn't live with himself if something happened to her.

That's probably how Maggie felt about those girls. She'd offered to help them, and then they ended up in a more dangerous situation than they ever could have found on their own. She'd never be able to live with herself if something happened to those girls.

*Dammit.*

The way Maggie's hand slowly slid inside her shirt —where her pepper spray was hiding—told him she was getting ready to strike. It told him he needed to ensure the girls came out of this unharmed. The girls were young, unarmed, and they needed his help.

Maggie did not.

He turned to Enzo, who had done an awesome job of standing back and waiting for instructions in the kitchen. Who knew a lawyer could be so agreeable? He whispered, "I'm going to get the girls. Stay here and help Maggie if she needs it."

Enzo nodded, moving forward while Chase slid along the wall over to the back door. He slipped out the back door and jogged around the side of the house.

Lacik was pushing the two girls into the backseat of a beat up car, the duffel bag nowhere in sight. "Come on, get in."

"You don't have to be so mean." Brianna was a feisty little thing.

Chase couldn't help but smile at that. It almost made him want to wait to arrest Lacik. A six-hour car ride with a mouthy tween would drive anybody crazy. Lacik deserved it.

"You haven't seen mean yet, little girl." He reached for his gun.

Oh hell no. Chase ran across the grass. Fifty feet to the car, more or less. The closer he got without Lacik seeing him, the better. Twenty-five feet. Chase lengthened his stride.

Ten feet. A twig snapped.

Lacik's head jerked up, and he turned toward Chase. "Who—"

Five feet. Chase dove for Lacik just as the gun fired. A shot sounded and Chase rolled, his head snapping forward and hitting the side of the car.

## TWENTY-TWO

"SIT DOWN." Creepy shoved Maggie toward the couch.

If she sat down next to Jessi, she'd lose what little chance she had of stopping this guy. Her agility was her only leverage. "Look, can't we talk about this?"

"I'm done talking."

Maggie inched her hand further into her bra. It seemed like such a good idea in the beginning, putting her pepper spray in there, but she was having a hell of a time getting her hand deep enough to wrap her fingers around the canister without looking suspicious.

It was do or die time—literally.

She tossed her hair over her shoulder and ran a tongue slowly over her lips. "Maybe we could trade?" Paired with the "fuck me" eyes, she was throwing her own Hail Mary and praying it would stick.

*Yuck.* Creepy had his own set of bedroom eyes,

practically humping her face. "What kind of trade?" This just might work.

Her voice dropped an octave. All throat. "Let us go, and I'll do whatever you want?" She pushed on her V-neck T-shirt, exposing just a hint of cleavage. Using her God-given gifts to get what she needed was SOP, but somehow playing with this guy made her feel dirty.

Maybe because the furthest thing from her mind, right now, was doing anything that would make him happy. Crappy? Now, making him feel crappy was something she could fully get behind.

That little push was all she needed to reach the pepper spray. She pressed her elbows in, giving him a show at the same time as she flipped the safety cap up. Anything to keep his focus off the covert action in her shirt.

Creepy's eyes bulged and his non-gun hand moved down to reposition his package. A little bedroom eyes and jiggle and the guy became a teen with his first Play-boy. *What a charmer, ladies.*

She slipped her thumb on the button and pulled the little can out of her shirt.

A gunshot rang out from the front yard, and Maggie twitched. So did Creepy. *Shit.* She jumped for him, reaching out for the gun and spraying the contents of the canister into his eyes at the same time.

Creepy screamed, which was good. What was bad was that she'd forgotten pepper spray didn't discriminate.

The fumes attacked her, clawing at her eyes. Tears dripped down her face, pooling on her shirt. She wheezed, snot sliding from her nose. Her throat burned. She held onto his gun hand for dear life. If she let go, she'd never be able to find it again.

Good news was, his breathing sounded like he was in the same situation.

A hand wrapped around her throat, cutting most of what little air she had. Her eyes cleared, if only for a second. Enzo was untying Jessi. Good.

"Help her," Jessi cried the second the tape came off.

"Get her out of here!" Maggie yelled as loud as she could. It might not have been all that loud, but she had a hand around her throat, after all.

Enzo hesitated. Probably thinking he could help. She didn't need help. She needed Jessi out of here.

Another gunshot. This time louder. Closer. Creepy had pulled the trigger. The bullet might not have hit anything important, but she couldn't risk another shot going off.

Maggie landed a low blow in deference to all womenkind. Statistically, women might not have the muscle mass to win the battle of the sexes, but they also didn't have an unshielded core that could be taken out with one swing. Her knee shot up, landing right between his legs with a thump. His hand disappeared from her throat.

"Go," she croaked at Enzo.

He and Jessi disappeared out the back door, leaving Maggie—once again—alone with Creepy. But this time there was no half-passed-out Jillian to interfere.

Creepy was bent over, gun still in his hand. She

hooked his ankles and he went down. Taking the gun and Maggie with him.

She kneeled on his chest and yanked the gun away from him. "Don't move!" She slid off his body and scrambled across the room. Her slime-drenched eyes and the muzzle of the gun never pointed anywhere but at him.

His head dropped to the floor and he coughed. Water dripped out of his eyes and mixed with the snot dripping from his nose. Yep, pepper spray was awful. But that's what he got for being a lowlife. He rubbed his face on the carpet.

"Don't rub that on my carpet." Creepy was gross. Creepy. She really should learn his name. "Who are you?"

"Screw you." He rolled over and coughed a mountain of phlegm onto the carpet. Now he was just being a dick.

She yanked a pair of cuffs from the pocket of her jacket. Moving slowly, she tossed them at him. "Put these on. Now."

"No."

Never negotiate with terrorists. She was going to learn her lesson one of these days. "Fine. I can't have you getting away." She aimed the gun at his leg. "So I'll just shoot you."

She got off one shot, aiming between his legs. Crap. That hole was going to be impossible to cover up.

"What the fuck? Are you crazy?" Creepy coughed as he jerked the handcuffs from the floor and snapped them on.

"Now, was that so hard?"

The front door creaked open. Maggie changed her stance to easily swing the gun at the door if Lacik walked through.

"Come outside. We need you." Enzo poked his head around the door jamb. "I'll take him."

"Make sure those cuffs are on nice and tight."

Enzo squeezed Creepy's wrists. "Let's go." He yanked him to his feet.

With Enzo handling Creepy, Maggie walked through the living room and out the front door. After all the drama and adrenaline inside, she forgot that outside they were fighting their own war. The girls stood in front of Maggie's Crown Vic, their arms wrapped around each other, crying. Crying.

No blood. No outward injuries. She walked toward them, and a head lolled side to side in the open backseat of her car. Blond spikes. Blood poured from his nose. He was probably rubbing it on the upholstery.

First the house. Now the car. Great, she'd need a Hazmat team.

Enzo brought Creepy out of the house and shoved him in the backseat of Maggie's car. Enzo was turning out to be a great help. Thank goodness she hadn't done this alone...

Chase. Where was Chase?

"Maggie, help." Jessi bounced up from next to the crappy car parked at the edge of the lawn. Her hands were dark—covered in something.

Blood. Maggie ran across the yard.

Chase sat on the ground next to the car, head

hanging forward, one hand pressing a bloody piece of cloth to the front of his scalp. He obviously needed help.

"We need to get you to the hospital." Jessi turned to Maggie. "He hit his head fighting. There's a nasty gash."

"I'm fine." His voice was gruff and annoyed as he tried to stand.

"Get down." Maggie pushed on his shoulder and he fell back down on his ass.

Maggie was on board for the whole hospital thing. The gash seemed bad—not that she was medically trained at all. But she knew blood. It looked like an awful lot coming from his forehead. "Did you call the cops?"

"No." Chase shook his head, and then groaned. Apparently, shaking his head wasn't a good thing with a brain injury. "If you call the cops, we'll have to report everything. Your dad will disown you."

Maggie looked at the man who weeks ago told her that *rules were in place to separate us from the gorillas.* Now, he was disregarding all the rules—completely ignoring them. She was the devil. She pulled out her cell phone and dialed. "Yes, I'd like to report a break-in. And we need an ambulance." She gave the address and clicked off the call.

If this situation wasn't another nail in the relation-ship coffin, she didn't know what it was. All she knew was that she didn't care about her father or anything else. She just wanted Chase to be okay and the drug dealers worrying about dropping the soap in the shower. She wasn't going to influence Chase to make bad decisions any longer.

---

CHASE LEANED against the front fender. He just wanted to stand up and get back home. Now they were going to have to deal with EMTs and questions. There would be hours of poking and prodding. Literally and figuratively. "Again, I'm fine."

"You're not fine." Jessi went to the trunk of the Crown Vic and unearthed another towel. "Put this on top. We need to stop the bleeding."

"It's not that bad." He added the towel anyway. It really was that bad. He knew he needed a hospital, but getting the drug-toting kidnappers back to Chicago seemed like a better use of their time. If he brought them in, he could control the narrative. He could keep Maggie's name out of it. She wouldn't have to deal with the wrath of her father.

She wouldn't be associated with this at all. But her phone call had made sure that wouldn't happen. The yard grew quiet. He turned to see Maggie running a hand down Brianna's back, calming her. Which wasn't exactly a newsflash. She'd been kidnapped at gunpoint.

He leaned back against the car. Spinning, whirling colors partied in front of his eyes. The sirens of emergency vehicles whispered through the air, slowly getting closer. The adrenaline keeping his eyes open must have spilled into the towel on his head. His lids drooped. His head throbbed. But the blackness clouding his vision felt so damn good—it almost dimmed the throbbing—well, at least made him not give shit.

Ow! Chase's eyes popped open. A burning pain twisted against his arm. He inhaled the putrid scent of dead grass. What he wouldn't give to smell oranges. He needed his partner.

"Wake up." Maggie stood over him, her fingers poised to pinch him again.

Or her. He needed Maggie. "I'm up, dammit." The pain in his arm almost made him forget the pain in his head. Of course, her yelling reminded him that his head fucking hurt.

Sirens screamed and then silenced. He wasn't thrilled that they were putting Maggie in a crappy situation, but he could admit he was glad for the backup. His eyes closed and the world went black.

# TWENTY-THREE

MAGGIE SAT in the interrogation room at the local police department. It had been hours. Hours at the house getting an unconscious Chase into the ambulance, documenting the crime scene, and taking statements. Hours of cops and questions.

At least she was out of the cold. The night had gone from chilly to downright frigid. Although, it might have felt worse since she was tired and just wanted to go home. Now all she wanted to do was check on Chase. He'd disappeared into the bus and that was it. No word —well, they said they'd send word if anything changed. Since she hadn't heard anything, she'd bet he was still passed out.

Passed out meant nothing worse was going on, so there was that at least.

"We have a few more questions, but we brought your car here so you can head over to the hospital. Detective Montgomery is still unconscious but stable.

Do you want some more coffee?" The local cop dropped Maggie's keys on the table.

The keys weren't a priority right now. She looked down at the empty Styrofoam cup. That was a priority. The coffee might've been bitter, but it was somewhat hot and simulated the caffeine lifeline she desperately needed. "Sure."

He nodded to his partner. "Get her some more coffee and a couple doughnuts."

Doughnuts sounded so good, even her stomach rumbled agreement. She had a feeling she'd been here longer than she'd originally thought. There was no clock in the room and her phone was DOA. If they actually let her see outside, she'd bet there was sunshine.

As they sat there in silence, the cop sifted through the pages in front of him.

She just sat there. Waiting. "Are there any more questions?"

"Yeah, I'm waiting for my partner." He sat there for a moment before standing up. "Let me see where he is."

Good idea. If he had an inability to ask questions without his partner, it was best to go find him. He opened the door and left it open a crack.

The sound of a familiar voice came from outside the room. "Where is she?"

"Sir, we need you to sign the guest list before you go back. It's policy."

Maggie got up and peered out the door. Her father's narrowed eyes looked down on the poor unsuspecting officers who had been asking her questions.

"Where is this list?" Her father followed the officer around the corner, to the front of the building.

"Make sure he hurries. We've kept her here as long as we can." Officer One nodded at Officer Two. "I'm going to my car for a cigarette. I'll be back." Officer One walked toward the back of the building.

Away from her father. Outside to freedom. With her car. She just needed keys. They sat on the table, but the cops hadn't necessarily said she could go. Not that they had to, she wasn't being charged with anything. And those keys just kept calling to her. *Run. Go to him.*

She knew the name of the hospital and she'd heard someone mention it was in Traverse City. Not far.

She wrapped her hand around the keys and slid out the door, hurrying toward the back of the building. The hallway made a turn, leading to a metal door with a small window. Light cut through the glass, bouncing off the scuffed white floor. Ten more feet and she'd be out the door and in the sunlight.

Outside in the parking lot, Maggie hit the key fob. Lights flashed, and she lengthened her stride to reach her car and freedom.

FORTY MINUTES later Maggie walked into Chase's hospital room. The heart monitor beeped. The nurses and doctors outside the door talked in hushed roars. And he sat there alone. She couldn't believe Enzo and Jessi had left him alone. She pulled out her barely-charged cell phone and texted Jessi. *Where r u? RU at the hospital?*

*Coffee. Want?*
*YES!!!!*

*k*

The phone vibrated after she slid it back in her pocket, but she didn't bother to check it. Jessi knew what coffee to get and Chase was here. There wasn't anyone else she wanted to talk to right about now.

Chase was so quiet. He just laid there. He had a bruise on his face and a bandage on the side of his head, but otherwise it didn't look like anything was wrong. And there was so much wrong. So many things needed to be said.

Watching him in that bed—knowing she put him there—made everything that needed to be said come to life. She couldn't be with him. She couldn't put him in danger. She couldn't bear to lose him.

But she had to.

"I'm sorry Chase—for so many things." She walked over to the side of the bed and wrapped her fingers through his. His hand was cold. So, so cold. Tears poked the back of her lids. "I'm sorry I got you involved in all of this. I'm sorry you're hurt. If there was anything I could do to fix this, I would do it. I just need you to be okay."

The circles she drew on his hands with her thumb were small but never ending. Around and around.

"I promise I'll stay away from you, just wake up." The pain radiating through her chest and making it hard to breathe would eventually go away. The tears that pricked her eyes and now fell down her cheeks would dry—someday.

At least that was what she hoped. Because this hurt way too much.

She rested her lips on his—maybe a little too long. But when you're giving a good-bye kiss, you want it to last as long as possible.

She memorized the feel of his lips, the smell of his skin. She pretended she could taste him, this one last time. Because really, she couldn't just molest an unconscious guy with a tongue down the throat. No matter how much she wanted to do it.

Her lips pressed a little harder and she swore he kissed her back. But that was impossible. He was obviously unconscious. If he'd woken up, someone would have contacted her.

She leaned away—too soon—and stepped away from the bed. "Good-bye." If thinking the word had been a knife to the heart, saying the word was like twisting that knife and lighting the grip on fire.

After everything they'd been through, she wanted, no, needed something more than one word and lingering peck. But who knew if he'd even want her anywhere near him when he woke up? If he was smart he'd blame her for what happened. If he was smart he'd want nothing to do with her. And dragging out that rejection would only hurt more.

So she pulled up those big girl panties she'd heard so much about—and walked toward the door, refusing to look back.

CHASE SWORE he felt lips and smelled oranges. Oranges? Flores better not be anywhere near him. He tried to open his eyes, but his body wasn't responding. Ever since he'd woken up from his head-trauma nap, he'd had a touch of fog-brain. The doctor said it would go away, but so far no go. It probably didn't help that he kept falling asleep again.

But there was no reason to be awake. Until now. He'd listened to everything Maggie had said. She blamed herself for what went down at the beach house. She shouldn't. It wasn't her fault he'd jumped into some metal spike sticking out of the car. How he'd continued to fight with Lacik and get his useless ass into Maggie's car, Chase still wasn't completely sure. All he remembered after the whack to the head was a fight, sitting on the ground, and an angel appearing at his side. Well, she might not have been an angel. In fact, she looked a lot like Maggie.

Those lips disappeared. And the sweetest voice said good-bye. Who was leaving? Definitely not Flores. Thank goodness. His eyes flew open. There was no Maggie. Just her back moving toward the open door.

"Why good-bye?" His voice was coarse gravel rubbing on pavement. At least it sounded like that to his ears.

"Oh—you're awake." She turned around, looking so sad. Her cheeks were flushed. Her eyes were welled with tears.

"Yeah." He tried to sit up, to get a better look at her, but his arms were dead weight and his head was pounding with any movement.

"Don't sit up." She ran back to the bed.

His brain throbbed, but at least she didn't leave. "Why good-bye?"

"Chase..."

"No. Why were you saying good-bye?"

"Look at what I did to you." Her eyes grew to saucers and the tears she had streaming down her face multiplied. "You're hurt. You're probably in trouble. You could lose your job. Your life."

"I have to agree with my daughter." Chief Lane stood in the doorway of the room. How he'd managed to appear out of nowhere, Chase had no idea. "Do you know how much trouble you're in? You could lose your badge."

Chase knew. He knew he shouldn't have followed Maggie, or at least enabled her to make the choices she'd made. He should have stopped her. "I made a mistake. When we realized Jessi was missing, my first call should have been CPD. When we received the call from the kidnappers, I should have gotten CPD involved immediately. When we found the drugs, I should have called. I didn't. That's on me. But we were afraid that CPD wouldn't negotiate and Jessi and those girls would be killed."

Maggie took a step toward her father. "Dad, it's my fault, not his. He was doing his job of protecting me, so he followed. I didn't give him time to contact anyone. If anyone should be blamed for this, it's me."

"You? You engaged in a drug deal without police involvement."

"I know. I'm sorry." Those tears in her eyes had

dried up, but the misery was clear on her face. "Please don't take Chase's job away. I'll do whatever you want. I won't talk to him. I won't go near him or any of your employees ever again. I'll come back to CPD."

"Now wait a minute." Chase planted his palms on the mattress and pushed himself to a sitting position. At least, more sitting then he had been. "I don't agree to not talking to you again."

A nurse in purple scrubs flew into the room, forcing the Chief to move closer to Chase. "What is going on in here?" the nurse demanded. "You'll all have to leave if you are going to excite the patient." She pushed a button on one of Chase's machines and glared from Maggie to her father. A high pitch beep stopped.

Chase had been so worried about the conversation going on in front of him, he hadn't even noticed the sound.

The nurse huffed as she walked out the door. "Strike one. Next one you're out."

Chase wanted to mention that wasn't exactly how strikes work, but he was afraid she'd kick out his visitors. Well, Maggie really.

Chief Lane was watching him, frowning slightly. "Why? Why don't you agree to that?"

To having Maggie removed from his life? He'd never agree to that. "I'm in love with her—um, sir." He almost forgot he was talking to her father and not just his boss. How do you make your speech double formal? Sir, yes, sir? That wouldn't work. He wasn't in the military.

"In love with her? You'd give up your job for her?" Her father looked confused. Did he really not know?

"Yes."

"It doesn't matter. I won't let him." Maggie sat on the edge of the bed and rested her hand on his. "You live the job," she told Chase. "You love the job. I can't let you lose your job. What would you do?"

"I don't care."

"But you do. And one day you'd care and you'd resent me. I saw it with my parents. I can't do that to you."

"What do you mean, with your parents?" Her father gripped the rail at the end of the bed.

"Dad, I know how much you had to sacrifice to be at mom's side when she got sick, and then after she died, taking care of us. I know you were set to be Super-intendent. I know they skipped you over and gave it to someone else. I know you still regret it." Maggie turned to Chase. "It's hard enough being the cause of my father's biggest regret. I can't let you regret choosing me, too."

Her father cleared his throat. "Margaret... Maggie, I have never once regretted my time with your mother or with you. Not once. I was devastated when I lost your mom. The only thing I wanted or needed was you and your brother. You're the only reason I made it through." Chief Lane ran a hand through his hair. "Do you love him?"

She was quiet for a minute—although it felt more like an eternity. It seemed like a simple enough question. Why wasn't she answering? "Honestly? Yes, I do love him. He makes me happy."

Chase knew that deep down she did. She was willing to sacrifice everything, so she must love him. But it felt really good to hear it. Of course the first time you hear it, you don't picture the woman's father looming over you.

Chief Lane sighed. "Since Brandi is over eighteen and takes responsibility for her younger sister, there are no kidnapping charges. And I spoke with the police chief here, apologizing for sending our police officer into their jurisdiction without prior notification." Sending our police officer? That implied CPD had knowledge. Wow—the chief was covering Chase's ass. "And since you did manage to find enough evidence to get Katsaros and Lacik off the street, I think we can overlook this one infraction."

"Thanks, Dad." She smiled, but it didn't light up her face. It was compulsory and cold. "What do I need to do to make this happen?"

"Nothing."

"Really?" Maggie looked as confused as Chase felt. She didn't have to go back to a job she hated at CPD? He was going to walk away with his badge?

"Yes, but I don't want you two pulling anything like this again. Montgomery, you said some things earlier that were wrong. Dead wrong. When you thought Jessi was missing and the kidnappers called, CPD was your second call. I should have been your first. In the future, I expect to be notified if things go sideways." His eyes moved to his daughter. "Got it?"

"Yes, sir." Chase could agree to that, even if he had to tie Maggie down and hold the phone to her ear.

"Yes." Maggie stood up from the bed and wrapped her arms around her father.

"You know all I've ever wanted was for you to be happy." His eyes closed as he brought her close. "I sometimes forget that. But that's really all I ever want for my children."

# TWENTY-FOUR

MAGGIE CARRIED Chase's overnight bag into her house as he hobbled in behind her. She'd left him at his place with Flores for an hour to get his stuff together while she cleaned her house. No embarrassing undergarments were going to be lying around today. No thank you.

The doctor said he needed to rest for two weeks. As the doctor talked about rest, the purple-scrubbed nurse glared at Maggie. Granted, the woman had snarled about Maggie being there for the two days Chase was in the hospital. But it wasn't like she wasn't going to let him rest. *Jeez.*

You get a man's heart rate up a few times, and suddenly you're some evil carnival ride. Maybe not the best metaphor—unless he wanted to ride her like a carnival ride, then...

Bad metaphor.

Chase was supposed to be resting. He didn't have

the time or energy for riding of any kind. She had to keep reminding herself of that.

He wrapped his arms around her waist as she dropped his bag on the couch—his hands slowly sliding down her body. Obviously he needed reminding too. "Stop."

She pulled away and pushed him down on the couch. "You're resting. If you're looking for something to fondle..." She picked up her unicorn pillow from the end of the couch. "Play with this."

"My favorite pillow." He tossed the pillow to the end of the couch. "But I'd much rather play with this." He hauled her over to him until her knees straddled his lap. He pressed his lips to hers.

Strong, powerful lips. And the tongue. His tongue slowly mapped out every dip and crevice in her lips. His hands joined the assault, finding the bottom of her shirt and slowly caressing a trail up her side.

"Not fair." She leaned her face back, but her body wouldn't leave him.

"Totally."

She steeled her spine and tried to get up. "You're supposed to be relaxing."

"I'm relaxed." He pulled her closer and slowly dragged his tongue from her neck to her ear. His teeth nibbled at her lobe as his body stiffened beneath her.

"You don't feel relaxed." The words left on a whimper as his hand splayed along her back. His mouth crushed to hers.

"I have a surefire way to get me relaxed." His hand roamed lower and lower. "You game?"

Was she game? Of course she was. They'd dealt with all the emotions of becoming a couple and had all the come-to-Jesus moments—without the fun. She liked the fun. She liked him.

"Let's go to bed." She stood up and pulled him to his feet.

"Are you sure you don't want to christen the couch?" He smiled. And didn't that smile just melt her heart.

"Next time."

"So there's going to be a next time?"

If she had her way, there'd be a next time and a next time and a time after that. They'd take their time and christen every square inch of this house.

"I love you." He leaned in and kissed that spot right below her ear.

She turned her head to let him closer. "I love you, too."

She wasn't afraid of those words anymore. She wasn't afraid of anything. With Chase by her side she felt like she could take on the world—not that she couldn't have taken on the world before Chase, but it was different, now. Complete.

That's what it was.

For the first time in a long time, her life was complete.

And wasn't that just amazing.

# EPILOGUE

## Danni

Danni sat at her desk, idly tapping at the keyboard in front of the monitor to her left. She had code to write and bad guys to catch. And a legion of PCs doing her bidding to get the information Leti and Maggie needed on a daily basis.

Right now she also had an order of Udon. She loved Japanese noodles. As a matter of fact, a delicious noodle dangled from her lips this very moment. Smooth and plump, it snapped back and forth as she sucked it between her teeth and into her waiting mouth. So good. So salty.

"Oh great." Maggie had somehow made it up the creaking stairs of Busted without Danni noticing. "Who let you have noodles?"

*You slurp down one noodle and you never live it down.* It may have been more than one noodle, but who was counting.

"Any luck with the tapes?" Maggie asked.

"I have the footage." Danni clicked on the file and moved the progress bar four hours into the standoff at the Michigan lake house. She'd managed to tape the whole night, which was mostly two morons sitting around scratching their heads—first the one on their shoulders, then the other one. Jury was still out which one they used for thinking.

"Did Jessi touch the gun?" The local law enforcement had a special report related to all the people who touched a gun at any crime scene—everything just short of DNA samples if you touched a weapon that had been discharged.

"I was waiting for you." Sort of true. Some intel on another case came in and Danni got a bit sidetracked.

"Let's fire it up."

"Got it, boss."

"Stop that. I'm not your boss." True. Maggie wasn't the boss. But starting up this detective agency had been her idea.

Getting Danni out of that soul-sucking police department had saved her life. She'd hated the boys club. She'd hated the politics. All she wanted was to do the job, but it was never easy playing law-abiding computer forensics examiner.

The CPD frowned on some of her more effective modes of gaining information, and you can take the disgusted looks from your co-workers only so many times before you start to question what side you're working on. She was a good guy. Why couldn't they see that?

"Ready?" Danni pushed the play button below the video and sat back.

The camera in the front yard showed darkness. No movement.

"This might be a little too early." Maggie huffed as she sipped the coffee in her hand. She always had a coffee in her hand.

Danni grabbed her own coffee. Yeah. She always had one too. *Sue me.*

The Katsaros girls stumbled out the front door, followed by Lacik. Yeah, this was way too early. She pushed the fast forward button and that night at the Michigan house went by in a blur.

A bright light pulsed across the yard.

"Stop." Maggie grabbed Danni's shoulder and Danni reluctantly hit stop. She remembered this part.

Chase rolled onto the ground as Lacik punched him in the face. The grunting and groaning was the stuff of nightmares, and she got to listen to it again.

"That son of a bitch." Maggie cringed as Lacik's fist hit Chase with a crack.

Danni didn't want to see this again. She didn't like blood. And despite the grainy picture, she could tell Chase was in pain. Who wanted to watch that?

His girlfriend, that's who. The masochist.

Danni focused on her coffee. "Can I fast forward yet?"

"Okay. Go."

The picture zoomed by. Blur. Blur. Blur. Jessi and Enzo. Enzo running around to the front of the house at breakneck speed.

*Play.* She hit the key and the picture moved at the speed of life.

Enzo dove for the gun on the ground and aimed it at Lacik.

With some hesitation, Lacik lifted his arms over his head. Jessi stood with the girls off to the side.

"See, Jessi didn't touch the gun." Danni knew she hadn't touched the gun.

"It's not over yet.

Jessi ran over to Chase, who was sitting on the hood of the car. He gave her a pair of cuffs. She walked over to Enzo and gave him the cuffs. Enzo gave her the gun.

"Dammit." Maggie shook her head as the sounds from the computer echoed through the quiet room.

"KEEP on HIM." *Enzo walked to Lacik and clicked the cuffs on his wrist behind his back.*

"*Ow. Not so tight.*" *Lacik whined and Enzo ratcheted the cuffs just a little tighter. "Owww."*

*Enzo pushed him in the back of the car and slammed the door shut. He turned to Jessi. "Watch him for one minute. I need to get Maggie."*

*Enzo ran across the yard and peeked into the front door. "Come outside. We need you. I'll grab him."*

"THIS IS WHERE I COME IN." Maggie shook her head.

"I can't believe I didn't notice Jessi was holding the gun."

"You were a little preoccupied with Officer Hottie bleeding all over the pavement."

Maggie rolled her eyes. "Thanks for the reminder." Maggie tried to hide that she was worried about Chase. But she was. He was still on leave with his gunshot wound. Danni could only imagine how protective the woman would be once he was back on the street serving and protecting.

They let the words hang over them as they watched the tape. The great Jessi-gun question was answered, but something kept them watching the tape. Probably the stress from the night. How much had they missed during all the excitement?

*"I'll take that." Enzo came up next to Jessi and she jumped, dropping the gun. He picked it up and tucked it into the waistband of his jeans. "It's okay."*

*His hand curled around her arm. She looked like she was the lone survivor in a Stephen King novel.*

*"Jessi, sweetheart." He ran a finger along the side of her face.*

*"What?" She looked up, frowning. But not angry. More like confused.*

*"I'm sorry," Enzo blurted at the same time Jessi said, "I should go."*

*Enzo shook his head. "I came all this way. I thought maybe we could talk."*

*She took a step away from him. "What's there to talk about?"*

*"Well, we could start with why you stopped taking my calls. Why won't you answer the damn phone?"*

*"Maybe because I'm the one who answers my damn phone—when I choose to answer it. I don't have some woman answering for me."*

*"What?" Enzo did an excellent imitation of a startled fish.*

*"Look, I don't want to fight..."*


MAGGIE TURNED TO DANNI. "Did you know they had a thing?"

"Nope." Jessi and Enzo were fighting. Danni wouldn't think they knew each other well enough to fight. They'd had a run in with the Mayor's mafia-squad about a year ago, but that was it. Danni couldn't wait to tease Jessi about this new development.

"We should shut this down." Maggie said the words but her eyes were taking in the unfolding drama. Danni just couldn't get her hand to move and click the X in the corner. This was way too entertaining.


*"I DON'T KNOW what happened between us, but I think you're being childish." Enzo's voice came over the microphone.*


JESSI HAD A SHARP TONGUE, which made Jessi fit in

nicely at Busted. But she wasn't childish. Not anymore. Not since she had her son.

*JESSI'S HANDS snapped to her hips. "I think you're being a jerk."*

OKAY. Maybe she acted a little childish, but who was Danni to judge—she was spying on her friends as their drama unfolded. Danni's hand hovered over the X in the corner. They had what they needed. They didn't need to watch anymore.

But this was like reality TV with people she knew. She felt guilty watching it, but she couldn't turn away.

*ENZO LEANED IN. His face serious. His voice soft. He looked like he was in physical pain. Poor guy. "It wasn't just sex for me. It was more. And you just left. A whole year without a word."*

DANNI SLAMMED the X in the corner and the screen went black. *Holy crap.* That was not something they was supposed to see. Sex? Twelve months ago?

"Twelve months ago?" Maggie had same shock-and-awe look that Danni felt. "How old is Matty?"

"Almost three months."

Jessi and Enzo were a thing. And that thing...

Danni could do the math. That thing might have produced an heir to their drama kingdom.

"Yeah." Maggie nodded. "Why didn't she tell us?"

Danni shook her head. She had no idea. They would have understood. Well, Danni would have understood.

Maggie took a deep breath. "We can't say anything to anyone. Not even Leti."

"No." Danni stared at the frozen screen. She couldn't move. "Jessi can't know we know. She would have told us if she wanted us to know."

"Yeah." Maggie nodded.

Enzo was Matty's father. He had to be. *Shit.* Danni swallowed. "I have to get back to work."

"Yeah." Maggie walked toward the stairs, and they squeaked as she made her way down.

Danni turned back to the screen. If she was going to invade someone's privacy, she should move on to the guy supposedly schtupping his wife's best friend and stay away from her own friends. She had an email to hack. And the code wasn't going to write itself.

If you enjoyed reading this installment of the Busted series, check out the other books in this series.

**Busted Series** (in order)
>   Busting In
>   Busting Out
>   Busting Through (coming soon)

Thank you for supporting an independent author. It would be great if you could leave a review or a rating wherever you purchased this book, or on Goodreads.

Would you like to know when my next book is available? You can sign up for my new release email list at http://www.vanessamknight.com or like my Facebook page at http://facebook.com/vanessamknightauthor.

# ABOUT THE AUTHOR

**Vanessa M. Knight** has always enjoyed writing, and once she found romance, she was addicted. She props her laptop in the suburbs of Chicago with her husband, son and menagerie of four-pawed claw-babies (AKA cats and dogs.) That laptop has partnered-in-crime to write contemporary romances with a dash of humor and splash of snark.

When she has a few moments to spare, you can find her singing off-key (but she assures everyone it's still considered singing), reading, kickboxing or killing a few brain cells as she stares at the many sitcoms and dramas available through the Internet and TV.

For more information on Vanessa, including her Internet haunts, contest updates, and details on her upcoming novels, please visit her website at www.vanessamknight.com.

**Other Books By Vanessa**

<u>**Contemporary Suspense**</u>

**Busted Series** (in order)

Busting In

Busting Out

Busting Through


**Chicago's Finest Series** (in order)

Second Time's the Charm

Stark Raving Mad

Stealing Vegas (Winter 2018)


<u>**Contemporary New Adult**</u>

**Ritter University Series** (in order)

Major Renovations

What Happens in College...

Christmas Breakdown

Rushing In

Sophomore Slump

The Makeup Test


<u>**Contemporary Romance**</u>

**Falling Pines Series**

Breaking the Fall